WHAT PEOPLE ARE SAYING

Unintended Consequences

"If you like strong, sassy women, suspense, and a good mystery, you will love *Unintended Consequences*. Kudos to Betsy Ashton for a great read."

—KATHLEEN GRISSOM,
  NYT Best Selling Author of The Kitchen House and
  Glory Over Everything

"The fast-paced writing style draws the reader into the action. Ashton unfolds a unique story that tugs on your heartstrings, clenches your fists at the injustice that happens to the characters, and then lightens with a humorous quip to release the tension and sadness. I laughed. I cried. I didn't want to put the book down until the very end."

—CHERIE REICH,
  Author of *Elements Of Untethered Realms* Series

"Ashton's attention to detail, coupled with a terrific plot line with surprising twists, makes this read a terrific thriller. This book is not for the faint-hearted; it is a story that will keep you fully engaged until the very end. The author's development of a strong, independent, female central character is refreshing and will appeal to men and women alike."

—KIMBERLY DALFERES,
  Author of *I Was In Love With A Short Man Once* and
  Magic Fishing Panties

"With *Mad Max: Unintended Consequences* Betsy Ashton has given us a fresh and original crime story. It's a study of how one woman's automobile accident sets in motion a series of events that no one could have anticipated (hence the "Unintended Consequences" of the title)."

—MAGGIE KING,
  Author of *Book Group Mysteries*

Uncharted Territory

"Mad Max is at it again—another "uppity woman" who can't leave well enough alone. Just the way I like it."

—MOLLIE COX BRYAN,
  Agatha Award Finalist for *A Cumberland Creek Mystery Series*

". . . a genre-bending tale of murder, suspense, chaos, and triumph."

—MICHAEL MURPHY,
  Author of *Goodbye Emily*

"I enjoyed the new characters here, namely the English tutor Max hired to homeschool the children and the two pastors from different sides of the track. The desolation of the area when they arrive is palpable, as is the menace that continually hovers over what's left of the town. Another winner from Ms. Ashton!"

—D.A. SPRUZEN,
  Author of *The Blitz Business*

"Missing immigrant workers, later found murdered, along with other violence and sinister stalkings require Max's sleuthing abilities. Much local involvement with two Baptist preachers, an abusive Catholic priest and two cowering captives in his manse add to the action. A fast, engrossing read highlighting social ills that seem to couple with natural catastrophes."

—SUSAN CORYELL,
  Author of *The Overhome Trilogy*

Unsafe Haven

by Betsy Ashton

© Copyright 2018 Betsy Ashton

ISBN 978-1-63393-549-5

Published by

 köehlerbooks ™

210 60th Street
Virginia Beach, VA 23451
800-435-4811
www.koehlerbooks.com

UNSAFE HAVEN

A Mad Max Mystery

Betsy Ashton

VIRGINIA BEACH
CAPE CHARLES

CHAPTER ONE

2008

"I CAN'T BELIEVE we're really at Uncle Johnny's ranch," my newly-minted thirteen-year-old grandson said. Alex clumped through the living room of the old Mexican-style adobe ranch house and stared through the rickety screen door.

I hugged him. "Happy Birthday."

"Is Uncle Johnny coming back soon?" Alex twitched away, all but dancing in anticipation of a day full of adventures and surprises. "I don't want to wait any longer to go on my first horseback ride."

"He'll be here when he's ready. Why don't you watch what he's doing?"

From where we stood, I could see a mountain range looming in the distance, a dark green smudge rising from the red desert floor—the Sangre de Cristo Mountains, as Johnny Medina, my best friend and life partner, called them. They were close to one hundred miles away, yet they looked near enough to touch.

Johnny's family could hardly have picked a prettier spot for their cattle ranch. Nearer Santa Fe than Albuquerque, it nestled in that junction where the desert rose gradually toward the mountains. We'd arrived at the Medina family homestead the night before, and already I felt cleansed by the dry air filled with the tang of juniper, sage, and greasewood. I'd never been in New Mexico, but the land reached out and drew me in. I thanked the gods for bringing Johnny into my life when I needed support most; I thanked Johnny for remaining.

Despite a tiring day of travel, Alex bounced out of bed right after dawn, impatient to start his birthday visit, with its promise of horseback riding, an overnight campout, and lessons in horsemanship.

Johnny came into view with a dancing dark bay mare on a short lead. He tied her to a ring on the trailer across the dusty yard.

"Oh, wow!" Alex forgot about using his indoor voice. "I want to go help."

Before he could push through the door and blast across the yard, I grabbed his arm and said in my most *don't-mess-with-me* voice, "Stop right there. Uncle Johnny told us to wait here. He had his reasons. We'll do as he said."

"But he needs help." Alex squirmed, but didn't try very hard to break my hold.

"And how do you propose to help? You know nothing about horses."

"At least I could pat them."

I was almost as excited as the boy. Johnny led a second horse to the trailer, a chestnut mare, and tied her to a second ring. I wondered if that was mine. She seemed much calmer than the snorting, fidgety bay.

Alex almost burst out of his skin when Johnny reappeared with a pinto.

"I bet that's mine," Alex shouted.

"Indoor voice, Alex, indoor voice." *Will the boy ever learn?* "Hey there, Captain Chaos, where's your jacket?"

Captain Chaos was one of our extended family's nicknames for Alex. He earned it—he was more likely to bolt in front of an angry bull or a giant earthmover than to sit on a fence rail and watch in safety. This one might live on a bit longer, but with him growing older, we had to retire my favorite nickname: *holy-crap boy-child.*

"Ah, Mad Max, can't I go just this once without a jacket?"

"No."

I'd had an ongoing argument with my daughter, Merry, over what name the kids should use for me. She wanted them to call me Grandma. No way did I feel like a *grandma,* a name I equated with blue-haired, doddering old ladies smelling of lilac talc. I hated *Nana, Grams, Noonie,* or any other cutesy name. My granddaughter, Emilie, told me not to be mad, thereupon forever anointing me Mad Max.

"As we say in New York, I'm having a Jewish-mother-sweater alert." I pointed toward his bedroom.

"You're not Jewish."

"News flash. All mothers are Jewish. It comes with the territory." I chucked Alex on the chin before he dodged away. He'd reached the age when any display of parental affection was humiliating, even in the privacy of a living room.

Boots scraped the mat on the worn wooden porch. The old screen door squeaked open, and Johnny entered. He looked every bit the real-life cowboy—broken-in, dusty jeans, black ropers covered with a veneer of corral dust, plaid shirt, jean jacket, and a Stetson. With his black hair graying at the temples, tanned skin, and dark eyes glinting with humor and warmth, he had never looked more handsome. Even with a smudge of dirt across his nose.

"What's a Jewish-mother-sweater alert?" he asked.

"If I'm likely to be chilly, you're going to take your jacket."

Alex stomped toward his bedroom. When he returned, he folded and stuffed his jacket into a half-empty backpack. He jammed on his ball cap.

I looked up at Johnny. "What? No sombrero?"

Johnny shot me a dark look. "You were expecting the second coming of Pancho Villa, maybe? Have you ever tried to ride in one of those damned things? Even with a chin strap, I'd spend the entire day chasing it if a gust of wind came up. My horse would buck and snort." Johnny removed the Stetson and slapped the dust off on his thigh. The sweat-stained hat had seen better days. "They're okay for festivals but not for real work."

I threw up my hands and quit while I was behind.

"Are you ready, Alex?" Johnny's question uncoiled Alex and sent him rocketing out the door, his backpack hanging over one shoulder and banging against his hip. He whooped and charged toward the three horses.

"Stop!" Johnny yelled.

"Don't run, Alex!" I cried out.

"Alex, I said *stop*!" Johnny's voice drowned out mine.

The bay mare tossed her head, flattened her ears, and snorted at the commotion approaching her blind side. She swung her hindquarters toward the noise and kicked.

My impetuous grandson skidded to a stop, inches out of range. Hooves flashed again. The bay kept her ears pinned; the whites of her eyes gleamed against the dark brown face. The other two horses snorted and tugged at their halter ropes.

I ran toward Alex; Johnny grabbed my arm and stopped me.

"Leave this to me," Johnny said.

"He's my grandson."

"My ranch, my rules. I'll handle it. Wait here." Johnny took Alex aside. I couldn't hear what he said, but Alex hung his head and nodded.

Johnny led him over to meet the horses, approaching from the left. Johnny showed him how to hold out his hand so that each horse could smell it, and how to reach up slowly to pat their necks. Johnny handed him several peppermint candies. After a sniff or two, each horse accepted Alex and lipped up the candies. Johnny nodded at me. I went through the same routine. Crisis abated.

"Which one is mine?" Alex was still wound up, but he used his indoor voice.

"You'll ride the little pinto. He's very gentle and fun to ride." Johnny fastened Alex's backpack behind the saddle, untied the black-and-white pony, and walked it into the trailer. "His name's Loco, but he's not."

Next in the trailer went the chestnut mare. "You'll be on Cherokee, Max. She's an easy mover, great gait, and responsive. I rode her for years until we retired her from ranch work. She's sweet and easy to handle."

Last to load was Johnny's dark bay. "This bad girl needs a lot of work. I ride her whenever I'm at the ranch, which is never enough to keep her in shape. Her name's Belle."

"Like Taco Bell?" Alex asked.

"Belle Starr, for the mark on her forehead." Johnny shut the back of the trailer and walked to the truck. "Although Taco Bell might be more appropriate. She's a handful, a real salsa gal."

"Gotcha," Alex said.

"Hey, wait a minute." I sped back to the house and returned with saddlebags filled with our lunches and a riding helmet.

"What the hell is that?" Johnny doubled over with laughter.

"Just what you think it is, funny man—my riding helmet." I drew myself up to my full height, all five feet four inches of it, and jammed it on my head. "I never get on a horse without it."

"You're not going to wear that. I'll be the laughingstock of the ranch."

I tossed the helmet in the backseat and climbed in front. "We'll see about that."

"Okay, is everybody ready? Anyone think we'll see an eagle today?"

Alex started to shout *yes* but caught himself. He settled for a head bob before he climbed into the back.

The dirt road unrolled beneath the truck's wheels. We left the ranch, turned onto a county highway, and climbed toward the mountains. Johnny kept a running commentary about the history of the area—the Native American nations that lived here; the Anasazi, who built pueblos in Mesa Verde and Taos; the national parks; the early settlers that came west along the Santa Fe Trail and built ranches around Albuquerque; and ranchers like Johnny's family, which had come up from Mexico and settled around Santa Fe. I glanced at Alex, who was texting as fast as his thumbs could move. I took his phone before he could howl in protest.

"Listen to Uncle Johnny. You might learn something." This vacation was supposed to be a way for Alex to relax. Texting and playing electronic games wasn't going to broaden his knowledge of anything. He needed to unplug, to disconnect.

Alex grabbed for his phone, but I held it out of reach. "I was telling everyone what Uncle Johnny's saying. Look at the phone if you don't believe me."

I scanned the messages. Indeed, many were to Emilie about what she was missing, about the horses and the Native Americans. A couple were to his father, Whip, and his teacher, Mr. Ducks, as well as to some friends back in Richmond, Virginia. More than a few were to Charlie, his first real crush. That fiery redhead had stolen all of our hearts, particularly my son-in-law Whip's.

"I'm sorry," I said. "I shouldn't have jumped to conclusions." I handed his phone back. Alex surprised me by putting it on the seat next to my helmet and looking out the window.

"Hey, what's that?" Alex pointed at a large bird riding a thermal high in the bright blue sky. "Is it an eagle?"

Johnny squinted. "No, too small. Probably a red-tailed hawk, or maybe a Ferruginous hawk. If it's hunting, you'll see it swoop down on a mouse or vole. One second it's in the sky, the next it's on the ground with breakfast in its beak."

Alex craned his neck to keep the circling bird in sight. He sighed when it didn't dive bomb an unsuspecting varmint. I had no interest in watching a hawk kill breakfast. It might be the natural state of things, but I'd rather not see it.

"The way a hawk eats is fascinating. Not very pretty, though. They literally peel the mouse, eat the insides, and then finish off the skin," Johnny continued.

I groaned.

"That's so, like, way cool," said Alex.

I was outnumbered. Two men, one woman. I shut my mouth and watched the dusty land fall away as we climbed through sage and greasewood toward tall pines in the distance.

"Are we going up there today?" I jerked my chin at the dark green horizon inching closer.

"Maybe some other day. That's too far, but we have some wonderful trails up ahead. We'll have a good ride and be home in time for dinner."

That would sit well with Alex. This boy never missed a meal. Neither did Johnny.

We passed a few small towns, dirt roads leading to Native American reservations, several roadside vendors with silver and turquoise jewelry, and a modern-looking building atop a hill in the middle of absolutely nowhere. Alex was keeping a lookout for more wildlife, the phone no longer his concern. The building passed on his side. He couldn't help but notice it.

"What's that? It looks out of place."

"It's a hospital, part of the Indian Health Service. The federal government built several on or near reservations to improve care and treatment of Native Americans. When this one was finished around 2000, it was supposed to be state of the art. I'm sure changes have come in since it opened, but it's so much better than the old hospital it replaced."

I hoped never to see the inside of it. I'd had enough of hospitals since I all but lived in an ICU for weeks when my daughter was in a coma following her auto accident.

"No reason for any of us to go there. We're going to have an easy ride for Alex's first time out, eat lunch, and return to the ranch."

"Works for me."

Johnny flipped his turn signal on, even though we hadn't seen a car in nearly half an hour, and pulled off the road. "We're at the head of the Navajo Springs trail. We ride from here."

He offloaded the horses, tightened the cinches, and exchanged halters for bridles. I knew how to put on English bridles, but Western tack was different. For one, Johnny wasn't using a martingale or tie-down strap. I recognized snaffle bits and the way the headstalls went together. The reins were different, because there were two of them rather than a single loop. Alex dogged Johnny's every move, listening to the running narration.

I reached into the backseat for my helmet, but at Johnny's glare I put it back.

"Good girl," he grinned.

"If I fall off and bump my head, it will be all your fault."

"I can live with that."

He showed Alex and me how to mount, how to neck rein, and how to ask the horse to go forward by pressing boot heels to its sides. Because I'd learned to ride English, I squeezed my legs to give Cherokee a silent command to move forward. She tossed her head and danced on her toes. Johnny gave me a look.

"Does she understand leg cues?" I asked.

Johnny gaped at me.

"Leg cues. You know, pressure from my legs telling her where to go and how."

"Where did you learn about leg cues?"

"I learned to ride English in Central Park. My step-daughter competed in dressage. She taught me how to sit still and give tiny cues either by squeezing my calves or twitching a finger. It comes natural to me." I rode Cherokee in a circle, reversing her course by squeezing one calf or the other. I left the reins loose on her neck. "I guess she does."

With one smooth motion, Johnny mounted his bay and led us at a walk. No way was I going to be a lump. I took hold of my horse and nudged her to follow Alex's pony along the wide trail. I looked around and enjoyed nature's quiet, hearing no man-made noise beyond the squeak of saddle leather and the soft jangle of bits. I listened to the movements of small animals and spotted a couple of rabbits disappear down holes.

The solitude and sun's warmth relaxed me as I observed Johnny in his native habitat. I knew him as a businessman in Richmond and as a road engineer in Mississippi. *Is this the real Johnny?* The man grew up on a ranch and sat a horse as easily as I sat in a box at the Metropolitan Opera.

Cherokee sidestepped and snorted, causing me to tighten my calves. She danced forward and swung her hindquarters halfway around laying her ears back. I didn't see anything to upset her, but she knew better. Johnny looked back when he heard the mare change her gait.

"I didn't see anything," I said. Of course, I was daydreaming.

"Well, she did." Johnny grinned. "Smallish rattler about ten feet off the trail. Alex spotted it. You'd have seen it if you followed our pointing fingers."

My grandson turned in his saddle and gloated. *Gad, I have to stay alert to keep from being outdone and outmaneuvered.* I patted Cherokee's neck and stuck my tongue out at the backs of the two men who mocked me.

CHAPTER TWO

WE FOLLOWED THE trail for about two hours. I imagined Native Americans walking along it, maybe moving to new hunting grounds, maybe visiting distant family. Stone outcrops rose around us; small pines and junipers, twisted and gnarled, grew in clumps across the open landscape. The scents of chaparral and sage grew stronger as the heat intensified. Crows and hawks soared overhead. On a ridge, a mile or so distant, a coyote raised his head to smell the air and stared at us for several seconds before evaporating into a stand of greasewood.

I kept a steady tension on the reins, ready to pull the mare aside if we disturbed another snake. Since Cherokee remained steady, I assumed any rustlings meant we hadn't startled something poisonous. I was about as far from my normal environs as I could be. Neither the constant energy of Manhattan nor the semi-isolation of the construction camp in post-Katrina Mississippi prepared me for the all-encompassing emptiness of northern New Mexico.

Alex and Johnny rode in front. Alex's endless questions covered the gamut of the boy's mind. "Why is Loco called a pony, not a horse? What is this buckle on the saddle for? What are those trees called? The birds? The small animals?"

Johnny answered each question patiently.

"Why did you bring a rifle?"

"I brought it in case we run into any large animals," Johnny said. "It's strictly for self-defense. It'll scare them off."

"You mean, like a mountain lion?" I didn't need to see Alex's face to know his eyes were round as Oreos.

"Don't get your hopes up. If we were to see a mountain lion, it would run away rather than attack three horses and riders."

"Have you ever shot a mountain lion?" Alex wouldn't relinquish hope of seeing a big cat.

Johnny shook his head. "I've seen a couple from a distance. I leave them alone, and they leave me alone. They have their place in nature. Unless one attacks a human or livestock, most of us ranchers just let them do their thing."

"What about coyotes?"

"Ah, coyotes are a different matter." Johnny slowed his horse, pulled his hat off, and wiped a sheen of sweat from his forehead. A layer of fine grit covered our clothes and skin. After Mississippi, I no longer noticed grit, having lived in an RV in the middle of a construction zone for two years. Johnny waved his hat in a wide arc before continuing with Alex's ecology lesson.

"Coyotes kill calves and lambs. They've adapted to feeding off livestock rather than deer and antelope, so most ranchers kill them whenever they can."

"Have you killed a coyote?"

"I grew up on a ranch, Alex. My brothers, sisters, and I all got rifles when we were kids. I learned to shoot before I was your age. Sure, I've killed coyotes." Johnny looked at the boy riding beside him. "We only kill those that attack our herds. They're hardly an endangered species. We never seem to run out of them."

"What about your Glock? You didn't bring it."

Relentless kid, my grandson. I understood where he was coming from, though. On the job site in Mississippi, his uncle Johnny and his father wore their guns in hip holsters. We had run afoul of a gang of escaped convicts. Most of the construction crew openly carried weapons to prevent attacks. Alex thought guns on hips was the norm.

"It's a Sig Sauer, not a Glock. Your father's is a Glock. It's made for shooting people. It has no use out here. Now, listen to the quiet all around us, okay?" Johnny's tone ended the conversation, and the set of his shoulders left no opening for more pestering.

Alex dropped back and rode in silence with me for a while. I was glad for the teachable moment. I watched him use all of his senses to pay careful attention to the land around us.

We turned off the trail onto what looked like a deer trace and rode single file, the path barely two feet wide. The vegetation was greener. A stream bubbled gently up ahead. Johnny pulled up in a small clearing and dismounted in a single fluid motion. I dismounted, my motion anything but fluid. I'd stiffened up in the past hour or so. Alex jumped off and followed Johnny's instructions, watering the horses at the stream before bringing them to a couple of pinyon pines. Johnny swapped bridles for halters and long ropes, and let the animals pick at what little grass there was.

"Time for lunch. Anyone hungry?" I shook out a blanket and spread it on the ground before opening the saddlebags and pulling out thick sandwiches, fruit, and water bottles.

"No chips?" Alex unwrapped a sandwich and took a bite.

"No chips. I left them behind because they were too bulky. You'd have had chip rubble after a few hours in the saddlebags anyway. I do have cookies, though."

Alex ate half his sandwich before jumping up and heading toward the stream.

"Hold up, bud. Where're you going?" Johnny called.

"I'm thirsty. I thought I'd get a drink at the creek." He was halfway across the clearing. "It looks clean and cold."

"Well, you thought wrong. It may look clean, but you don't know what's upstream. It could be a dead animal or something equally gross that pollutes the water. I don't want you to get sick." Johnny sipped from his water bottle.

"Gee. I thought water would taste better if it came from the ground." Alex threw himself back on the blanket and snatched a bottle.

"It does, but all kinds of bacteria and parasites live in water, no matter how clean it looks. *E. coli* is one bad one. Comes from drinking water contaminated with feces, human or animal."

"*Eww.* I thought only fish pooped in streams."

"So do cattle, horses, and deer. Nearly anything that comes

to a watering hole or stream to drink." Johnny paused to finish a bite of his sandwich. "Other bad things, like cholera and *Giardia*, give you the runs, make you puke your guts out, and make you feel like you want to die."

I'd had enough. I didn't need the conversation dwelling on illness or poop. I finished my apple and stood. "Can I give the core to Cherokee?"

When she heard her name, the mare raised her head and blew gently.

"She'll love it." Johnny leaned against a rock, his hat pulled low over his eyes. He looked for all the world like a professional cowboy in the Westerns I'd devoured with my brothers. His DNA was all ranch. His movements and general posture put him naturally in this environment. I may have grown up on an Eastern farm and knew how to kill chickens for the pot, milk cows, and help birth calves, but I would never look relaxed propped against a rock.

Alex went off to explore the rock outcropping upstream.

"Don't climb on anything. Your new boots are too slippery. You might fall," I called.

Johnny only moved the muscles needed to call a warning when he added, "Remember what I said about snakes. They'll be out sunning themselves, so give them plenty of room. Go no more than half an hour up the trail, turn around, and come back. By that time, we'll be ready to ride down to the truck."

A wave of one hand told me that Alex had heard Johnny's instructions but made no promise to follow them. I wandered around the clearing and picked up a handful of small, pale-yellow seeds that looked somewhat familiar. I brought them to Johnny, who peeled one eye open.

"Pine nuts."

"Like those I buy in the store and pay a fortune for?"

Johnny nodded. "We've had a decent snow pack for the past couple of years, so the Native Americans are harvesting bumper crops. Also explains the hawks."

"How so?"

"Small rodents eat pine nuts, and the hawks eat rodents. Classic food chain. That's why we saw so many today. Lots of food."

With Alex off exploring, Johnny pulled me down to lean on him in companionable silence. I squirmed until I made a groove for my hip in the dirt under the blanket, and then I snuggled against his shoulder. He smelled of horse, dust, and sweat. We napped. After almost an hour, Johnny sat up, checked the sun's position, and said we should head home. He wanted to get to the ranch before dark.

"You'll be surprised how quickly the temperature drops up here. We're a hell of a lot higher than we were in Mississippi."

"Alex is late. He should have been back by now," I said. "I'll go find him."

While Johnny tightened the horses' cinches, swapped halters for bridles, and watered them one more time, I hiked up the trail and looked for Alex. I didn't see him, so I followed his footprints. I saw where he'd stopped and disturbed the dirt as if digging something up. He left a hole behind.

"Alex. Time to leave."

I assumed he was hiding, waiting to jump out and scare the bejeezus out of me. I braced myself for his *holy-crap-boy-child* sneak attack. I turned a bend, heard pebbles fall from a rock ledge about fifty yards off, and looked up. Alex balanced on a narrow ledge, thirty feet above the main trail, waving his arms at me.

Didn't Johnny warn him about staying off the rocks? His new leather soles weren't broken in enough for him to be climbing ledges and hiking nearly non-existent trails.

He saw me and yelled, "Hey, Mad Max. Look what I found."

"Alex! Get down from there before you fall."

I took a step toward him. Alex lost his balance and tumbled off the ledge. He bounced off the rock face before landing behind a boulder. I couldn't see him, but I heard him land.

Snap.

Oh, shit! I knew that sound. Broken bones.

"Johnny!"

CHAPTER THREE

MY PULSE GALLOPED in my throat. Alex lay face-down in a dusty heap, his right leg twisted unnaturally underneath him. I didn't see blood. I placed two fingers on his neck, over the carotid artery. Strong. *Maybe he had the wind knocked out. Maybe he didn't break his leg. Maybe that crack I heard was his head hitting the boulder. Maybe he has a concussion.*

I knelt next to him and rolled him over, careful to support his head and not jostle him. His face was covered in scratches and dirt. His eyelids quivered. One eye peeled open.

Where the hell is Johnny?

I opened my mouth to yell again when Johnny materialized beside me and pushed me out of the way. He squatted in the dirt and ran his hands over my grandson's torso, feeling for injuries. With little warning, Alex gulped air and coughed violently. He tried to sit up. Johnny held him down.

"Easy there, pal. Don't move."

"It hurts." Alex coughed again and drew in several shaky breaths.

"Where? Your head? Your chest?" Johnny lifted each eyelid. I'd seen enough television to know he was checking for signs of a concussion.

"My chest. It hurts when I breathe." Alex proved his point by taking another quick breath and coughing. He groaned.

"What about your head? Do you think you hit it? Does it hurt?" Johnny ran his hands around the back of Alex's head, but he wouldn't find any blood—I'd already looked.

"You probably have a broken rib or two." Johnny turned his attention to Alex's legs. "Your dad and I have had several. The bad news is, you'll hurt like hell for a couple of weeks. You won't want to cough, sneeze, or laugh."

I moved to Alex and brushed bits of dirt and small rocks from his face and hair.

"Don't let Em near me. She'll tease me to death." Alex sneezed and groaned. He was right about his sister. Emilie had honed teasing into a fine art form.

"Where else do you hurt?" Johnny felt along Alex's left leg.

"My—my right leg. I think I broke it." Alex sucked in air and screwed up his face, close to crying.

How can Johnny be so damned calm? I wanted to scream even though I knew that wouldn't help. I opened my mouth, but Johnny cut me off. He looked at the twisted leg.

"Max, will you go back to my horse and bring my saddlebags? I need my first-aid kit," he said calmly.

I ran down the deer trail, damning the slippery soles of my new boots. *What I wouldn't give for sneakers.* I remembered to slow before I rounded the last bend, so as not to spook the horses. Cherokee nickered and stamped a hoof. I patted her neck in passing before I untied the saddlebags on Belle and rushed back. I heard Johnny's voice before I reached the scene of the accident.

"Yes, about ten miles up the old Thomas Mine road."

Johnny fell silent. He was on his cell. At least we had coverage here. I reached into my jacket pocket and pulled out my phone. Two bars. I needed to call Whip, Alex's father, but he'd ask questions I couldn't yet answer. Better to wait. After all, what he didn't know at that moment wasn't causing him any worries.

"I left my truck and horse trailer at the trailhead . . . You can get an ambulance that far, but we rode two hours up to Navajo Springs. We're probably half a mile north of that now."

Silence.

"That's the one. Our horses are at the spring."

Silence.

"He fell about thirty feet off a rock ledge, knocked the wind out of him. Right leg's broken."

Silence.

"Multiple fractures of the lower right leg. The tibia erupted through the skin."

Silence.

"That's what I said. Open fracture of the tibia."

I listened with one ear and looked at Alex's legs. Johnny had pulled off the new boots and used the knife from his belt to slit Alex's new jeans, exposing a bloody tear in the skin.

What does Johnny mean about an open fracture? Then I saw it. A jagged piece of bloody bone poked through Alex's shin. I gulped, determined not to be sick.

"I have a first-aid kit," Johnny said. I held out the bags. He motioned for me to set them on a flat rock next to his hat. "Yes, I can sterilize the skin break and put on a splint."

Beneath layers of dust, Alex's face was pale, his breathing rapid and shallow. Shock. I took off my jacket and draped it over his chest to keep him warm. I wished I'd thought to bring the blanket. The sun was hot, but Alex fell in the cool shade. His teeth chattered.

"No, that'll take too long. He's going into shock, but I don't think he has life-threatening injuries." Johnny listened again.

"You can cry if you want," I whispered as I brushed hair from his forehead.

The head under my hand moved from side to side. Alex didn't say a word. He caught a lip between his teeth and bit it hard. A single tear escaped and left a muddy track to his hairline.

I reached for the backpack, found the first-aid kit, and pulled out a gauze pad, which I slipped between Alex's teeth. "Bite on this. It won't bleed like your lip will."

"Great. That's even better. I'll watch for it." Johnny flipped his phone closed.

"EMS?"

"They know roughly where we are and will be here as soon as they can. I don't want to move Alex." Johnny reached for the kit, ripped open a couple of sanitary wipes, and scrubbed his hands. "I need your help, Max. We have to stabilize the leg while we wait for the cavalry."

I didn't have time to think about what Johnny was getting ready to do. I'd never been good around blood, and Alex's leg was bleeding freely.

Johnny spoke to us both at the same time. The more we knew about what was going to happen, the better prepared we'd be to help. "We're going to take care of your broken leg so that you don't get an infection." He nodded to me and at the leg. "Max, I want you to hold Alex's knee while I pull on his foot. I have to get that bone under the skin."

While he was talking, Johnny put on Latex gloves and swabbed the wound with alcohol. "Alex, this is going to hurt like hell. I can't help it. Yell all you want. Heck, I'd be screaming if I broke my leg like you did."

Alex shook his head again. I'd never seen him so stoic. *No, he's not being stoic. He's scared speechless.* I wished I could hold him in my arms, but neither Johnny nor I wanted to lift him until a doctor checked him for head injuries. Right now, we could work on the leg, nothing else. I gripped Alex's knee like a vice. No way was that leg going to move.

"Ready, Max?"

"Yes."

"Ready, Alex?"

Alex nodded, sucked in a breath, and held it. I followed his lead and held my breath, too. Johnny knelt at Alex's feet and held the ankle between his large hands. He gently pulled it toward him.

I watched the bone slide under the skin, gulped, and whispered, "Johnny put the bone back in place."

Blood oozed from the slit in Alex's shin. Johnny swabbed the wound with more alcohol. Alex barely flinched. Johnny laid a thick gauze pad over the tear, taped it in place, and fashioned a splint out of fallen branches. He wrapped an Ace bandage around the leg and sat back. Sweat ran down his face. He wiped it on his sleeve and scanned the sky.

"Where did you learn to do that?"

"In the Army. I was a medic."

"A medic? You're too young to have been in Vietnam. Where were you stationed?"

"Panama. We had lots of stupid kids fall off motorcycles and break legs. Some troops had bullet wounds, too. I learned to set bones, suture gaping wounds, and keep soldiers with concussions quiet."

How odd that I didn't know that.

Johnny stood and retrieved his hat. He replaced the depleted first-aid kit in his saddlebags and squinted south, back the way we came, probably watching for dust swirls from the ambulance.

Before long, I heard an unnatural sound. I too looked south. And up.

Thwapita, thwapita, thwapita.

A blue-and-white Medivac helicopter sporting a stylized sun logo flew straight toward us, covering the distance in seconds. It circled once before hovering over our little tableau, and threw up a cloud of grit and debris when it landed a few hundred yards away.

"Figured you could afford the helicopter." Johnny flashed his lopsided grin. If the situation weren't so serious, I'd have punched his shoulder. Instead, I smiled and gathered Alex's boots.

"Don't forget the fossil I found." Alex's voice was breathy, but loud enough for me to hear. He pointed toward a black rock with something embedded in it. His hand fell back on the ground as he gasped.

"This?" I held it up. "It looks like a cockroach."

"It's a trilobite," Johnny said. I tucked the fossil into my pocket. I didn't care what Johnny called it. It looked like a cockroach.

Two medics ran up. While the younger one fired questions at us, the other took Alex's blood pressure. He called out numbers; the younger EMT made notes. I turned to Johnny for assurance that they knew what they were doing. He squeezed my shoulder.

Some questions we could answer, others we couldn't. I didn't know if Alex hit his head. We knew he couldn't talk when I first reached him, but that could have been from having the wind knocked out of him. Or he could have been unconscious with a concussion. One medic fastened a neck collar to stabilize his head.

"Just in case, ma'am."

I nodded. The younger medic unwrapped the Ace bandage and peeked under the gauze. He whistled when he saw Johnny's work and looked up, questions unasked.

"Army medic," Johnny said simply. He gave the medics a thorough, professional update on Alex's condition. The medics fetched a gurney, strapped Alex onto it, and pushed him toward the helicopter.

Johnny put his arm around my shoulders and kissed the top of my head. I leaned into him as we hurried behind Alex. "Go with him, Max. I'll join you when I can. I have to take the horses home first."

"Bring my handbag when you come, will you? It has Alex's insurance card in it."

"He'll be all right." He gave my shoulder another reassuring squeeze and half-lifted me into the helicopter. I grasped the hand of the older EMT, who helped me to a jump seat. The pilot revved the motor. Johnny stepped out of the rotor wash and turned his back, hand on hat, as the younger medic shut the door. The helicopter lifted, a cloud of dust hiding Johnny from sight. The racket of the helicopter and smell of hot engine oil replaced nature's tranquility, the clean smells of horses and greasewood. The older medic handed me a headset to communicate as he monitored Alex's vital signs.

Alex lay still, his skin grayish and clammy.

"Is he unconscious?" I asked.

"No, ma'am," said the older medic.

"I asked because he should be peppering you with a million questions about what's happening, about the helicopter, and if he'll have a cast."

"Oh, he'll have a cast. It's better if he doesn't talk. Don't worry. He's in good hands."

"Where are we going?'

"Our base is the hospital on the San Felipe reservation. It's the nearest emergency room."

"Is it any good? I mean, can't you take us as far as Albuquerque?"

"Ma'am, we may be Native Americans, but our health care is top notch," he answered.

"I didn't mean it like that. I'm a city girl, so I thought a bigger hospital might be better equipped. That's why I asked." My face flamed from embarrassment.

"Well, ma'am, your tax dollars built the Indian Health Service to provide health care to Native Americans. San Felipe is state of the art. Your son—"

"Thank you, but he's my grandson."

"Your grandson will be fine. I take my kids there. So does Bill, here. And Martin, our pilot."

Bill, the younger medic grinned. "We fix broken legs all the time. We've even been known to fix a couple of horses with broken legs. Your grandson's will be a piece of cake. After all, he can't kick us like horses can."

I wanted to feel better about going to the local hospital, but I couldn't. I tried to keep my tone light. "I've known Captain Chaos to hit, but I've never seen him kick anyone. You should be safe."

"Good. Rumor has it that some of our doctors actually went to medical school." Bill smiled wickedly at me. I nodded and shut up.

I sat in the jump seat and tried to force some tension from my back and shoulders. I could do nothing for the moment except mentally prepare for Alex's next steps. He seemed to be in good hands.

Below, the land rolled away, leaving Johnny and the horses far behind. In less than half an hour, the roar of the rotors changed. The pilot checked our airspeed and circled. With a tiny bump, he set us down at a heliport adjacent to the hospital we'd passed on the way to Navajo Springs. I was going to see the inside whether I liked it or not.

The EMTs offloaded the gurney, and nurses and orderlies wheeled Alex through the desert heat and double doors marked *Emergency*. I followed them at a slightly slower pace. My back ached from the uncomfortable jump seat, and my butt was sore from hours in a saddle. A blast of air-conditioning hit me. The team moved Alex into the examination area, where they closed the curtains. In seconds, the EMTs were pushing the empty gurney out of the emergency room and waving at me. I nodded and mouthed "Thank you." I'd call Whip once we were inside.

The pocket of my jacket vibrated. Two text messages.

One from Ducks, our so-very-British home-school teacher: *What happened to Alex?*

One from Emilie: *He'll be all right.*

I sent twin texts before sagging in relief. My two spooky watchdogs were on duty.

CHAPTER FOUR

A HOSPITAL ADMINISTRATOR approached. "Right this way. We'll take care of your son."

"Grandson." *Son! Do I really look young enough to have a thirteen-year-old son? No way.* Perhaps the administrator was being polite.

"I'm sorry. I assumed. At any rate, you need to meet with our admissions clerk to get him registered."

She led me to one chair beside of an opaque, plexiglass partition. The clerk asked about as many questions as Alex did. I recited every detail of his health for the three years I'd been a daily part of his life.

No, no previous broken bones.

Yes, he's current on his vaccinations.

Yes, even tetanus. We made certain he was protected when he, his father, and his sister went to Peru a couple of years back.

No, no known serious illnesses.

Yes, he'd run the gamut of childhood illnesses: measles, mumps, and chickenpox. No, no chronic illness like asthma.

No, no family history of cancer, heart disease, pulmonary problems.

And then came the tricky part. The clerk asked for Alex's insurance card, which was in my handbag. On the sofa in the living room at the ranch.

"I didn't take our ID with us on the trail ride, so I don't have it. My friend Johnny will bring it as soon as he gets back to his brother's ranch. Will that be acceptable?" I asked.

"Don't worry. People come in all the time without their insurance cards. When do you think your friend will get here?"

I explained about the horses, how far up the trail we were, how far we drove from the ranch. "Johnny will have to walk the horses down that trail, so he said he'll need two hours just to get back to the trailer."

I stared at the clerk when she laughed.

"I live out that way," she explained. "I've ridden that trail since I was a kid. I can judge times and distances like birds can find their navigation routes. He'll need more time than he estimated if he's leading a pair of horses. What's the rest of your friend's name?"

"Johnny Medina."

"Richie Medina's younger brother?"

"Yes."

"I used to have the biggest crush on him in high school. He was the cutest guy."

"He still is," I said.

"We never dated, but hey, a girl can dream, can't she?" The woman, who was no longer a girl, grinned and winked. "Let's give him three hours. That, plus rush hour traffic, and he should get here around seven, maybe eight."

"Rush hour?"

"There's a plant about seven miles south. It lets out at four-thirty, so he'll get caught in the backup, likely as not." She clicked her mouse a few times. "Come back to me when Johnny arrives. I'd like to see him again."

"Can I go to my grandson now?"

"Down the hall and to your right. Follow the red arrows to the emergency room."

In the examination area, a nurse pulled the curtain aside when I approached.

"Mrs. Pugh?"

Mrs. Pugh? Alex must have told them his name.

"No, I'm Mrs. Davies, Alex's grandmother. How's he doing?"

His face washed clean, his wiry, gawky body in a hospital gown, and a tent over his broken leg to support the blankets, he was pale but no longer gray-tinged.

"I'm okay, Mad Max. I'm not cold anymore."

I touched the oven-warmed blankets. Merry had similar ones during her coma. I held Alex's hand. Sure enough, his normal body temperature had returned.

"Now that you're here, we can take him to surgery. You can have a few minutes."

"Did you check him for a concussion?" I didn't worry about the bones, but after Merry's brain injury, I prayed—to a god I was no longer sure I believed in—that Alex had no such problem.

"The emergency room doctor doesn't think he has one. Alex passed all the tests and doesn't remember hitting his head. He hit his chest when he fell off the ledge. He thinks he hit the ground flat on his face and knocked the wind out."

"I didn't see him land, but from what I observed when I found him, he's probably right."

"He was lucky. A concussion could have complicated the operation. Follow me. You can stay in the waiting room outside of surgery until Dr. Running Bear comes out."

"What kind of a doctor is he?" I put my hand on the nurse's arm. I wanted an orthopedic surgeon.

"He happens to be a really good doctor who will fix your grandson." The nurse grinned before she left the curtained-off area.

Alex beckoned me over. He smiled through the pain. "What's going to happen to my vacation?"

I smoothed his hair. "Let's get that leg fixed. We'll ask Uncle Johnny for a rain check."

Alex stuck his tongue out. I laughed and stuck mine out too.

"When did he last eat?" the nurse asked as she returned with an orderly, who moved to the bed and unlocked the wheels.

I glanced at my watch. "About three hours ago. Why?"

"If he gets sick, we don't want him aspirating vomit into his lungs."

Yuck!

"Let's see. He had a sandwich around twelve-thirty, along with a bottle of water and an apple. Nothing else."

"I ate three cookies," Alex corrected me.

"Three?" I demanded.

Alex grinned. "Yup."

"He should be all right. I'll call up to let the anesthesiologist know," the nurse said.

So many moving parts. I'd had no reason to think about the risk of surgery on a full stomach for a long time.

"You didn't answer my question about Dr. Running Bear," I said.

"Why don't you ask him when you meet him?"

The orderly pushed the bed along a tiled corridor, adobe-tan walls painted with colorful murals of children playing against a sweeping panorama. They served their purpose; they soothed me as I followed Alex's bed to the elevator.

We exited the elevator into the surgical area. No peaceful paintings here. Nothing but plain, tan walls and a pair of heavy doors marked *Surgery* in red. The squeak of one off-kilter wheel brought back an unpleasant memory of the first time I saw Merry after her accident. She too was on a gurney, but so heavily bandaged that I didn't recognize her.

"Why don't you wait in there?" the orderly suggested, nodding toward the surgical waiting room. He swung his hip at a pad on the wall. "You can't go any further."

Alex disappeared. I carried his now-scuffed boots and a plastic bag with his clothes into the waiting room. A man in sky-blue surgical scrubs stood at a window, watching the lowering sun, his hands clasped behind his back.

"I love sunrises and sunsets. Don't you?" he asked.

"Yes, the promise of a new day and the promise fulfilled at day's end have special power." I dropped the bag and boots before standing next to him. The slanting rays tinted my face pinky-orange and his, a deeper, golden tan.

"I never tire of this view. The mountains hold such mystery." He didn't turn his head.

"I just got here, and already I'm in love with the land."

"Once it takes hold of you, it doesn't easily let go." The man finally turned and held out a hand. "I'm Dr. Running Bear."

"Maxine Davies."

Tall and lean, with high cheekbones and a hawk-like nose, he wore blue booties and a cap over his hair. He walked me through what he was going to do.

"All routine, Mrs. Davies. The procedure would take roughly two, maybe two and a half hours."

"I asked the nurse about your specialty, but she said to ask you. I know you're going to operate on Alex, but with all due respect, I need to be assured that you're the best, not just the best on duty." As soon as the words left my mouth, red replaced pinky-orange. Even though I had a right to question the man operating on Captain Chaos, I could have been more tactful. I started to apologize when Dr. Running Bear held up a hand.

"If it will make you feel more comfortable, Mrs. Davies, I studied pre-med at the University of New Mexico, medicine at University of Arizona, and trained in general surgery at UCLA. I've fixed over a thousand broken legs, so you have nothing to worry about."

"Thank you. I didn't mean to sound like I was vetting you."

"You were, though. I'd do the same if I had a child in a strange hospital. Anyway, he should be in recovery in a couple of hours. Are you going to wait here?"

I nodded. I had no place to go and no means of getting anywhere, and nothing could drag me away from Alex. The doctor gave me a reassuring smile, slapped the door pad, and walked into the surgical unit. I decided to go downstairs to find the cafeteria and get coffee, much as I had when Merry was critically injured. At least I wasn't worried about Alex's chances of survival.

I asked a passing orderly for directions to the cafeteria.

"Follow the green feet decals."

I did as instructed and entered a quiet, nearly empty room filled with brightly-colored chairs and tables. Wrapped food items lay on trays or were stacked in refrigerators. I saw healthy snacks, drinks, and the all-important, never-empty pot of coffee. No one was on duty at the cash register, but a couple of nurses came in and told me how the cafeteria worked outside mealtime.

"We're on the honor system. Everything has a price on it. Just toss money in the jar next to the register."

I picked out a carton of raspberry yogurt (seventy-five cents) and a cup of coffee (one dollar). I reached for my handbag, only to remember I didn't have it. *Oh well.* I'd feed the jar after Johnny returned. I sat beside a window. The sun filled the room with warmth and light. For several minutes, I stared out at the landscape and emptied my mind. Then I closed my eyes and listened.

Every hospital had its own rhythms, its own voice, and yet all hospitals were essentially the same. People came to get treated. Some were born; others died. Hospitals encapsulated the cycle of life within their walls.

This one felt safe. Nurses and orderlies squished in and out on rubber soles; snippets of conversation floated my way; sudden bursts of laughter rang out; refrigerator compressors clicked on and off; overhead lights whispered in their own secret language.

But I couldn't sit idly when I had calls to make. I finished my yogurt, topped off my coffee, and called Whip, who answered on the first buzz.

He and Emilie were home in their Richmond townhouse, on a break from the construction project in Mississippi, now approaching its third year. It took me a few minutes to fill him on the fall, the break, and the surgery.

"I knew something was wrong, because Em's in her secret place."

Whip had finally accepted Emilie's special gift, even though he didn't understand it. Neither did I. When she was tuning in on someone's feelings, when she was putting her empathic gift to work, we called it going to her "secret"—or "special"—place. She retreated into herself, meditated, and invited what she was feeling from others to tell her what was going on.

"Tell me the truth. Is Alex going to be all right?" Whip asked. I imagined him running his hand through his hair, as he always did when he was upset.

"Yes. He broke his leg. Johnny did a terrific job in trail triage. Dr. Running Bear—"

"Did I hear you right?" I imagined Whip's eyes popping wide open.

"You did. We're in a Native American hospital with a mostly Native American staff."

"Shouldn't you be in Albuquerque or Santa Fe?" Whip demanded. Like me, he wanted the best for his son. "Hold on. Em told me not to worry about Dr. Running Bear."

"She's right," I assured him.

"Let me put Em on. She's glaring a hole in my forehead." The phone changed hands. I went through the same information dump, such as it was, with my granddaughter, certain that I was doing little beyond confirming what she already knew.

"He'll be all right. Dr. Running Bear will take good care of him. Please don't worry," Emilie said. The familiar rush of warmth from Emilie enveloped me, letting me know she was on the job. We talked for many minutes before I thumbed the cell off. An unseen feather brushed my cheek, demanding answers, too. I called Ducks, my other sensitive, who manifested his unseen presence as a soft touch like a feather on my cheek.

Time to refill my cup and check in with my best friends, Eleanor and Raney, to tell them what happened.

"You won't believe it," I said as soon as I was connected with both of them. "I'm in a hospital outside of Santa Fe."

Raney cut in before I could continue. "Are you all right?"

Eleanor added, "What happened? You've been in New Mexico, what, a couple of days?"

"Isn't it a little too soon even for you to get in trouble?" Raney teased.

I told them about the ride, the fall, the helicopter trip, and Dr. Running Bear.

"And yes, that's his name. Em says he's good."

"She would know," Eleanor said, ice cubes clinking in her pre-dinner cocktail.

"Alex is in surgery right now because the break was pretty bad."

"Sounds as though you have everything under control," Raney said.

Past experience reminded me they'd be on the next flight if I needed them. More than once, these Great Dames, part of my Manhattan bridge and 'tini group, held me up when I needed help. I'd played bridge and consumed gallons of martinis with four women for years. While I loved them all, Raney and Eleanor were special. I could always turn to them. My alter egos, they formed a Greek chorus in my life.

"I'm fine." I assured them Johnny and I were handling everything.

When I'd satisfied them, and caught up on the gossip of the last two Great Dames who weren't on the call, I took my coffee and retraced my steps to the waiting room.

A worried couple came in right as I finished texting Whip and Emilie again. I was bored and wanted to chat about normal things to keep my mind occupied with something other than Alex's surgery. The couple paused in the doorway until I closed my phone and smiled at them. We exchanged pleasantries in Spanish—I'd become fluent after two years living and working around Mexican-American construction workers. Their three-year-old daughter had a ruptured appendix, which required emergency surgery. Like me, they would stay with her until she could go home.

I sat in an unforgiving plastic chair, Alex's filthy clothing in a bag beside me, his scuffed boots on the floor. Those boots led directly to Alex's injury. But I couldn't blame them, any more than I could blame the curiosity of a thirteen-year-old on the beginning of a new adventure. I wished more than once that his boots had rubber soles, though.

###

Johnny had stopped at Hillson's Western Wear on the way from the airport to his ranch to buy Justin boots, "the best brand and the one most ranchers wear." Alex had run directly to a display of fancy dress boots.

"Hey, Uncle Johnny. I want these." He held up a pair of carved leather boots, black with red inserts.

"Put those back. They're dude boots. You want to look like a real cowboy, don't you?"

"Well, yeah." Alex cast a last loving glance at the display before sulking his way over to the flat-heeled boots Johnny held up. "They're so boring," Alex said.

"And they're just what you need." Johnny called to a salesman to measure Alex's feet.

While the men discussed the demerits and merits of flat-soled versus high heels, round toes versus pointy, I was in Alex's camp—fancy boots. A pair with fringe screamed, *Buy me!* But I wouldn't indulge myself when my grandson couldn't as well. I tried on several pairs of *ropers*, as Johnny instructed us to call them, before settling on a pair of oxbloods.

"I know you want the fancier boots, but your new ones will be more comfortable," Johnny said. "Hey, what do you think I wear? I sure don't wear dude boots to work."

We walked to the cashier, and Alex froze in front of a wall filled with every model of hat imaginable. "Can I have that one?"

He pointed to a wide-brimmed rodeo hat.

"No." No matter how Alex wheedled, Johnny didn't budge on the Stetson. "You don't need a cowboy hat. Besides, you have to earn the right to wear one. Your baseball cap will do just fine."

When Alex turned to me, I raised one finger before folding my hand into a clam shape. He shut up.

On my coffee and snack run, I found a tiny kiosk and perused the three books offered—a romance, a Western, and a thriller by one of my favorite writers. Luck was with me. I hadn't read this one yet. I left with a promise to pay for it in an hour or so. At least I'd have something to occupy my time until Johnny got there and Alex was out of recovery. I read a few chapters. I must have dozed, because the next thing I knew, Johnny kissed the top of my head. I sat upright, my neck popping.

"Hey, pretty lady. How's Alex?"

"I don't know, funny man." I looked at the clock. Seven-thirty. "The surgeon said the operation should take about two hours. It's been over four."

Johnny put his arm around me. "He'll be fine. I brought your bag, your overnight kit, and Alex's iPod. I figured he'll want his tunes when he wakes up."

"Yes. I wouldn't let him take anything electronic except his cell on the trail ride."

As if he'd been waiting for Johnny's arrival, Dr. Running Bear pushed through the double doors. He walked over, smiling. I introduced Johnny.

"I reset the bones. Whoever pulled them inside the skin did a terrific job. The tibia was nearly back in alignment." He gestured for us to sit.

I jerked my head toward Johnny. "He did."

"Are you a doctor?"

"Army medic. I set more fractures of all kinds than I care to remember."

The doctor processed the information and gave us the rundown. "Alex did fine. I put some permanent screws and a plate in his tibia, plus a couple of large, temporary screws to keep everything in place. They poke through the skin, so I don't want you to be surprised when you see him. It's standard operating procedure. The fibula will heal without screws."

"Standard operating procedure? Surgeon's humor?" I liked this doctor.

Dr. Running Bear laughed. "I didn't even realize I said that. But yes, to the humor and to my standard practice."

"The operation took longer than you anticipated." I glanced at the clock again.

"In spite of the good job Mr. Medina did, I had to clean a lot of debris out of the wound. Several small blood vessels suffered punctures. We closed them." Dr. Running Bear pulled his cap off, shaking shoulder-length black hair free.

"What else?" I asked. The surgeon was holding something back. Had Emilie been here, she'd have asked the question. The tiniest flush of acknowledgment rippled through my body.

"Alex had some difficulty breathing once we got him under, probably due to his broken ribs and any dust he inhaled when he fell. We had to continually adjust the oxygen-gas mixture to keep him sedated."

"He'll be fine, though?" Johnny asked.

"He will."

"How long will he be here?" I asked.

"I'd like to keep him for a day or two. Inhaling dust can lead to pneumonia, so I'm starting him on intravenous antibiotics just to be safe." Dr. Running Bear looked at me. "Do you live around here?"

"We don't. Right now, Alex, Johnny, and I live in RVs with the rest of our weird extended family on a construction site in Mississippi." I gave Dr. Running Bear the short version of our living arrangements. For the past two years, the extended family lived in a series of RVs, plus a retired John Madden bus where our home-school teacher lived. The RVs were surrounded by construction equipment, smaller trailers, and large tents housing the crew of highway engineers and contractors that helped rebuild after Katrina. I thought about the impossibility of keeping Alex quiet and his wound clean.

"Taking him to an RV park is not an acceptable option," Dr. Running Bear said.

"It's not even an RV park. It's a group of RVs and trailers in a fenced enclosure adjacent to a major construction zone."

"Even riskier. We'll talk about release protocols after we see how he progresses." The doctor rose to leave. "I'll send a nurse to bring you to the recovery area. He should be waking up in little more than an hour."

"Good. That'll give me time to go through the insurance business downstairs," I said.

"The cafeteria stays open all night, if you're hungry." Dr. Running Bear shook my hand and then Johnny's before he returned to the surgical suite.

"We might be here longer than we planned, huh, pretty lady?"

"Maybe I should take Alex to Richmond or New York. I could have my company send our corporate jet. Or I could charter a plane." *Commercial aviation is out of the question.*

"Here's pretty nice, too. If you had to, you could stay at the ranch. My brother wouldn't mind, and my sister-in-law would be glad to have you," Johnny said.

"Let's see how everything goes. I don't want to be a bother, funny man."

"Fat chance of that, pretty lady." Johnny put his arm around me, and we went down to admissions to make Alex's stay legal.

"By the way, one of your high school admirers is looking forward to seeing you again." I winked. "I forgot her name, but she remembers you as being really cute."

Johnny turned red as a desert sunset.

CHAPTER FIVE

I'M SURE I looked as fatigued as I felt, because after leaving admissions, Johnny led me to the side of a corridor, where we paused.

"Alex will be fine." He pressed me against the wall, moved in close, and kissed me.

I took a deep, albeit shaky, breath. "I hope so." During the wait, I'd tried to shrug off my concerns, but my mind was having none of it. I rested my head against his chest and listened to his heartbeat, strong and steady.

"It's seems like I can't plan anything, or go anywhere, without something happening to a member of our family, or something happening to upset our plans. I'm so tired of it."

"I understand. This was supposed to be Alex's grand adventure. None of us planned for him to break his leg and spend a night or two in the hospital. Am I right?"

"You are. I looked forward to getting away and kicking back for a while. I wanted Alex to be a free-range kid while I loafed and left some of my duties behind." I looked up at Johnny. "And now this."

"It's only a small setback. We'll reschedule."

I nodded but wondered how we would fit in Alex's birthday gift again. Our schedules were squeaking tight. The last time we did anything just for the hell of it was when Johnny and I escaped the construction site for a weekend in the French Quarter. That trip ended in a pillow fight. I grinned at how silly we'd been.

"Do you remember Eleanor's advice after Merry's funeral?" Johnny turned me gently and led me down the corridor toward the lobby stairs. The only light coming through the tall front windows was from halogen lights in the hospital turnaround. Full dark shrouded the hospital.

"You mean about leaning on others and not feeling I have to do everything myself?"

"That's the one." Johnny kept his arm across my shoulders. "Let me help."

We walked the corridors between wards to give me sorely needed exercise. My body craved the endorphin rush a strenuous workout offered as much as it craved coffee, good food, and good sex. Alex wouldn't be in the hospital long enough to need a workout room, but the corridor in front of us presented a straightaway perfect for roller blading. I'd done plenty of that in Richmond and Mississippi, as well as biking.

"Dr. Running Bear said Alex will probably be able to leave tomorrow or the next day. There's no need to set up a shift schedule," I said.

"If he's here longer, we'll alternate. You take one night, and I'll take the next," Johnny said.

"That would work. We can't both stay. His room's pretty small." I planned to commandeer a reclining chair for the night.

"I don't want you to get overly tired, pretty lady." He hugged me. "This is supposed to be a vacation for you, too. Besides, I want some quality time with you alone."

"And it's all right if you get overly tired, funny man? Where would that leave me?" I tapped his chest.

"We both need to stay alert, but I'd rather be here with you. We have to focus on Alex's wellbeing."

"Alex and I aren't going anywhere. You should go back to the ranch for the night," I told him.

"Okay. Do you want me to bring anything special in the morning?"

"Call me before you leave. I'll need a change of clothes and another book. I put a couple on the table next to our bed. I'll know what else after I've talked with Dr. Running Bear." I rubbed my temples.

Johnny kissed more than the top of my head before leaving for the ranch. I walked him out to his truck and watched until his taillights faded into a faint, pink smudge.

Regardless of posted warnings against the use of cell phones anywhere on hospital grounds, I noticed them poking from staffers' pockets. When I made a dozen calls throughout the course of the evening, no one paid attention.

I checked in with Alex before trying to settle in to wait for morning. A blood pressure cuff on his right arm pumped itself up every thirty minutes, a clip on his right forefinger monitored his pulse oxygen levels, a cannula looped around his ears with plastic prongs in his nose delivered oxygen to his lungs, and an IV bag for fluids and medications dripped into his left arm. Had he been more aware, he would have pretended to be a super hero, or at least thought that all the tubes and gadgets were way cool. Had he not been monitored so closely, his room might have been quiet enough for me to concentrate on my new book. As it was, I was just too restless to sit and watch a child sleep.

I did another walkabout an hour or so after Johnny left. I paced corridors and checked in to see if the cafeteria was open all night, as Dr. Running Bear promised. It was, but I discovered I wasn't hungry. I was coffee-d out as well.

I stepped outside and sucked in fresh, unfiltered air. The hospital was far enough from human density that I detected no traces of city pollution, no light smudging the sky. A highway of stars stretched across the night sky; the moon was a sliver; the planets winked and laughed in the void. *Are there sentient beings up there looking down at us, wondering if there's intelligent life here? Or would they think the planet is populated by idiots and blowhards?*

I sat on a carved bench beside the door, my back to the emergency entrance, and imagined I was sailing away on the Milky Way. Other than when my last husband and I were on our sailboat in the middle of the Atlantic, I was rarely in a place where I could so vividly see the galaxy. In the distance, flashing red lights heralded the approach of a silent ambulance.

On my return to the medical-surgical ward, where Alex had been transferred, I met another restless parent, the father from the waiting room. He and his wife had slipped out while I was dozing and were gone when Johnny woke me.

"How's your little girl?" We stopped in the middle of the corridor.

"She's going to be all right. She goes home tomorrow after the final tests and check up with the doctor." He stretched his shoulders.

"That's great."

"Yes. Her sisters miss her. They're staying with their aunt," he said. "How is your grandson?"

"Groggy, but doing all right. Thanks for asking." I continued on to Alex's room, where I found him asleep. He'd been in and out of consciousness, still under the effect of the anesthesia. I sat by his bed and called Whip. It might be close to the middle of the night in Richmond, but we'd spoken an hour or so earlier. He and Emilie would still be awake.

"You and Em should come out." I massaged one temple, where a persistent headache had moved in rent free. "Alex is going to be here for a day or two, nothing long-term or frightening. Nothing like it was with Merry, but he's still a kid. He'll want to see you two."

Smells of disinfectant and alcohol, the snap of vinyl gloves, and the not-quite-silent rubber-soled nurses' shoes threw me back to our long vigil at Merry's bedside. Either Whip or I had stayed with her around the clock while she was in a medically-induced coma to reduce swelling in her brain.

I sat straight. If the small of my back didn't touch the back of the padded chair, I would stay alert and on guard against any bogeymen that might threaten my grandson.

"I agree. Em's checking flights as we speak." Whip's pacing echoed through the phone. His habit of bouncing off walls when upset or nervous might have been compounded by his incarceration—after he was wrongly charged with Merry's murder—but he had always been antsy.

After a minor shuffle in the background, Emilie took the phone from her father.

"Mad Max, I have the flight information." Emilie booked seats from Richmond through Houston and into Albuquerque the next day. She read off the details. "I'll text you and Uncle Johnny."

"Terrific. Do you need Uncle Johnny to pick you up at the airport?" I asked.

"No. Dad said we'll rent a car. I called Mr. Ducks. He's leaving New York about the time we leave Richmond. We'll meet him at the airport in Albuquerque."

"He doesn't need to come."

"He knows that."

Whip came back on the phone after another muffled conversation with Emilie.

"Talked with Johnny. Got the coordinates to the hospital. Be there as soon as we can. You staying the night?"

I explained my concern about Alex waking up in a strange room. Hospitals were bad enough for adults, but for children they could be terrifying.

"After the first night, I'll return to the ranch," I said.

"Good."

"I want to be sure Alex isn't scared if he wakes up alone in the middle of the night."

"I'm not scared." Alex opened his eyes and tried to focus. "Hey, way cool."

"Your son just woke up and saw the pins sticking out of his soft cast. He's in traction," I narrated for Whip.

"My leg hurts," Alex said.

"I don't doubt it. I'll see if you can have something to help. Do you want to talk with your dad and Em?"

Alex held out his hand for the phone.

I found a nurse, told her Alex was in pain, and stood in the doorway while she gave him an injection through the intravenous line. Alex mumbled "mooph" and dropped the phone on the bed. I stepped into the hall to finish my call.

"Are you all right, Mad Max?" Emilie asked.

"I am, but being in the hospital brings back so many bad memories. I'm trying not to think about all those hours I spent at your mother's bedside." *As if trying not to think about something works.*

"It's not the same, though. Alex broke his leg. Mom broke her head," Emilie said.

She was right. Alex's broken bones did not compare with the traumatic brain injury my daughter had suffered. I reassured Emilie that everything would be fine. I'd see her the next day.

"I love you," Emilie said.

"I love you, too, dear child." I thumbed the phone off. No sooner had I done that than the phone buzzed again.

"Hello."

"I say, how is Captain Chaos?" Ducks never failed to cheer me up.

I gave him the twenty-second post-op update.

"I'll be there tomorrow afternoon."

"You don't have to come," I said.

"I want to. Where the hell is—*Al-byu-kwer-kwee*?" Ducks' British accent completely butchered the word.

"It's *Al-beh-kerk-key*." I was laughing so hard I could barely speak. "Well, since you made flight reservations, you know it's in New Mexico, silly."

"Oh my. I'm about to go into the Wild Wild West, am I?"

I leaned against the wall outside Alex's room. "You are. And before you ask, there are lots of Indians around here. Alex's surgeon is named Running Bear."

"Right. Anyway, I get in an hour earlier than Whip and Em. We'll come out together. Be thinking about what I can do to help."

"Bring his lessons and homework."

"I will."

CHAPTER SIX

BREAKFAST AND LUNCH passed without Johnny arriving, although we talked or texted at least twice an hour. I knew where he was and what he was doing, and he knew where I was and what I was doing. After I talked with Dr. Running Bear, I changed my mind; one of us would stay with Alex around the clock. Johnny promised to bring the things I needed for a couple of days at the hospital. He grouched at not having me all to himself. I grouched at me for the same reason.

Just past one, Johnny walked in with a bag of my necessities and Alex's Game Boy. Alex and I exhausted the limited morning television schedule, which was designed for stay-at-home women and not restless thirteen-year-old boys. The Game Boy would keep him in bed until Dr. Running Bear told him he could move around the ward.

"How was last night?" Johnny sat with me at a cafeteria table, where we found fresh iced tea. He already knew the medical details, so I assumed he was asking about me.

"Fitful."

"For whom, you or Alex?"

"Yes." Both of us twitched and fidgeted all night. When Alex's pain medications wore off, he moaned and thrashed; I couldn't get comfortable in the recliner an orderly had rolled in to replace the straight-backed chair.

We took our tea back to the ward to wait for our extended family. The sixty-mile drive from Albuquerque to the hospital would take less than an hour at the speed Whip normally drove.

The wall clock in the room ticked three. Johnny had commandeered a chair from the waiting room and stretched out his legs, pulling his ball cap over his eyes to doze. I used the time to get lost in my book. I was smack in the middle of a tense standoff between an assassin and the feds when I heard a commotion in the hallway. Emilie threw herself into my arms as I stood.

"Mad Max! How is he?"

"Awake. He's eating a little, but the antibiotics are upsetting his stomach."

Right on cue, Alex retched. Johnny woke and held a metal pan under his chin to catch the discharge.

"See?"

"Yuck."

"He's still on antibiotics?" Whip asked. He and Ducks brought up the rear. Both men kissed my cheeks, earning a mock-jealous glare from Johnny.

"Hail, hail, the gang's all here," I said. I hugged Whip and Ducks. Their arrival shifted responsibility from my shoulders to theirs. Even if the shift was temporary, I'd take it, accustomed as I'd become to sharing duties with the men in my life.

Johnny explained the possibility of infection from the open wound. "It's just in case. He's been on them since he came out of surgery."

"Hey, thanks for helping, Johnny. Glad you were there to take care of his leg." Whip lightly punched his best friend on the bicep.

Whip and Emilie approached Alex in time to see him cough, gag, and vomit a string of bile-flecked gruel. He fell back on his pillows and smiled wanly at his father and sister. Ducks remained in the doorway with Johnny and me.

"Double yuck." Emilie took the metal, kidney-shaped pan from Alex's hand and put it in the sink. She looked around for another one. When none was in sight, she washed the soiled pan and returned it to the bedside table.

"I hate this medicine." Alex wiped his mouth with a tissue. He sipped his water, waited to be sure it would stay down, and took a second sip. "It makes me so sick. Dad, can you tell them to stop it?"

The nausea often caught him unawares. He was suffering as much as his mother had with morning sickness when she was carrying him, although in her case nausea continued all day for nine months.

"Dr. Running Bear should be in soon to check on you. We'll ask him if he can order a different antibiotic," I said.

Emilie looked at the contraption suspending her brother's leg. She ran a hand over the soft cast and half shut her eyes. She headed for Ducks and me and we moved into the corridor, out of Alex's hearing and line of sight.

"His leg is infected. I can feel more heat than should be there." Emilie closed her eyes again. From her secret place, she examined her brother. "There's something else. I can't figure out what it is. Mr. Ducks, what do you feel?"

Ducks nodded. "I agree. Something isn't right. That cough needs to be monitored."

I'd attributed my concern to the general apprehension I endured whenever anything threatened my grandchildren or Johnny. But I also worried about the cough. He didn't have it when we brought him in—I assumed his body was fighting off the dust he inhaled, like Dr. Running Bear suggested, but during the night I'd dreamed about heat in Alex's shin and something crawling in his lungs.

None of us said anything more. We'd wait for the doctor before scaring the shit out of anyone but each other.

Within an hour, Dr. Running Bear came through on his afternoon rounds. I was in the bathroom when he arrived, so Johnny introduced him to the family. I returned in time to see the doctor shake hands with Whip before grasping first Emilie's and then Ducks' hands. He stared deeply into their eyes, a flicker of awareness passing between them.

Dr. Running Bear opened Alex's cast to look at the wound. "There's some puffiness around the incision, maybe a little more than is normal. We have him on antibiotics to prevent any possible infection. I wouldn't worry, but I'll order a blood test, just to be safe."

Another "just to be safe." Is it more than that?

The doctor replaced the cast and pulled the blanket up to Alex's chest, but not before Emilie and I had a good look at the incision. It was more than a little puffy and red. *The leg shouldn't be that color.* Warmth flowed through me, and a feather attacked my cheek. I was not alone. The doctor gave Emilie an infinitesimal nod. He knew that we knew he was downplaying the seriousness of the infection to keep Alex quiet and calm.

"Tell me how you're feeling." During the early morning hours, a nurse had hooked Alex to a more complicated machine to monitor his vital signs. Dr. Running Bear scanned Alex's medical chart on his laptop and glanced at the new screen.

"Can you change my antibiotics? These make me really sick," Alex said. "I don't feel like eating because I puke."

The doctor reviewed the chart, noted the elevated temperature on a monitor, and assured Alex he'd order a medication that was easier on the stomach. "How's your pain?"

"Okay, most of the time."

"Don't be a hero. If your leg hurts, ask the nurse for something. I would. Broken bones hurt like the devil, and bone surgery is one of the most painful you can have."

Alex gritted his teeth.

"Where does it hurt?" Dr. Running Bear asked.

"My chest. It's hard to breathe. I can't seem to get any air deep in my lungs. I want to cough, but I'm afraid I'll puke." Alex looked for the pan in case he needed it.

"Go ahead and cough. That's your brain telling your body it needs to get rid of any gunk in your lungs. I'll prescribe some medication for the nausea, although that should pass once we get you on a different antibiotic." Dr. Running Bear had Alex sit up and listened to his lungs. He didn't say anything. He put his stethoscope away. "Does anyone have any questions?"

Whip jerked his head toward the door. He, Johnny, and the doctor walked into the hall and nearly out of sight. Emilie plumped the pillows, and I pulled the blanket back up to Alex's chest. Ducks placed the kidney pan on the bed.

"Hey, Alex, Mr. Ducks said you could spend your recovery time getting a head start on the next round of lessons. Aren't you the lucky one?" Emilie teased her brother, who laughed and fell into a coughing fit. "I'm afraid your vacation is over."

"Don't make me laugh. My chest hurts too much." Alex gagged and pressed his hand to his ribcage.

I edged closer to the door to watch the hallway conversation. Their words were too low for me to hear, but when I saw Whip smile and shake the doctor's hand, I relaxed and glanced at Emilie, who was also a little calmer. We'd wait to see how the new medication worked.

A sandy-haired technician squished into the room.

"I'm Toby, your happy vampire, here to drain all of your blood. Once we find out what germs are running around in your veins, Dr. Running Bear can zap them." Toby pointed at Emilie and glared. "You, off the bed."

He set a tray on the sheet and wrapped an elastic tourniquet on Alex's right arm. Smacking the inside of the elbow, he slid a needle into the pumped-up vein and extracted several vials of blood. I looked away.

Alex crooked his elbow around a cotton pad. Toby put a Band-Aid over the pad, picked up his tray, and left.

"That chirpy vampire routine is going to get really old, really fast," I said. "I prefer my technicians competent and silent."

"Wonder why he puts on that façade," Ducks said.

CHAPTER SEVEN

WITH WHIP ON the scene, I changed plans once again, leaving Alex in his care for the night. Father and son could use some bonding time; I could use some quality Johnny time.

On the way out of the medical-surgical ward—or Med-Surg, as the nurses called it—a bustle of activity two doors away shattered the calm. Johnny elbowed me and jerked his head back down the corridor. Orderlies wheeled gurneys into two adjacent rooms. Nurses followed, as did a doctor; Toby the Vampire wasn't far behind, followed closely by two pairs of parents.

"Wonder what happened," Johnny said. He had an almost uncontrollable curiosity about wrecks and ambulances.

"I don't know." Both rooms had been empty—the girl with the rotten appendix was released early in the morning.

"Maybe we should check." Ducks half-turned back.

"Not yet." Emilie said. "We can't do anything, because there's nothing the nurses will be able to tell us."

"If it's anything, we'll find out tomorrow." I pinched Johnny's jean jacket and steered him toward the stairs. "Hey, you guys are on East Coast time. Aren't you hungry?"

"Are you kidding? I'm starved," Emilie said. She rushed ahead of the adults and skipped down the stairs.

"I could eat a horse." Ducks' appetite was a match for Johnny and Alex. When I cooked for the family, I increased the food by half again what I thought would fill them. Some days I was still a little short.

"You're out of luck, Ducks," Johnny said with a wink at me. "We ride horses out here. We don't eat them, but I know a great steakhouse near the ranch. We can be carnivores."

"Not Mad Max," Emilie called over her shoulder. If the men were carnivores, I was the opposite most of the time. While not a vegetarian, I typically ate grains and vegetables with a small amount of meat, preferring chicken or fish over beef and even pork.

On the way to the steakhouse, Johnny once again played tour guide, providing a running monologue. Ducks swiveled his head to take in as much of the vastness as possible. Emilie locked herself in her special place; I was somewhere in between. I breathed a silent thanks to Johnny for taking our minds off the injured boy we'd left behind.

We settled into a booth and placed drink orders, alcohol for the adults, iced tea for Emilie. "Okay, guys, thoughts?" Johnny said.

Ducks and Emilie shared a look that didn't include Johnny and me. I may have dreamed that Alex was in danger, but that didn't put me in the same psychic realm as my two spooks. I needed them to warn me if greater danger was present. And Johnny? He was a what-you-see-is-what-there-is kind of guy. He could analyze any situation but wouldn't go into the "Twilight Zone," as he called it. "One of us has to be grounded in reality," he often said.

"I don't like Toby," Emilie said, looking up from her menu. "I didn't like his fake behavior."

"I don't like him either," said Ducks. "There's something odd about him. I can't decipher it, but I will. He has something to hide. He's all swishy, but his behavior is too over the top to be real." Ducks closed his menu.

"What do you mean?" Johnny asked.

"He acts effeminate, with the lisp, the limp wrist, and fake swish, but it's just that—an act. He uses it to be invisible or to be dismissed by people he meets for the first time."

"Why?" Johnny set his menu aside.

"I haven't figured that out yet. Maybe he thinks if *you* think he's gay, you won't look beyond the façade. His behavior keeps people at a distance." Ducks took a long pull from his beer glass.

"And you know this because your gaydar didn't go off." I, too, closed my menu, ready to order.

"Partly," Ducks said. "I have several friends whose normal behavior is exactly like Toby's, but they're gay like I am. He isn't."

Emilie stared into space. "Why would he pretend?" Ducks also sank deeply into thought.

Meanwhile, Johnny smiled at the waiter hovering just behind his left elbow. "I'll have the T-bone."

"And how do you want that cooked?"

"Make it a cow with a fever."

The waiter nodded. "Miss?"

Emilie ordered a filet, medium rare; Ducks picked a New York strip, also medium rare. I was the odd man out as usual.

"I'll have the salsa-covered chicken breast."

The waiter left. Ducks buttered a warm sourdough roll. "You almost never order beef, Max, unless it's in stew or burgers. I never asked if you have a particular aversion."

"It has nothing to do with cows having faces, if that's what you're thinking. Chickens and pigs have faces, and I eat them. I ate too much red meat when I was a kid. We raised milk cows and beef cattle, so we had beef several times a week. One day I woke up and found I'd really lost my taste for it. The steaks smell good, but I want something that once clucked."

Our salads arrived, and I dove into mine like a starving refugee. I could have eaten twice as much of the "plants," as Johnny called greens.

"Back to Alex—we'll watch that Toby guy, but I don't think there's anything to worry about. When my niece was in here with pneumonia, he treated her really good. He's been at the hospital for maybe a dozen years. He probably got distracted by your beauty, Max, and wanted to reassure me that he wasn't a threat," Johnny said.

I punched his shoulder and blushed. The man had a way with words that led to a way with me.

"Mr. Ducks and I will check on Alex from time to time. If anything happens, we'll know it before Dr. Running Bear does," Emilie said.

She leaned across the table and speared carrots from Johnny's salad. He only ate them under duress, which meant heavy chiding from me. Johnny once told me that he didn't eat carrots because they had souls.

Emilie winked at me. "How did you find a doctor named Running Bear?"

"I didn't find him. He found me. Several nurses assured me he's the best surgeon in the hospital." I laughed. "You had the same initial reaction I did, but I like the way he talks to us. Blunt."

"I like the way he includes Alex in all decisions. He treats him with respect." Ducks ate silently for a few moments. The conversation flowed around him until he rejoined. "He didn't tell us the whole truth, though."

"Who didn't?" I asked.

"Dr. Running Bear."

"He did outside of Alex's room," Johnny said, relaying the gist of the medical update. Dr. Running Bear confirmed that they were knocking down the infection in the leg. He thought the cough would resolve itself and not turn into something worse. He planned to run tests to rule out pneumonia.

"Like I said, we need to keep an eye on Alex's leg and lungs." Ducks had said all he was going to for a while.

"You know, Em, you and Ducks should take your show on the road," said Johnny, his eyes twinkling. "Spooks R Us. Think of the money you guys could make."

Emilie had no interest in exploiting her gift. She worked with a therapist for several years to learn to control it. When she used it to help people or protect them from danger, she was fine. If she ever tried to use it for profit, her therapist said she'd become deathly ill. Right now, her brother was her complete focus.

We chatted about their flights into Albuquerque. Emilie said theirs was really bumpy just before they landed. Ducks' plane had slewed sideways as it approached the runway.

"You hit the afternoon thermals," Johnny said.

"And how. The plane bounced all over the sky for about ten minutes. Several people screamed, and a couple of children got sick." Emilie cut a bite of filet. "I didn't do either. I'm getting really good at flying."

"We had a couple of sick passengers as well. I say, I vastly prefer flying in your private jet, Max. At least I have legroom and the coffee and tea are always hot," Ducks said.

"My plane would have slewed, too," I said.

"True, but I'd have ridden out the slew in comfort."

Ducks often accompanied me on my corporate jet from Biloxi to the general aviation airport at Teterboro in New Jersey, just outside of New York City. After my third and last husband died in an experimental plane crash, I inherited his engineering business, which was invested in determining alternate fuels that could be used safely in transportation. I went home for monthly board meetings; Ducks went home to shop and visit friends.

"So, tell us, Ducks, are you set to sail with Max and Em?" Johnny shook Worcestershire sauce on his steak.

"I'm ready to pack. As soon as Max says it's a go, I'll meet them in Key West. I'm looking forward to getting back on the water. Maybe do a little scuba diving when we reach port in the Virgin Islands."

Johnny shuddered.

"What? You don't like scuba diving?" Ducks asked.

"I don't like the ocean," said Johnny. "I stay out of salt water."

"Come to think about it, I've never seen Uncle Johnny swimming," Emilie said, attacking her baked potato with a gusto normally reserved for Alex.

"And you never will."

CHAPTER EIGHT

THE NEXT MORNING, Johnny, Ducks, Emilie, and I arrived at the hospital to find families milling around in the lobby and an ambulance idling in the emergency bay, lights flashing. The day before had been quiet until we left. My initial impression was that San Felipe served a steady stream of routine injuries and ailments, but little else unless there was an accident on the highway. This hubbub seemed unusual. I shot a look at Emilie and Ducks, who responded with small nods.

"Whatever it is, it's getting worse." Sweat beaded on Emilie's upper lip, a sure sign that she was in her secret place.

Ducks stared at the family, evaluating their concern. He jerked his chin toward the crowd. "They're terrified."

Johnny's eyes clouded. "The sooner we get Alex out of here, the better. He'll be safer at the ranch."

Safer? We left the lobby to see if Alex had made enough progress to leave. We found Whip in his room, looking tired but relieved.

"Had a good talk with Dr. Running Bear," he said in greeting. Alex was out of traction, although the screws still poked through his cast. His temperature returned to normal, and the swelling diminished around the incision.

"He's responding well to the different antibiotic," said a mousy nurse, who'd followed on my heels. "You just missed Dr. Running Bear. He's living up to his name today. We had a rush of admissions last night."

"It looks like another one came in just now." The nurse moved back down the hall and I moved to Alex's bedside, and leaned over to kiss his cheek.

"Alex has a date with the physical therapist within the hour." Whip stretched cramped shoulders. I should have warned him that the reclining chair wasn't very comfortable.

"We're here to give you a break," Johnny said. "Come down and have a cup of coffee."

The three men left Emilie and me alone with our now restless boy, who said he hadn't vomited once on the new medicine.

"Mad Max, hospital food sucks," Alex complained. He picked at the cast, and I swatted his hand away.

"Yesterday you didn't give a crap about the food," Emilie said. "Nothing tastes good coming back up."

Alex stuck his tongue out at his sister and laughed before falling into a coughing fit. Emilie moved to the side of the bed. She watched Alex's face contort, his chest heave, as he tried to clear whatever was in his lungs. He tried to draw a deep breath, but stopped.

"My chest hurts so bad."

"Don't forget you have two broken ribs," I said. "Uncle Johnny said it could be a couple of weeks before they stop hurting."

Emilie and I shared a look of concern over his head. The antibiotics worked on the infection in his leg, but not on his lungs.

The physical therapist came to exercise Alex. She put him through a series of leg lifts, which caused him to groan. "I know it hurts, but you have to strengthen the muscles."

"My chest hurts worse than my leg does."

"I'll teach you how to tighten your tummy muscles to help with the exercises. I'll be right back with a pair of crutches. No matter how much your chest hurts, you need to get out of bed. It will help with that cough. We don't want it to turn into pneumonia, do we?"

When we were alone again, Alex bitched about how much it hurt to raise his leg. I ignored him. Emilie stared into the distance as if the windowless wall were transparent. Five minutes passed before the therapist returned with kid-sized crutches.

"Okay, I want you to clench your abdominal muscles." She laid her hand on Alex's stomach. "Tighten here. Good. Now swing both legs off the bed slowly. You can put your good foot under the cast and lift if that hurts less."

Alex bit his lower lip and did as he was told. The therapist adjusted the length of the crutches and showed Alex how to put his weight on his hands and not his underarms.

"Your hands are tougher than your armpits. They'll get sore, but if you bear all your weight on your underarms, you'll irritate the skin and get a rash."

Alex took a few tentative steps to get used to swinging the dead weight of his cast.

"Keep the cast in front of you," the therapist said. "Lead with it. You'll be better balanced than if you keep it behind the crutches."

"And no being the terror of the ward." I didn't want him barreling down the hall until he was steadier. Strike that. I didn't want him barreling down the hall. Period.

"Hey, Captain Chaos, no racing," Emilie called.

Dr. Running Bear turned a corner in time to see Alex shuffling along as fast as he could. "I see where you got your nickname."

"Yeah, well." Alex returned to his bed. He was sweating from the effort.

The therapist praised him. "I want you to walk every two hours, but don't try to get out of bed by yourself yet. Call a nurse to help you. We don't want you to fall. Walk to the end of the hall and back. Walk slowly."

"Let's not break any more bones, okay? Much as I like you, I want you to go home," said Dr. Running Bear.

Toby slipped into the room and chirped, "Time for your daily bloodletting."

We held a family council in the hospital cafeteria to talk about the next steps in Alex's recovery. Dr. Running Bear planned to release him in another day or two, but he wouldn't allow him to return to the construction site. We had to be in a cleaner environment, closer to doctors who could monitor his recovery. He'd need outpatient surgery to remove the screws in a couple of weeks.

"We have great doctors in New York," I offered. I'd been on the losing end of the bring-the kids-to-New-York argument many times in the past. After their mother was murdered, I felt the best place for them was my Manhattan apartment. The novelty of living in a huge city would be good therapy. Their father wanted nothing to do with that. "They'll live with me," he'd said.

Again, Johnny volunteered his brother's guest house. "Max, stay at the ranch until his incision heals. Once there are no open wounds, you can come back to Mississippi. My sister-in-law would love to have you. She's really good with kids, too."

"That's not a bad idea," Ducks said. "He can continue his lessons through the Internet and email while he recuperates. We can text and talk by phone to get a jump start on the next term."

Emilie remained in her special place. When she re-emerged, her brow was creased, her eyes dark and troubled. Ducks stared at her. Had I not been looking directly at her, I'd never have noticed Emilie and Ducks sharing an unspoken message.

"What?" I said. "You feel something. I can see it."

She shook her head. "I do, but I don't know what it is. I don't feel right about something, but it's just too vague to have a name or face."

"A name? A face? You mean, like a person?" Whip asked.

"Yes." The word came out in a long string of syllables. She shook her head again. "I don't know. Maybe it'll become clearer soon."

Over a second cup of coffee, we decided as a group that it made little sense for all of us to sit around and watch Alex heal. Whip and Emilie would return to their townhouse in Richmond, and Ducks to his New York apartment. Johnny would stay with me until Alex was released, then he would go back to the job site where he'd eventually be reunited with our extended family. I'd stay with Alex at the ranch until he was cleared to travel.

Whip decided to spend his last night in New Mexico with Alex. The rest of us returned to the ranch, where Johnny arranged for his brother and sister-in-law to loan me an old truck so that I could come and go as I wished. I protested that I could rent a car, only to be rather summarily smacked down. The nearest rental agency was close to sixty miles away, at the airport. Western hospitality demanded I accept the loan of the truck.

"I hope you can drive a stick," Johnny said.

"No problem." I'd learned to drive on my dad's farm truck. Nothing fancier than a three-speed standard transmission. But I had more recent experience, too. "My first Jag was a five-speed manual."

CHAPTER NINE

THE NEXT MORNING, Ducks and Emilie left to visit with Alex before heading to the airport for their late-afternoon flights. I planned to follow Johnny to the hospital to acquaint myself with the peculiarities of the old truck, whose name was Gabby. The column shift had to be wiggled three times to go from second to third, and the brake pedal was loose, but regardless of its assorted squeaks and squeals, the truck seemed sound. I parked in the visitor lot next to Johnny's truck.

When we entered the hospital together, we immediately sensed a change in atmosphere. Nurses rushed around the lobby, most with cell phones glued to ears. Orderlies ensured that the emergency room was stocked and ready to receive patients.

Is this urgency because more patients have arrived? Or is something unknown causing the apprehension I feel?

Johnny took my hand "Upstairs. We need an update from Ducks and Em." We rushed for the staircase.

"I don't know what's going on, but something significant has changed. Even dense me can feel it," I said as we turned the corner toward Med-Surg.

"Hey, guys," Ducks said, heading toward us. He pointed a finger back the way we came. "Cafeteria."

Johnny and I spun on our heels and trotted downstairs with him. We drew cups of coffee and threw money in the jar before Ducks led us to a table in a far corner. He was edgier than I'd seen him, even distraught.

"Is something wrong with Alex?"

"No. Hear me out before you rush in." Ducks blew on the coffee. I stirred cream into mine until Johnny took the spoon from my hand.

"If you stir that any more, you'll have butter."

I put my hands in my lap. Ducks sipped the coffee and wrinkled his nose before speaking. "You can feel the difference, can't you, Max? Something bad is beginning."

"Beginning?" Johnny asked.

"Yes, but I don't know what it is . . . "

Ducks had been in and out of Alex's room all morning. At one point, he and Emilie left Whip and went on a walkabout, much as I had the first night. They poked into every ward except maternity, which needed a wristband to get in. They strolled through the attached medical center where the doctors had their offices. They peeked through doors into physical therapy, located the lab where our chirpy vampire held court, and found several more general wards, each with individual patient rooms. Gone were the days of open wards. Gone were the days of double rooms, unless they were needed to accommodate a sudden influx of patients.

"We stumbled into the ICU without knowing what it was at first. That's when things got weird," Ducks continued.

"Weird? How?" Johnny asked.

They'd seen two patients in the ICU, both children, and both surrounded by medical personnel.

"Dr. Running Bear was there, as were two other doctors I didn't recognize, and several nurses. The lab tech passed us on a run with a fistful of blood samples. He smashed through the door and disappeared down the hallway. The parents hovered outside the rooms, the mothers wringing their hands and crying."

"Was there an accident?" That seemed like the most logical explanation to me.

"I don't think so. You wouldn't need blood work for an accident, would you?"

"Not usually," Johnny shook his head. "Unless there were severe injuries requiring transfusions."

"No one will give us information. A couple of nurses brushed me off with 'some children are sick.'"

"No shit," Johnny said. "From what you saw, they must be really ill. Otherwise, why the urgency?"

Ducks had run out of details. We looked at each other, rose, and carried our stale, burnt coffee upstairs, where Emilie, Alex, and Whip played cards. We needed Emilie to give us her take.

"Hey, Mad Max," Alex called as soon as he saw me. "I've been up and down the hall six times since you left. Want to see me?"

Of course, I did. Alex tossed his cards on the bed, swung his legs to the floor, and grabbed his crutches. In his excitement to show off his newly-round freedom, he forgot to call a nurse for assistance. He moved out into the corridor faster than he should have, tripping Toby in the process. Ducks jumped in time to catch Alex, but Toby dropped his tray of syringes, which rolled away or shattered.

"Goddamn it, kid, watch where you're going!"

"Hey, don't swear at my son," Whip cried, jumping to his feet—not to help with the cleanup but to confront Toby. He grabbed his arm. "It was an accident."

"Get away from me," Toby's voice rose. He shook Whip's hand off. Gone was the fake cheer. "Get back in your room until I clean up the mess you made." Johnny leaped to help.

"Don't touch anything."

Johnny and Ducks exchanged glances, as did Emilie and I. Toby's reaction was way out of proportion for a simple spill of syringes and vials. If an influx of patients caused Toby to abandon his chirpy façade, I wondered how he'd react if the situation exploded out of control.

Toby's shouts brought an orderly on the run with mops and brooms. Before Toby could warn him, the orderly swept the broken glass into a pan and dumped it. The orderly pulled a sliver from his thumb and wiped a smear of blood on the hem of his shirt.

Whip helped Alex back into his room. Alex called an apology to Toby's back, to no avail. He turned toward Ducks and his father.

"I didn't mean to trip him." Tears formed in the corners of his eyes.

Whip put an arm awkwardly around his son. Alex got tangled in his crutches and stumbled. "I know you didn't. I'll talk with Toby before I leave. He needs to apologize for his language."

Ducks and Whip helped the upset boy into bed. I promised I'd watch him walk in the evening or the next day. He had plenty of time to show me how strong he was getting. We headed out for a late lunch after Alex assured us he'd be fine alone for a couple of hours. He'd play with his Game Boy while we were gone.

We slipped out to a small mom-and-pop restaurant. We needed time to talk. Homey smells of meatloaf and macaroni and cheese welcomed us.

Emilie started with, "Something bad is coming. I don't know what it is. I keep trying to feel the source of danger, but I can only get so far. I have jumbled impressions of one or more people involved. Everyone's general unease gets in the way. You're getting in my way, too, Mr. Ducks."

"Me?"

"You're partly blocking me."

"I see. Sorry."

Emilie closed her eyes.

"You described what I sense perfectly, Em. It's like a dome fell over the hospital, trapping something evil inside." Ducks scanned a menu and decided on his meal.

A bead of sweat formed on Emilie's upper lip before she answered. "It's not just in the hospital. It's outside, too."

"What's outside?" I shoved the menu aside, no longer interested in food.

"Something evil," Ducks and Emilie said in unison.

CHAPTER TEN

WHIP HAD ONE last, long talk with Dr. Running Bear after lunch. Alex was making progress and should be released the day after next. The doctor stood firm against releasing him before his lungs cleared, however.

"You guys can go on home," Dr. Running Bear told Johnny and me. Johnny insisted that we'd stay.

I was comfortable with the family leaving. We agreed they should catch their flights as planned. Emilie could do nothing here that she couldn't do from Richmond or Mississippi. Ducks wanted to get ready for Emilie's birthday sailing trip, even though it now looked like it, too, would be postponed until Alex could leave New Mexico. That wouldn't matter—sailing season in the American Virgin Islands lasted all year unless a hurricane was brewing.

"We won't be far away," Ducks said.

The odd urgency in the hospital didn't seem to bother Alex. It wasn't centered on him. Unfortunately, his cough worsened the following night. He complained of muscle aches, ran a fever, and wasn't interested in eating. I worried his leg had become infected again, so I asked one of the nurses to look at the wound.

"It's healing well. No swelling. Does that hurt?" she asked, pressing near the incision. Alex shook his head and coughed wetly. She pulled her stethoscope from a pocket and listened. "I want Dr. Running Bear to check your chest again."

"I don't like this, Johnny," I whispered in the lounge down the corridor from Alex's room. The parents whose children had arrived two days before huddled inside themselves, eyes stricken. I nodded at them, but they didn't respond. I probably wouldn't have either, were I in their position. *Except, I am.* "He's never sick. Do you remember him ever turning down food, the first day notwithstanding?"

"No. He'd rather try to out-eat me," Johnny said affectionately.

"No matter what the nurse said, could the infection Em felt in his leg have returned?" I paced a circle. "Alex doesn't know what's wrong or where it's wrong. He just feels crappy."

Johnny made a pest of himself trying to find someone to talk to us. Most of the nurses were swamped, and Dr. Running Bear needed roller blades or a Segway to move any quicker. Johnny returned alone. Even though Alex was sleeping, I wasn't sure he couldn't hear us. When Merry was in her coma, Whip and I assumed that she could hear us, so we talked with her all the time. In this case, Johnny and I left the room to speak in private.

"What's wrong?" I didn't like his expression. My big, strong friend looked worried. Very worried.

"I don't know. I asked one nurse if Alex could have MRSA, but she said if there's no rash or other skin discoloration near the incision, we shouldn't worry." Methicillin-resistant Staphylococcus aureus, or MRSA, had come to the public's attention recently through several high-profile cases of professional athletes sickened or felled by this new drug-resistant bacterium. According to the newspapers, it flourished in places where groups of people lived or worked in close quarters. College dorms, nursing homes, health clubs, and hospitals were fertile breeding grounds.

A circuit completed, we returned to Alex and peeled back the blanket to see for ourselves. The bandage showed no bloody seepage, and the skin above and below it felt cool to the touch. Alex groaned and coughed deeply. I grabbed the kidney pan and caught a stream of vomit just in time. Johnny gagged.

"You are not allowed to vomit in here. Do you hear me?" I called over my shoulder. With my hands full with Alex, I didn't need Johnny getting sick as well.

"I feel awful," Alex said as he fell back, his skin pale and clammy.

I laid a hand on his forehead. Hot. I looked across the bed at Johnny. Without a word, he turned and left the room. I sponged Alex's face and gave him water to rinse his mouth. His stomach convulsed with dry heaves.

An unfamiliar nurse bustled in, Johnny close on her heels.

"Let's see what's going on," she said.

I stepped aside and watched her go through her routine. Temp: two degrees above normal. Breathing: raspy. Blood pressure: elevated. Nausea and vomiting.

"If it's any consolation, young man, you're not the only person in this hospital who feels like this. We admitted three more overnight. I'll send one of the doctors in to see you as soon as one is free."

Three other cases? "Is this some kind of flu?" I demanded.

"We're not sure. We're taking blood to see if it's viral or bacterial, but cultures take time to grow. We're pretty sure it isn't food borne, though, since no one ate at the same place. I'll bring something for Alex's fever. I'll also let Dr. Running Bear know to stop by."

She returned a few moments later with Tylenol. The pills stayed down about five minutes.

I laid wet towels on his forehead and the back of Alex's neck—my grandmother's tried-and-true method for bringing down fevers. Johnny brought me ice water to keep the towels cold. More than an hour later, an orderly arrived, followed by the lab technician.

"I have orders to draw a blood sample before we transfer him," Toby said. "I need a cheek swab as well."

"You're transferring him? Where? Why?" I asked, awaiting an explanation. I also waited for an apology for his boorish behavior yesterday.

"I don't know. Decisions like that are above my pay grade."

Well, the question wasn't above my pay grade. Time for tiger mom to appear. I blocked the bed, folded my arms across my chest, and thrust my chin out, my most *don't-mess-with-me* pose.

Toby was having none of it. He pulled on gloves, laid out his tools of the trade, and filled several vials of blood. He pressed a bandage on Alex's arm and ran a cotton swab around Alex's mouth, causing him to gag again. All he brought up was a smear of bile.

"Off to the lab," Toby said, whisking away the samples.

The orderly unlocked the wheels on the bed and moved to its head. Knowing he couldn't answer my questions, I let the bed ease me out of the way. I fell in behind.

"No one's told us he's moving. In fact, he's supposed to be discharged tomorrow," I told the orderly.

"I don't know about a discharge. I have orders to move your son—"

"Grandson."

"Grandson. Dr. Running Bear wants him closer to three other patients until he knows what's going on."

"What do you mean, 'until you know what's going on?'" My heartbeat quickened, and I felt lightheaded. Johnny grabbed my arm, but I shook him off. "I'm not going to faint."

We followed Alex and the orderly through several unmarked, automatic doors. At the end of another long corridor, the orderly wheeled Alex into a private room. Not totally private, since one wall was made of glass. I'd been in my share of ICUs before; this sure as hell looked like an ICU.

"Johnny?" Before I could finish, Dr. Running Bear rounded the corner and beckoned to us. "Alex, we'll be right back."

Alex had dozed off.

"What the hell is going on?" Johnny burst out before I could. My alpha male left me to recover my composure.

"We don't know, Mr. Medina. We have several cases of what looked at first to be bronchitis, but this isn't the season for upper respiratory ailments. We've called around to private doctors, but no one has seen an uptick. Right now, it looks like we have a cluster of flu-like illnesses. I just don't know which one." Dr. Running Bear rolled his head around, vertebrae creaking like rusty hinge. "I want Alex close by. If we treat all the patients in one place, it's easier on the nursing staff."

"But why is he in the ICU?" Tiger mom surged. "Is he in any danger?"

"Don't read too much into being in the ICU, Mrs. Davies. The suite was empty. When you think about it, it makes the most sense. We can watch all the children at the same time and in the same place. We'll have a single, rotating nursing staff keeping everything in order. We're going to hook each child to a series of machines to monitor vital signs."

When Merry was in a coma, she'd looked like the bionic woman. I tried to smile. "Alex will think that's way cool once he feels better."

"It is way cool. Our medical facility is state of the art, so don't worry." Dr. Running Bear looked around. "By the way, did you granddaughter leave?"

My pulse jumped. "Why? Is she in danger?"

He forestalled my panic with a hand. "Not at all."

"You thought if she were still here, you could use her help, didn't you?" I stared at the tall Native American. I saw a flicker of recognition in his eyes.

"Yes."

"Don't worry," Johnny said. "She and Mr. Ducks are on duty. They're there if you need them."

I was too distracted processing the situation to realize that Johnny had taken charge again. Had I not known him as well as I did, I'd have felt shoved aside, even marginalized. I didn't, however; I welcomed his help. Dr. Running Bear patted my shoulder, shook Johnny's hand, and responded to a bell-like code over the loud speaker.

"That's me. See you later."

CHAPTER ELEVEN

JOHNNY WENT BACK to the ranch after a skimpy cafeteria meal. I walked him to his truck, patted Gabby on the fender, and waited until taillights faded to black. The Milky Way beckoned. I circled the building, pulled dry, dusty desert air deep into my lungs, and cleansed my spirit. I noticed two dark shapes slip out of the back exit and disappear toward the employee parking lot.

Since I was walking that way anyway, I followed at a discrete distance. A man climbed into a truck; a woman stood talking to him before vanishing back into the hospital. I continued my walk. An hour later, I re-entered the hospital through the main door and climbed to the second floor.

"Why don't you change into something better for sleeping?" A nurse held out a pair of scrubs.

Grateful, I shed my own clothes and got ready for my recliner. My thriller failed to keep my attention, however; I dozed.

Sometime in the middle of the night, the atmosphere in the hospital shifted. Not fully awake, yet not asleep either, I sensed the change, but had no frame of reference as to what caused it. I kept my breathing deep and steady as if still asleep, while my hearing picked up tiny sounds; my skin detected air currents that didn't come from the overhead vents. Fighting the urge to shiver or scream, I waited to see what would happen. My teeth ached in my effort to prevent my jaws from chattering.

Alex rolled over and got tangled in his tubes, setting off a low, beeping alarm. Quicker than a jiffy, the hospital came back to normal. My cell buzzed with an incoming text.

The evil left for a while, but it will be back. Stay vigilant. I'm here, Ducks wrote.

Stiff thumbs worked the keys. *Ducks, who is it and what does it want?*

I don't know.

A nurse I hadn't seen before responded to the beeping alarm.

"Now, don't pull this out. It'll help you breathe," she told Alex, who had briefly roused but was already asleep again. She glanced at the rest of his vital signs, tapped a few keys on her laptop, and turned toward the door. "I'll be back in a few minutes with some things to make him more comfortable."

The nurse left before I could read her nametag. Alone, I had nothing to do but wait and fret, fret and wait. An hour after dawn, I called Whip.

"Dr. Running Bear says he has everything under control, even though they moved him into the ICU. He thinks the fever could just be a temporary setback," I said.

"But I thought it broke when Alex started responding to the antibiotics for his leg."

"So did I, but what if the two aren't related? What if this fever wasn't caused by the leg infection, but by something else?" I wondered.

"By what else?"

"I have no clue."

"How was he last night?" Whip asked.

"He was about the same when Johnny left around nine. The medical staff didn't expect any change in Alex's condition, nothing serious enough to warrant both of us staying."

"Do you think he made the wrong decision? Maybe you both should have stayed?" Whip's tone carried his disapproval of the "casual" way we were caring for his son.

"No."

"I'd have stayed," he said.

I sat in silence for several moments. *Is Whip right? Are we somehow shirking our responsibilities?* He'd shirked his to Merry often enough before her accident; he once equated being a good husband and father with being a good provider. That didn't absolve me of laxity, except I hadn't been lax. I closed my eyes and drew in a single deep breath. "I know you would have, but Johnny's no more a doctor than you or I are. We deferred to the medical staff about Alex no longer being in danger. I will be here all the time."

I stared at the green-and-black LED display and tried to decipher what each blip meant. Temperature, pulse, blood oxygen level, and a couple more I couldn't interpret. Five separate lines and blips that should tell me if Alex was getting better or worse. *If worse, how* much *worse?*

"I'll come back."

I could hear Whip pacing, boots swishing on the thick carpet, clacking on the hardwood floors. "Whip, be reasonable. I'm perfectly capable of taking care of Alex. We've been over this."

"I know. I'm sorry. I shouldn't have implied you aren't doing as good a job as I could. I was thinking about Merry." Whip backed away from what could have turned into a useless, full-blown argument. "You shouldn't have to shoulder the responsibility alone."

"I'm not alone. Johnny's with me. And I accepted part of the responsibility after Merry died. Let me do my job, okay?"

"Johnny's not Alex's father."

"It's true. He isn't. But he's competent in ways Alex needs right now." I rubbed the back of my neck. Worry kept knotting the muscles in my shoulders. "You're not a doctor, either. We have to trust Dr. Running Bear's opinion."

"You're right. It's not as if I can do anything, medically." Whip, who hated not being in control of everything, was helpless. He entered a muffled conversation with Emilie. The only word that came through clearly was "Ducks." I was certain she was reassuring her father that she and Ducks were monitoring the situation. My son-in-law returned to our conversation, sounding defeated. "At least when Merry was in a coma, I could sit and read to her."

An incoming text buzzed. Emilie. *Call me five minutes after you hang up with Dad.*

"You still can, in a way. Text Alex often. I'll keep his cell charged," I said.

"But you can't use a cell phone in a hospital, can you? Particularly not in the ICU."

"Well, du-uh. Where do you think I am?"

Whip chuckled. "Point taken. Keep me posted."

I texted an update to Ducks, although he probably knew everything already. He responded that he was "on call" as needed.

Emilie picked up on the first buzz. "I'm in my room. I didn't want to upset Dad. He's upset enough already."

"I know. He wants to come right out and take over," I sighed.

"Don't worry. I won't let him. So tell me what happened last night," she said, all business.

"I don't know. Mr. Ducks said something evil came and left, but he told me to be alert. I don't know anything else."

"Neither do I. I slept through everything."

"How did you do that?" I asked, surprised. Emilie had never been shielded from my emotions.

"Mr. Ducks blocked me."

Hmm. "On purpose? Has he done that before?"

"Not that I know of."

The longer we talked, the less it seemed we knew what was going on.

"Mr. Ducks is going to follow Dr. Running Bear. I'll stay with you and Alex," Emilie assured me before we hung up. I could never explain to an outsider how comforting it was to have those two watching over me. With them, I was never alone.

A nurse, not the one from earlier, entered and apologized as she flipped on the overhead lights. I blinked to adjust my eyes. She set an armload of packets and a washbasin on Alex's table.

"Let me change his bed before I walk you through some things you can do to help him," she said.

"Anything. I'm not a nurse, but I raised two kids and two grandkids." I stepped aside to let her change the sheets. Her sure movements told me she'd been doing this for quite a while. She was somewhere in her mid-forties, I guessed, with braided, black hair drawn up in a bun at her nape.

"We haven't met," I said. "Everyone calls me Max."

"Alex calls out for Mad Max. That's you?"

"That would be me."

"I'm Leena," the nurse said. Nurse Leena laid a warm blanket across the lower half of the bed. When she glanced at me, her dark eyes glistened mysteriously in the overhead lights. "Let me show you what I brought. We don't do sponge baths anymore." She pulled the wash basin over and piled packets of wipes on the table.

"That's probably for the best, because Alex just turned thirteen. He'd be mortified if I bathed him."

"He's the same age as my younger brother. He'd rather die than let me see him naked," Leena said. She added cotton towels and alcohol rubs to the stack. "These will help bring down his fever. Follow me and I'll show you where to find ice. Good, old-fashioned cold compresses on his forehead and the back of his neck will help, too."

I walked with her to the ice machine, where I half-filled the blue basin. "When my kids were little and ran fevers, I gave them cool water enemas to help keep them hydrated." I remembered how much water my babies absorbed through their colons. A lot of water went in; very little came out.

Leena nodded. "I'll talk with Dr. Running Bear. We don't want him to get dehydrated."

We returned to Alex's room. Leena made additional notes on her laptop. At the doorway, she paused. "Um, I may be out of line, but you aren't alone."

An electric shiver crossed my shoulders, and both Emilie and Ducks reached out to me in comfort. I raised an eyebrow.

"My grandfather is one of the local medicine men, what some call a shaman. I grew up around people with sight," she explained, calm and composed. "I have it, too."

"My granddaughter and her teacher both are special. Em told me she found helpers here. I should have realized she meant people with the gift, not only nurses and doctors."

"I talked with Mr. . . . umm, Ducks, isn't it? We had an immediate connection. He asked me to keep watch, too," Leena said.

I relaxed a bit. "Great, three spooks."

"Oh, many more than that," she assured me. "Several nurses and a couple of doctors are very close to Great Spirit. Researchers have yet to prove that modern medicine and the old ways can't work together. We'll do our best for the kids."

A machine beeped across from Alex's room. She laid a hand on my shoulder before leaving to checking on another child.

I called Eleanor, only to find her unavailable. Raney wasn't, so I filled her in on what was happening.

"Whip's angry with me. He thinks I'm shirking my duty," I said.

Raney dismissed Whip's attitude. She'd been critical of him when Merry was recovering. "That's crap. You aren't. He couldn't do any better."

"He knows that. He lashes out when he's scared."

We talked until the battery in my cell complained of abuse.

Three hours later, when Johnny walked in, Alex looked worse than ever. Johnny read the green monitors, frowned, and kissed me. Alex was drowsy but able to communicate.

"Hey, Captain Chaos. You look like one of the X-Men, all hooked up to those way cool machines," Johnny said.

Alex tried to grin, but grimaced instead. He coughed. "It hurts."

"I can see that," Johnny said. "I brought a couple of new games for your Game Boy."

Alex's lack of interest was a mute testament to how sick he was. I led Johnny out of the ICU and to a balcony, where we could see light and shadows painting the distant mountains with purples and lavenders from a mad artist's palette. Another day dawned.

"He's been down for X-rays, but they haven't found pneumonia. He's scheduled for a CT scan later to see what's going on in his lungs."

"What can I do?" Johnny held me tight against his strong chest.

"Just this. Be with me."

I told him about Nurse Leena. "It seems many Native Americans have gifts similar to Em and Ducks. They're all working to help. We need them," I said.

"I agree. We're not alone."

Once again, I felt Emilie's presence. Johnny jumped away and waved his hand around his face. He looked around the corridor, but no one was near.

"Something touched me."

"That would be Ducks. He's letting you know you should follow your instincts."

It was my turn to hug a trembling Johnny. His death grip on my hand showed how shaken he was by Ducks' touch. I turned the subject away from the twilight zone. "Let's talk with some of the other parents. Maybe they know something we don't."

We tracked down two mothers and a father, all of whom had children in the ICU with Alex. We introduced ourselves and compared notes, but none of us knew anything definitive. Symptoms ranged from fevers to rashes to body-shaking chest congestion. One had swollen lymph nodes. The children had only one thing in common—they were desperately ill.

"I sent my husband home to take care of the younger ones. They need their father," said one of the solitary mothers. The other mother had done the same. The women were the parents of the two children who'd checked in on Alex's first day, the ones Johnny, Ducks, Emilie and I had seen arrive.

"I'm all Belinda has, so I'm staying. She's my only child," the father said.

Sirens approached the hospital, and we glanced at each other, shoulders tense, faces drawn with new worry. *Another sick child?*

Johnny and I argued over whether he should stay the night or not. Although I needed his strength, I thought we should alternate. Johnny wanted to take the watch. My phone rang. Emilie asked to speak with her uncle Johnny. After a minute of listening, Johnny handed the phone to me.

"Mad Max, Alex is really bad. Mr. Ducks agrees. We don't know what it is, but you need to stay with him. Uncle Johnny can go back to the ranch." She muffled the phone. I heard the ping of an incoming text. "Mr. Ducks wants you to call him."

"I will as soon as I hang up. Is your dad there?" I asked.

"He's working late at his office. He'll be home later."

"Ask him to call me as soon as he arrives."

"Will do. Stay strong."

No sooner had I ended my call with Emilie than my phone rang again. "Hi, Ducks," I said.

"Tell me what you're seeing."

I gave him a quick update on how Alex looked and acted, what tests had been run, which were still waiting, current treatments, and what Leena suggested. He already knew about the midnight apparition.

"Good. I'm sensing the same things," Ducks said. "I've been doing a bunch of research on the Internet. Have you heard of hantavirus?"

I hadn't. I asked Johnny.

"They used to call it Navajo flu. It's not flu, but it can—" Johnny broke off and turned away. "It can be pretty bad."

Ducks learned that it was prevalent in the Southwest and was found in mouse urine and feces. It caused upper respiratory symptoms similar to what we were seeing, according to various websites.

"How serious is it?"

"Caught early, it can be treated. Alex fell ill in the hospital, so Dr. Running Bear began treating him immediately," Johnny said.

I heard Ducks shuffle through papers. "Symptoms include fever, racking cough and gastrointestinal complications sometimes. Alex has some of these symptoms, right?"

"Check, check, and check. I'll ask Dr. Running Bear about hantavirus. Thanks."

I asked him to "stay on this channel."

"Don't worry, Max. I'm here."

CHAPTER TWELVE

JOHNNY PREPARED TO leave shortly after dinner, but only after I crossed my heart and promised to call if Alex's condition changed for the worse. We walked downstairs.

"I can at least lend moral support if I'm here," he said as he hugged me at the front door. We stepped outside, where the heat of the day had given way to an evening bordering on chilly.

"I'm having my Jewish-mother-sweater alert, but the night air and freshening breeze feel wonderful. I don't want to go inside just yet." Johnny and I sat on the hand-carved bench beside the entrance, me resting against his chest. He put his arm around me for warmth.

No matter what he said, I needed more than moral support. I needed the damned medicine to work. Hell, I'd take a miracle if it meant Captain Chaos could breathe easier.

With Emilie and Ducks on remote watch, and Johnny on his way back to the ranch, I ambled, deep in thought, through the all-too-familiar corridors to the ICU. Patients were bedded down for the night; nurses squished by; voices were hushed. Back in the room, I alternated between reading and dozing in the recliner. Each cough, moan, or restless tossing brought me to full wakefulness. I hadn't been this alert since my own kids had been down with various childhood diseases. Strep and croup had been the worst.

Alex's temperature spiked and dropped and spiked again. I changed the damp towels on his forehead, offered cracked ice, and used alcohol rubs to cool him. No matter what the doctors and nurses tried, he remained inexorably ill.

When Alex's breathing labored, Dr. Running Bear ordered inhalation therapy with cortical steroids. Toby brought in a nebulizer and taught Alex how to use it.

"We should see an almost immediate change," Toby said. He wasn't his normal, chirpy self, sounding distracted and exhausted, albeit not angry this time. "This stuff works really fast."

I didn't see any improvement by the time Dr. Running Bear dropped by an hour later.

"Antibiotics took care of the infection, but they aren't having any effect on his lungs. Let's give him a couple more treatments with the steroids and monitor him," he said.

For all practical purposes, Dr. Running Bear lived in the ICU. Four more children came in, and one left to a funeral home—the first death. It wasn't one of the first three children. The child who died was already sick when she arrived by ambulance; her case was discovered too late.

"What else can we try?" I tamped down fear, trying to shove it in a box and lock the lid. It struggled free.

"Right now, we're treating his symptoms. I think he has a virus, which would explain why antibiotics aren't doing anything."

Dr. Running Bear ran his hand through his hair. His high cheekbones were more pronounced, and his black eyes had sunk deeper into his skull. "If Alex and the rest can avoid secondary infections, their bodies' natural immune systems should take over."

He steered me out of the ICU and away from the patients. We walked to a bank of windows and watched a thunderstorm rise as if by magic.

"You don't know what kind of a virus this is, do you?" I asked.

"No. I sent blood samples overnight to a CDC lab for testing. We should have the results in a couple of days."

"Don't you have a lab here?"

"We do, but we lack special equipment to isolate one virus from another. That takes very expensive stuff we've never needed before," he sighed.

"So, you can do basic tests, but you need the CDC's help isolating this virus from all others out in the world?" I leaned my back against the railing to better to watch Dr. Running Bear. "Em and Ducks found your lab in the basement, but they didn't go inside."

"Probably a good thing they didn't. Toby reigns over it like it's his private kingdom." He smiled down at me. "Anyway, the lab has the basic equipment to let us handle the routine problems we face in the population, but this outbreak isn't routine."

He shook his head, releasing hair from behind his ears. "My hair's getting too long, but I don't have time to get it cut."

I laughed. "In New York City, you wouldn't have this problem."

"I've been there. Your health department frowns on long hair for medical staff unless it's tied back. Ours does too, but it allows Native Americans to follow our traditions as long as we maintain proper hygiene." His gaze shifted to the world outside. "Do you know one of the families wants to bring in a local shaman to smudge their son?"

Nurse Leena had told me about the shaman.

"It might help with those families that put more faith in traditional healers than in modern medicine. I have nothing against trying anything. I'd try voodoo if I thought it would work."

"You and me both. Anyway, the uncle of one of the boys burned dried grasses and sage in an attempt to smudge the evil from the child's room and from his body before his parents brought him to the hospital. Given how sick that little boy is, I didn't think the ceremony helped."

"If you bring in a shaman, Captain Chaos will think it's pretty darned cool," I said, to show that I had nothing against these families seeking comfort in traditions.

"He'll do a ceremony tomorrow. He'll start outdoors before moving into the ICU. In the meantime, let's hope more children don't come in." Dr. Running Bear's fatigue deepened the creases around his eyes. He looked much older than he had five days earlier.

"Life was so much easier when you operated on Alex. Smooth sailing until he got sick." A feather tapped my cheek—I couldn't forget what Ducks told me about this hantavirus thing. Dr. Running Bear looked sharply at me.

"You met Ducks, didn't you?" I asked.

Dr. Running Bear nodded. "He just reached out to you, didn't he?"

"He did."

"Spooky guy. Not as spooky as your granddaughter, but spooky enough. What's he thinking about?"

"Hantavirus."

Dr. Running Bear seem to stare through me. "Hmm. When did Alex arrive? Not at the hospital, but at the ranch?"

"Late the day before we went riding. That would be five—no, six days ago," I said, mentally counting back.

Dr. Running Bear watched the cloud shadows continue transforming the mountains with different colors. *Could the Great Spirit, embodied in the Sangre de Cristo Mountains, hold the answer? Is he looking beyond modern medicine, beyond scientific diagnostics, for help?*

"Rare that symptoms show up so quickly. The incubation period for hantavirus is usually between one and five weeks," he said.

"He said this virus usually strikes children. Is that true? Other than their ages, I don't see much else in common."

"If it's hantavirus, it can strike healthy people of all ages, but those at greatest risk are often younger than twenty-five. Try not to worry, Mrs. Davies. We'll find out what's going on. We have to." Before he could continue, his cell buzzed. "Shit! Gotta go."

He broke into a run down the corridor, stormy sunlight turning his hair blue-black.

"What do I do now?" I asked the empty corridor. Neither Emilie nor Ducks had an answer.

Before dawn, Alex broke out in a rash.

CHAPTER THIRTEEN

CLOSE TO FIVE the next morning, I hit the panic button next to Alex, my hands trembling on an adrenaline surge. I slid aside when two nurses ran in and scrutinized the beeping machines. I couldn't detect a change in the various graphs from the day before; perhaps the machines kept secrets they didn't want me to understand. If that was what they were trying to do, I'd wring the truth out of them. The nurses turned to look at me.

"I was changing a wet cloth on his forehead when Alex's gown slipped off his shoulders and exposed a mean-looking rash. It wasn't there when I sponged him at ten last night. He cried out when I touched him. When I saw the rash, I called you," I said. I pointed to a swollen area along his neck covered in red bumps.

One nurse exited into the hall. The remaining one updated Alex's data on her laptop. I paid little attention to what was happening in the hall until I saw the first nurse tie a gown over her scrubs, cover her hair with a cap, and add gloves and a surgical mask before checking first one room, then another. The nurse with Alex waved for me to leave.

"Too late. If he's contagious, he's already infected me," I said, tired of being waved off in general. I stayed, unable to imagine anything or anyone prying me from my grandson's bedside. Deep in my illogical heart, I knew that if I stayed, I could prevent him from getting any worse. I didn't consider that he could die. I refused to go down that rabbit hole.

It's bad, but the doctors are doing everything they can, Emilie texted.

I know, I texted back.

Try not to worry.

As if.

An on-call doctor arrived half an hour after I hit the alarm. He too had donned protective clothing before he steered me out of the room by my elbow. I tried to pull away, but his grip only tightened. "Wait outside," he said firmly.

He slid the glass door closed, leaving me to watch everything he did, note every place he touched, and watch as much of Alex's reaction to the prodding as I could see. I knew from how he twitched when the doctor probed his neck and under his arms that his condition had worsened. Until now, his lymph nodes hadn't been swollen.

I texted Johnny. *Please come back. Alex is much worse.* I needed someone to lean on. I needed him to be with me.

An hour later, I met Johnny downstairs. He dropped a small duffel bag before I threw myself into his arms.

"I'm so glad you're here." I squeezed a grunt out of him.

"I knew I should have stayed last night," he said.

"And done what?"

"I could have taken a turn by Alex's bed." He kneaded a knot in my neck.

"You couldn't have prevented the rash any more than I could."

"No, pretty lady, but I could have done this." Johnny held me close and I took solace from his beating heart.

"I'm sorry, funny man, but the scene in the ICU has been one step short of chaotic." I gave Johnny all the information I had, which turned out to be practically nothing. Every doctor and nurse on duty had rushed from room to room upon the discovery of Alex's rash. The ever-present Toby drew blood from each patient. The medical staff sent family members like me out of the unit to fume and fuss elsewhere.

Panic left my mouth as dry as a wad of cotton. Johnny led me into the cafeteria, where we bought the last bottle of water in the cooler. We shared it. No one had restocked the cafeteria for breakfast.

"I texted Ducks and Em. Hell, they already knew something is badly wrong," Johnny said. "Maybe they can find something the doctors haven't thought of."

I kicked myself for not contacting Ducks immediately. "Thanks. Em sent a 'don't worry' text. All I can do is worry. It's not like I can focus on anything outside what's happening upstairs."

We walked down the long corridor that connected the emergency room, maternity and pediatric wards, and the main lobby to the medical and surgical wards and the ICU. The corridor was strangely dark; it should have been filled with early morning sunlight. I looked through the wall of windows facing the desert beyond. Heavy overcast lent an ominous feeling to the start of the day. I shivered.

"Did you sense something?" Johnny tightened his hold on my hand.

"I'm not sure what it was, but yes."

Just outside the ICU, we met Dr. Begay, the night physician, who had bags under his eyes as big as mine. I pointed at his face. "Try Preparation-H. It'll reduce the swelling."

He looked startled before he grinned. "That's the first piece of useful advice I've heard all night. Thanks. I will."

Before he could escape, Johnny stepped into his way.

"What's going on with Alex?"

"He has new symptoms," I reminded the doctor. I had to speak, or I'd explode. "So, what is it?"

"Is Alex the only one with a rash and swollen lymph nodes?" Johnny asked.

Dr. Begay shook his head.

"From what I've been reading, Alex has most of the classic symptoms of hantavirus, doesn't he?" Johnny set his hook and refused to let the doctor wriggle away.

"Yes and no. The chest congestion, body aches, fever, and gastrointestinal symptoms can be caused by influenza, hantavirus, Legionnaires' disease, or any of several other viral, fungal, or bacterial infections." The doctor pulled off his surgical mask. "We're waiting for results from the CDC. Until we get them back, we're pretty much in the dark."

"What about the rash?" Johnny asked. "Nothing I read said anything about a rash."

"All the more reason to wait for the CDC response. Rashes aren't part of the syndrome." The doctor rubbed his face against his sleeve.

"But if it's something else, what could it be?" My pulse beat heavily in my throat; I took another swallow of water.

"We just don't know. Right now, we have more symptoms than belong to any single disease." He stretched his shoulders and rolled his neck to loosen taut muscles. His neck clicked.

"How many can be transmitted from human to human?" I jumped in.

"A lot of them, but if it's hantavirus, it doesn't jump from human to human, only from mice to us."

Johnny eyed the doctor. "You're wearing protective gear because whatever this is could be contagious, though, right?"

"Until we know for certain, Mr. Medina, Dr. Running Bear ordered us to follow contagious or infectious disease protocol and err on the side of caution. We'll gear up whenever we treat one of the children, just in case. We don't want to spread it from child to child if it turns out to be contagious. You and the rest of the parents need to take similar precautions or stay out of the ICU."

"Fat chance of that," I said.

The doctor leaned against the wall, his eyes moving from room to room, monitoring what the nurses were doing. Seemingly satisfied, he shed his mask and gloves like a snake molting, throwing them toward a trash bin marked with a screaming red bio-hazard warning. He missed. He sighed and picked them up. "Figures." He turned back to us. "I emailed the changes to the CDC a little while ago. We should know something soon."

"Which children have the rash?" Johnny slipped a paper cap over his black hair.

"Right now, Alex and two of the children who've been here the longest have similar symptoms. Not counting the child who died, we have eight children in the ICU and several more in the Med-Surg unit, which we turned into an isolation ward until we know what we're dealing with and how it's transmitted. All the children have serious chest congestion."

That explained the body-racking coughs I heard up and down the ICU. "But they don't all have the same symptoms, do they?" Like a terrier with a new squeaky chew toy, I wasn't about to give up.

"It could still be the same syndrome with some children further along in the disease's progression," Dr. Begay said. "We're treating the symptoms."

Out of the corner of my eye, I saw Toby enter the ICU. He wore protective clothing and pushed a caddy with more nebulizers on it.

"I have a meeting with Dr. Running Bear in a few minutes. Either he or I will come back when we have something to report. Until then, try and keep Alex quiet and comfortable. Use the nebulizer to help him breathe."

Leena approached and showed us how to put on the protective clothing. "I know you've both been here all along, but you need to do what we do." She held out a paper gown.

My hands trembled again when I tried to tie the gown on. Johnny moved my hands aside and tied the strings behind my back. He put his on as well. We had entered a medical twilight zone.

What the hell is loose in the ICU?

Morning passed with no sign of Dr. Running Bear. The night physician didn't return, and the nurses changed shifts. Alex's cough deepened. I gave him a breathing treatment—he was allowed one every four hours. Toby arrived to take him to X-ray to rule out pneumonia again.

"You've been here most of the night," I said. I'd seen Toby nearly everywhere I looked.

"We're short-staffed. I pull double duty as an orderly when I don't have to take lab samples," he said. With that, he pushed Alex's bed into an elevator and disappeared.

"Let's get some food. I'm starving," Johnny said.

"You're always starving."

No sooner had Johnny and I exited the ICU than a page sounded from the intercom: "Dr. Running Bear to the lobby."

It was repeated three more times. Odd, because most of the doctor's pages came through his cell. Or through a coded chime. Gone were days of pages for "Code Blue." Television had overused it as a warning for all medical personnel to head to a specific room immediately. Originally designed as a way of calling for assistance during a crisis, it had become synonymous with, "Need a crash cart STAT!"

"*Now* what's happening?" I looked up at Johnny. "I hope it's not more patients."

Johnny's brow wrinkled. "I doubt it. They'd come in through the emergency entrance, not the front door, don't you think? Admitting a new patient hasn't involved loud speakers before."

Several nurses sprinted past us. As one, Johnny and I trotted along behind them. Through the tall windows lining one side, we saw a line of black SUVs and a limousine.

"What the hell?" Johnny picked up speed until he was running.

"What's going on?" I asked, keeping pace.

Men in dark suits, white shirts, ties, and earpieces on leashes tucked into their collars, stood around the limo and faced outward. One opened the right-hand passenger door to allow an elegant though casually-dressed woman to step onto the sidewalk. Three men walked ahead of her; two followed. The automatic door swooshed open. Dr. Running Bear extended his hand in greeting.

"What the fuck?" Johnny blushed and looked down at me. "Sorry."

"Don't be. What the hell is the vice president's wife doing here?"

CHAPTER FOURTEEN

"YOU RECOGNIZE HER?" Johnny asked.

"She's often in the news," I explained, wondering why she was coming to a hospital so far from big cities. She didn't look like she needed medical attention.

We joined several nurses hanging over the railing on the second floor, gawking like teenagers when the Beatles performed so many decades ago at the Ed Sullivan Theater in New York, but without the screaming and hysteria. We peered down at the group just inside the door, a curious fan base watching an unanticipated spectacle.

"Dr. Running Bear sure doesn't look at all happy," I said.

He stood with arms crossed. The vice president's wife held both palms outward to soothe the situation. Secret Service agents stood by impassively. I assumed they were watching the crowd from behind their reflective dark glasses. *What do they see? Do they think baddies are hiding at San Felipe?*

"Looks like we have a standoff," Johnny whispered.

"We forgot she was coming," a nondescript nurse said quietly. "The advance team was here about eight weeks ago to check everything out. When the kids started getting sick, none of us thought to call her office to cancel."

"Dr. Running Bear is going to lose this argument," Leena said. "That doesn't happen often."

"At least she's a doctor, not a civilian, so if any of us get to meet her, we can behave normally and answer questions without worrying about terminology," another nurse said.

"It doesn't look like she's going away." I turned to Johnny. "Do you think her visit will interfere with treating Alex and the rest of the children?"

Leena shook her head. "We're operating as if the kids in the ICU are infectious. It wouldn't be safe for her to roam around there."

"I can't imagine the Secret Service letting her anywhere near the ICU. I bet she gets a quick tour, shakes a few hands, makes a statement about exciting it is to visit such a state-of-the-art facility as San Felipe, and leaves for her next public event," Johnny said.

"I'd agree if our ICU wasn't a poster child for how an ICU should be run," Leena replied. Two nurses shared a look before one slipped away.

Downstairs, Dr. Running Bear bowed his head, stepped aside, and led the group away from the ICU. Several Secret Service personnel stayed outside with the cars.

"Détente wins out," Johnny said.

The nurses returned to their respective workstations. Johnny and I retreated down our now familiar corridor. As soon as I finished putting on my gear and pushed into the ICU, I heard crying from a room across from Alex's. Johnny peeled off to check on Alex; I looked around the room, where I saw an empty bed, vital monitoring equipment gone dark, rubber gloves, and bloody towels abandoned on the floor.

"What happened?" I asked the woman sitting crumpled in a chair. She had spent every hour with her daughter since she was brought in two days earlier. The girl wasn't one of the original patients.

"My daughter sat up in bed, threw up blood, and died. Just like that." The grieving woman stared at the stained, rumpled bed as if hoping that her daughter would somehow appear. "The doctors tried to revive her, but she was gone."

I held out my arms. She leaned her head on my shoulder

and sobbed. I rocked her gently, secretly relieved that her pain wasn't mine. I turned to Johnny standing in the doorway. "Is Alex all right?"

"He's not in his room. Neither is his bed." He took a step toward the nurses' station to ask.

"We haven't been gone more than an hour, if that. Johnny, how could a child die and be removed in such a short time?" Tears trembled on my lower lashes before they spilled over. I laid my cheek on the woman's head. Her grief made my heart ache.

The elevator dinged. Toby pushed Alex's bed down the hall and into his room.

"Did you know he was going down for tests?" Johnny demanded.

"No one told me," I said, mystified. I continued to pat the sobbing woman on her back. Like a baby, her sobs gave way to hiccups, slowed, and stopped. She pulled herself upright and went in search of the bathroom.

"Seems like Alex is getting a lot of tests," I suggested as I stood in the door to Alex's room and tried not to appear judgmental—I didn't trust anyone at this point. Toby hooked up the oxygen line and leads for the monitors before leaving, frustratingly silent. Alex slept. I passed worried and closed in on a full-throated temper tantrum. "What the hell is going on?" I looked at my grandson, so still and small in his bed, not the hyper-active Captain Chaos we all loved. "What do we do?"

"We wait." Johnny put his arm across my shoulders. "Together."

"If waiting is all that's left, it's feeding my panic. I need answers, and I need them now." I squeezed my eyes shut, trying to block the memory of the empty bed in the other room and the grieving face of the mother who'd just lost everything. "Yesterday would have been better, but right this damned minute will have to do. I feel so damned helpless."

"We all do, pretty lady. We all do."

I couldn't use my normal response of calling Johnny "funny man" right then. Comforting as Johnny's strength was, it wasn't enough. With Alex asleep, I sat by his bedside and texted updates to Emilie and Ducks, anxious to discuss my concerns and not simply set them aside. Johnny went on a coffee run.

Nothing new to report, except Alex is getting all sorts of tests, I texted Ducks. *I don't understand why*

Ask Dr. Running Bear. Emilie added to the conversation. *Either he ordered them, or someone is acting on his own.*

Someone? The only person who took any of the patients to X-ray is Toby, I texted.

Watch him, Ducks texted.

Yes, Emilie agreed.

I updated the Great Dames. True to their natures, Raney and Eleanor offered to take the next flight out. I assured them that a trip was unnecessary. "All you could do is sit and watch me fret."

"We could fret together," Eleanor said.

"If you're sure . . . " Raney didn't like not being able to help me.

"I am. Just be there when I need someone to talk to."

They promised. "Although, if you need us—"

I broke off the direction the conversation was heading— they'd been my solace after Merry was murdered. "We're not going to bury anyone this time. No way, no how."

The day dragged on with no change in Alex's condition. I was desperate enough to take no change as a good sign. We didn't know anything about his most recent X-rays—no one had come to talk to us. An unfamiliar doctor treated a child on the other side of the ICU, but no one was rushing around. There didn't seem to be an emergency. The next time I glanced up, the doctor was gone.

We entered a period of stasis. Sometime later, Leena approached Johnny and me. We were cloaked and covered lest a germ attack us. I wished I could find my sense of humor, because we looked like we were prepared for an alien invasion.

"I'm kicking myself for forgetting we had the vice president's wife coming on a goodwill visit," Leena said. "One of her main interests is the Indian Health Service. She's the first Native American—and the first surgeon—in such a visible position. From what I hear, her grandmother was Choctaw and a traditional healer."

The vice president's wife was touring several IHS hospitals and spent a lot of time at the headquarters in Maryland. Leena went on to say how excited the doctors and nurses had been when they heard about the visit.

"Is this her first trip?" I asked.

"Yes. Our facility is one of the newest hospitals. Her coming here gives us publicity. Maybe we can expand what we can do."

"I hope I get to meet her," said a nurse in passing.

"Being blunt, her timing sucks," Johnny said. "I mean, this is a state-of-the-art ICU, and she won't be able to see it."

By now, the ICU had ten Native American or Hispanic children and one white boy, all of whom were gravely ill, all of whom were being treated for an unknown biological predator or predators.

No one counted on how strong the vice president's wife's commitment to Native American health care was—an hour later, the doors to the ICU swung outward, and Dr. Running Bear led a small entourage into a now-crowded space. Over his surgical mask, his eyes told everyone who knew him not to interrupt.

Leena murmured observations while she finished her check on Alex's condition: unchanged. "Watch how he shepherds our guest straight through the ICU, even though her presence is a gross imposition in what has been a smooth process for caring for the children. He'll never let her know he doesn't want her here, never let his emotions show. He has polished that stoic expression until it's a masterpiece."

"I hear you. I wouldn't want to mess with him when he's being his implacable strongest. As for me, my chin is my warning sign. When it's thrust out, either get out of my way or duck," I said.

"I'll remember."

Two Secret Service agents, distinctly uncomfortable in their gowns, guarded the exit door, their collective rigidity screaming disapproval. The vice president's wife, fully dressed in the same clothing we wore, a mask hanging loosely around her neck. On her, the clothing looked natural; on the detail, it looked like something they wanted to rip off before ushering their charge the hell away from harm.

"Everyone, may I have your attention, please?" Dr. Running Bear repeated his statement in Spanish and what I assumed was a local Native American language. His voice reached every corner of the unit. The patients may have been oblivious, but parents poked their heads out of rooms. Nurses gathered at the central station. Johnny and I drifted over.

"It is our great pleasure to have Dr. Sharon Anderson, the wife of the vice president, with us today. As you know, Dr. Anderson is a strong advocate for our work here. I'd like you to answer any questions she may have about what we do here in the ICU."

"With all due respect, Dr. Running Bear, I know how an ICU works. I'm still a surgeon." She smiled to take any harshness out of her words. "Thank you, though. I can see how busy you are, so I'll try not to be an impediment."

Dr. Anderson moved into the nurses' station and perched on the edge of a desk. With records in electronic format, the clutter of bygone eras was absent. After a few starts and stops, the nurses talked about their jobs, the good they were doing in the community, and how educational outreach was making slow but steady inroads to chronic lifestyle problems.

"Good," Dr. Anderson said. "What do you need?"

"Another care-flight helicopter and EMT team for bringing patients to the hospital. A trauma surgeon. Sometimes, we have too many injuries for Dr. Running Bear to handle by himself."

The nondescript nurse I'd talked with over the lobby railing called out from the back, "More nurses and orderlies, too. We often pull double shifts when we have a wreck, a series of accidents, or a flu outbreak."

I could attest to needing more staff. I rarely saw more than two nurses on at the same time in a unit with eight beds. That ratio was too great, especially with the cases coming in quickly. When Merry was at the Virginia Commonwealth University hospital, the ratio was one nurse to two patients. At San Felipe, one to four was the norm. I didn't know whether this ICU generally handled as high a volume as the one in Virginia. Perhaps it was normal not to staff it so heavily.

"And we need to do more with community outreach," the nurse continued. "Drug counseling, nutritional education, diabetes and obesity counseling, alcohol treatment. We can prevent many negative life-choice conditions if we just had enough outreach counsellors."

Another nurse added to a growing laundry list of needs. "We need some sort of community-wide communications network. This would help us better manage an outbreak."

One of the doctors moved into the nurses' station. "While our patient-focused equipment is state of the art, our alert system uses last-century techniques. Emails to all doctors, hospitals, clinics. That sort of stuff. The local television and radio stations help, but nothing reaches everyone. If we could set up an automated system to send broadcasts to all cell phones, which most people have, we could help more people that you could imagine."

"More and better diagnostic equipment for our lab," Dr. Running Bear added. "As you could see coming in, this part of New Mexico is pretty remote and has a widely scattered and diverse population. If we had better diagnostic equipment, we wouldn't have to ship blood samples to the CDC and wait days for test results."

"What's wrong with these children?" Dr. Anderson moved from the nurses' station and peered into a couple of the rooms, but didn't enter.

"We don't know." Dr. Running Bear edged toward his distinguished guest and her detail, a clear indication she should move along with the rest of her tour and leave. "Once the CDC responds, we can target the pathogen directly. Right now, we're using broad spectrum antibiotics in case this is a bacterial infection and treating the symptoms with inhaled cortical-steroids for the congestion."

"We're wearing protective clothing, so you think they're contagious?" Dr. Anderson stopped in front of Alex's room and glanced at me.

"As I said, we don't know. Antibiotics aren't working with some patients, so we may be dealing with a virus. Until I know for sure, we're following CDC protocols for an infectious outbreak."

"We created the IHS to serve Native Americans because their level of health care was abysmal," Dr. Anderson said, her gaze still on me.

"We treat everyone in need, Dr. Anderson," Dr. Running Bear said. "We don't discriminate."

"I'm sorry if I implied that. It wasn't my intention. Forgive my rudeness, please." She smiled at me.

"I'm really glad the hospital is here. We were staying at my friend's ranch before Alex was injured and then got sick," I said. I gave her a brief sketch on how we got here and why we were still in the hospital.

Johnny exited Alex's room, standing next to me long enough to say, "Before you ask, I'm Mexican-American from Albuquerque. Might have some Apache or Navajo in me, but who knows. We're here because that boy in there was injured closer to San Felipe than any other hospital." He grinned before pulling his mask back over his face. "If you'll excuse me, I want to get back to him."

"Me too." I followed Johnny. My place was with my grandson, not a celebrity.

"Of course," Dr. Anderson said.

The Secret Service detail collected their charge and ushered her through the door, Dr. Running Bear accompanying. Alex was sleeping, so I went to the cafeteria. Everyone exiting the ICU paused to throw gowns, masks, and gloves into the bio-hazard barrel.

The entourage had barely reached the end of the corridor when angry voices rose from the lobby. Dr. Running Bear rushed toward the staircase, the Secret Service hustling the vice president's wife along behind him.

Several new white-and-blue vans and trucks barricaded both ends of the semi-circular drive leading to the front door, trapping the black limo and SUVs. With no clear view of what these new vehicles were, I shamelessly eavesdropped from the balcony.

"Stop right there." One of the Secret Service agents tried to block a group of people from coming inside. "This hospital is closed until further notice."

A tall, regal black woman with a shaved head stepped forward, speaking with a light accent. "You are right. It is. Until further notice."

The door behind her whooshed open. People unloaded equipment from a van, piled cases on the sidewalk, and walked around the men in suits.

"Don't give us orders," the lead agent said, taking an aggressive stance, arms slightly away from his body. I could see the bulge of a gun tucked into the small of his back. I wondered if we were about to have a shootout. "We have priority. We're protecting the vice president's wife."

"So I see. Keep your men outside." The woman's voice was commanding but low. A confrontation was brewing until Dr. Anderson walked up with Dr. Running Bear.

"What's going on, and who are you?" Dr. Anderson asked before Dr. Running Bear could open his mouth.

The woman flashed her credentials. "Dr. Nathalie Duval, CDC."

Leena appeared next to me to watch the confrontation below. "I wondered how long it would take to get someone out here. We need help."

Dr. Duval motioned to a stranger, who slapped signs on the doors. "Under my authority as head of the infectious disease unit at the CDC, this facility is quarantined until further notice."

"All the more reason to remove the vice president's wife immediately," the agent said, shoving his way into Dr. Duval's space with his chest puffed out and his countenance dark and glowering. He stood close enough to intimidate a mere mortal, but Dr. Duval didn't flinch. My first impression was that she was no mere mortal.

The doctor didn't move, standing eye-to-eye with the agent. "Did you not understand what I said? This facility is under quarantine. This means you and everyone else here are quarantined as well. No one leaves. No one enters."

"This is the vice president's wife—"

"You have established that fact. I recognize her, but if you contact your superiors in Washington, you will learn I have jurisdiction under certain conditions. This disease outbreak constitutes one of the 'certain conditions.'" Dr. Duval turned toward Dr. Anderson. "With all due respect, madam, we cannot let you or anyone else leave until we know what is infecting patients in this hospital. You could be at risk yourself, or you could risk spreading a disease of unknown origin."

"We can't stay here," said the agent, still trying to reassert a modicum of control. "We'll move her into a hotel."

"Let me ask you this. Does this hotel have an isolation suite?" Dr. Duval asked.

The agent shook his head.

"Do you have a portable isolation unit for Dr. Anderson?"
The agent shook his head again.

"Then she stays here. As do all of your men who are inside. The rest will remain outside." Dr. Duval turned her back and gave orders to her staff.

"May we have a word alone?" Dr. Anderson asked her, gesturing toward a section of the lobby right under where I was standing. Leena and I stepped back, out of eyesight should anyone look up, but not out of earshot.

"Dr. Duval, how serious is the danger to the community? I'm not an infectious disease specialist, so I don't know much beyond the courses we took in med school." Dr. Anderson lowered her voice, but the acoustics in the lobby projected her words.

"Until we know exactly what we're dealing with, we consider the danger to be high. We have tested samples Dr. Running Bear sent in. Some of our results do not make sense, so we do not know what precisely we are dealing with." Dr. Duval's soft island lilt did little to mask her concern. "Right now, we have a cluster of cases at the hospital, a few more in the community beyond the hospital confines, two on a ranch, and one in a remote settlement."

"You said the test results were inconclusive. Dr. Running Bear just asked for proper equipment for elaborate tests, so I know his lab is inadequate," Dr. Anderson said.

"We brought our portable lab in that large truck. We'll either operate out of it or offload what we need into a separate room. We will release you as soon as it is safe for you and the community."

"I understand."

Dr. Anderson returned to her detail, and Dr. Duval moved to speak with Dr. Running Bear. I stepped closer to the railing. I couldn't hear what she said, but the agent's angry expression told me they were joining Johnny and me as guests of the Indian Health Service.

"May I ask the detail outside to fetch my overnight case and tote?" Dr. Anderson called to Dr. Duval.

"Of course. Have them leave them outside the front door. We will send someone out to pick them up." Dr. Duval stood straighter, if that were possible. The situation was under her control.

CHAPTER FIFTEEN

WORD PASSED QUICKLY that the vice president's wife was trapped with the rest of us. I fetched Johnny to deliver the news.

"Quarantine, huh?" He rubbed a bristly chin and his eyes narrowed before a smile took control. "Guess you're stuck with me for the duration, like it or not, pretty lady."

I lightly slapped his arm. "I'm glad we're in this together, funny man."

Several nurses gossiped about the near donnybrook between the CDC director and the head of the Secret Service detail. The lead agent contacted headquarters in Washington to demand a contamination chamber be flown to the hospital. When none was immediately available, he demanded a trailer be sent to quarantine Dr. Anderson.

"You should have seen his face. He was yelling at his boss just outside the cafeteria door. What did he think? That he could snap his fingers and get one delivered in half an hour?"

"It's not like there are decontamination chambers available at the local pharmacy."

"I heard the vice president's wife called her husband to tell him what was going on. I think they had a similar conversation, only they weren't yelling like the Secret Service agent was."

I ambled over to the nurses' station. "Dr. Anderson have any better luck?"

"From what I heard, she and the Secret Service are our guests, so I guess not."

"I'd be a lot happier if the head of her detail had been left outside," I said. "He reminds me of a Rottweiler." Laughter rippled around the ICU, and I ran my hands through my hair, thoroughly mussing it. A few minutes later, a page requested that family, visitors, and the staff not treating the sickest patients come to the cafeteria.

Dr. Running Bear opened the meeting by explaining why no one could leave the hospital until it was cleared by the CDC. The quarantine was absolute. The vice president's wife sat alone at a table for two near the CDC doctors, while the Secret Service detail arranged itself along one side of the room and glowered at the head of the hospital. Dr. Running Bear paid no attention to them. He thanked everyone for their understanding.

"You can make me the bad guy here. I sent blood samples to the CDC for analysis, because we couldn't figure out what was making people sick. That triggered the arrival of the team from Atlanta to help us keep you and the rest of your families safe. And now, I'd like to introduce Dr. Duval."

The black doctor rose. Her height made her impressive, but her calm expression brought a moment of comfort. "I am Dr. Nathalie Duval, chief of infectious diseases for the CDC. Before you ask, I am from Haiti and trained in medicine here in the United States. With me are Dr. Meenu Gupta, our top virologist, Dr. Jerome Klein, one of our pathologists, and Dr. Gretchen White, our best epidemiologist. We will be working with the doctors and nurses here to identify the source of the illness." Dr. Duval outlined her initial plan of attack. "Our top priority is to identify the organism. We could be dealing with a parasite, a virus, or a bacterium. It could even be a fungus. Our initial lab tests were inconclusive, leading us to think the samples may have been contaminated in transit. Dr. Gupta will explain."

Dr. Gupta rose. "It is my understanding some patients are not responding well to antibiotics."

"That's correct," Dr. Running Bear said.

"Then either we aren't using the right drugs, or we're dealing with a virus. I'll be drawing fresh samples from each of you."

"All of us?" One of the mothers raised her hand. "Why do you need our blood?"

"We need to be sure none of you is carrying the organism."

"Like Typhoid Mary?" a man called from across the cafeteria.

Dr. Gupta smiled. "Exactly. One of you could be a carrier and not exhibit any symptoms."

The man glanced around the room. Several people smiled at him. Since I'd spoken to him many times up in ICU, I gestured that I believed what the doctors were saying and would roll up my sleeve.

"Think of yourselves as what we call control samples. If your blood is clear, terrific. If not, then we'll treat you as well."

"But for what?" countered an upset father. "You just said you don't know what the problem is."

"That's true, but you belong here, where we can monitor your health. If any of you fall ill, we can move you into isolation immediately." Dr. Gupta looked around after concluding. "Back to you, Dr. Duval."

"Dr. Klein will be doing autopsies if we have any casualties. If not, he's also a terrific scientist who will assist in the lab. He'll be looking for the disease reservoir." Enough people looked confused for Dr. Duval to explain. "A disease reservoir is the source of the organism. It's where it hides. It could be an animal, something in the natural world, an inanimate object, even the ventilation system. Nearly anything carries viruses and bacteria, including our own skin and our guts—er, intestinal tracts. One part of our analysis is to find where the organism is hiding."

Dr. Klein took the floor. "Call me Jerry. We're going to get real close to each other in the next few days, so I see no reason for you to stand on ceremony with me. Think of what I do as going on a scavenger hunt. I'll poke into everything, take samples, and swab a lot of surfaces. I'll analyze everything under a microscope, and eventually figure out what is making your family members sick. I work very closely with Dr. White."

More parents shifted in their uncomfortable chairs, worried but silent. A nurse shot a glance across the cafeteria, but from where Johnny and I sat, we couldn't see who caught it.

Dr. Gretchen White stood next—all five feet of her. My gut told me she brooked no nonsense from anyone. "You can call me Tick."

Johnny raised his hand. "Sorry for the interruption, but why Tick?"

"I work with disease vectors. That's how diseases get from the reservoir or carrier into you. I map where the outbreaks are, how people become infected, and identify the active carrier. Fleas, ticks, and mosquitoes are frequently the culprits. Mosquitoes carry diseases from dengue fever to West Nile virus to different types of poxes."

"This is the desert. We don't have mosquitoes," Nurse Leena said.

"I understand. Fleas and ticks still carry plague, Lyme Disease, and a bunch of other very unpleasant illnesses. My colleagues at the CDC think I'm weird because I have a huge collection of insects that transmit dangerous organisms we call pathogens," Tick said.

I leaned over to whisper to Johnny, "Did you hear her say plague?"

"I did. Dengue fever, too." Johnny stared out the cafeteria windows, jumping slightly right before I felt Ducks' touch. For the first time, I wondered just how closely Ducks could monitor a remote situation. *Could he actually be eavesdropping in some strange way?* Johnny and I shared a glance.

Dr. Duval reminded us that the CDC had absolute authority—growls from the Secret Service floated over the heads of the worried audience—but would work closely with the staff to minimize disruption. All remaining doctors and nurses would be called back to duty immediately, even if they hadn't treated the patients in the ICU.

"This is precautionary. We don't want the hospital to go into crisis mode should it be swamped with new cases. The emergency room will be closed until further notice except for patients who present with symptoms similar to the current patients. All others will be sent to Albuquerque or Santa Fe."

"Have you notified the adjacent hospitals? Do they know what to expect?" Toby the vampire asked.

"Yes, we have excellent communication protocols in place.

Someone from my office has been on the phone or e-mailing every doctor, clinic, and hospital in a fifty-mile radius."

"Good," Dr. Running Bear said. "I've been too busy with the outbreak itself to do much along those lines."

"Why such a large catchment area?" asked Nurse Leena.

"As I said, we don't know what the organism is. Therefore, we don't know how it's transmitted."

Dr. Klein spoke up. "We don't know where it's hiding."

Toby asked a question many of us hesitated to ask. "But you said you ran tests. What did you find?"

"Right now, we think this may be a localized outbreak of hantavirus, a relatively rare virus that cropped up in the Four Corners region in 1993, but we found bits of something else."

"A lot of people died from that," said a woman I recognized from the ICU. Her son was a couple of rooms down from Alex. "People called it Navajo flu."

"You are correct. The Four Corners outbreak had a high mortality rate, but if we catch it soon enough, we can treat the symptoms. We need to find out what the 'something else' is," Dr. Gupta said.

"What are the symptoms of hantavirus?" One of the Secret Service agents shifted his attention away from threats to the vice president's wife toward something that could harm him.

"Fever, muscle aches, shortness of breath. It sounds like the common flu, but it isn't," Dr. Gupta said. "The common flu makes you sick, but this virus makes you sicker by a factor of at least four."

"You said something else was in the sample." Toby again. "What was it?"

"As I said, our results were inconclusive. That's why one of the first things we will do today is take fresh blood samples from everyone in the hospital, sick and healthy, to try to isolate it. From there, we hope to identify it. Whatever it is, something causes a rash, which is not part of the hantavirus symptoms." Dr. Gupta stepped back to sit with the rest of her team.

"But rashes are part of dengue fever symptoms," Johnny breathed in my ear.

"In a way, it is good that the outbreak struck at this time," Dr. Duval said. "While we never wish for an outbreak, the common flu season is weeks away. We will not have confusion from it in the diagnosis."

"With so many extra people living at the hospital, is there any chance we'll run out of supplies?" I asked. Neither Johnny nor I took medications beyond multiple vitamins and baby aspirin, but I was sure others weren't in such good health.

Dr. Duval assured everyone that the CDC was prepared to continue supplying everything the hospital required. "We will establish a system for restocking. Food, medicines, and everything else we need will be delivered to the loading dock in the back of the hospital. After the delivery team leaves, we'll send someone out to carry everything inside. Please set up a meeting with Dr. Klein and let him know what medicines you take. Either we will have someone pick them up at your home, or we'll supply them to you."

One of the men twitched at the back of the room. "Can we smoke out there? I need a cigarette."

"We have nicotine patches if anyone wants to try them," Dr. Running Bear said. "We use them in our smoking cessation clinic and for any smoker about to undergo surgery. Please let me know if you want to try the patch."

The man looked skeptical. He shrugged and patted the pack of cigarettes in his shirt pocket. "But if we want to smoke, can we?"

Dr. Running Bear and Dr. Duval had a quick conference. The Haitian doctor beckoned the head of the Secret Service detail to join. After a couple of minutes, all three nodded. Dr. Duval told the group that smoking would be allowed on the loading dock when no deliveries were expected. "You can also ask your families to drop off anything you need there. The Secret Service will keep a log of who goes outside and what enters."

Relieved looks bounced around the room, as did murmurs of approval. Dr. Running Bear raised his hand. "Good. One question resolved. Now, on the bad news side, we admitted four more children with symptoms similar to those we've been seeing. They came in overnight. Two are on the critical list.

"Drs. Gupta and White will take charge of analyzing blood samples. So far, healthy adults show no symptoms of disease, but without knowing the cause of the illness, we don't know what the incubation period is. Until we can put a name to this, we remain in quarantine."

Several women grumbled about not being able to go home to their husbands and other children. They felt fine and didn't understand why they couldn't leave. Dr. Running Bear promised to explain the situation to their families.

He stepped forward. "We'll meet here daily at four in the afternoon for updates. I promise to keep no secrets. Now, please see Nurse Gilligan for sleeping assignments. Each of you will have a bed in a private room unless we need it for patients. Then some of you will have to share. Please, work with us. We'll get you out of here as soon as it's safe."

With that, Dr. Running Bear and the CDC team exited the cafeteria.

"Why don't you go back to Alex? I'll talk with Nurse Gilligan to get us a berth on the SS *Minnow*." Johnny stood and stretched.

"As if she hasn't heard the jokes most of her life," I said with a mock-scowl.

"I'll be good. I promise." Johnny chucked me lightly under the chin.

"Yeah, right." I tried not to show how worried I was. Johnny left to call his brother. He wouldn't be returning to the ranch any time soon. I left to call Whip, the Great Dames, and the watchdogs.

CHAPTER SIXTEEN

"THAT'S WHAT I said, Raney. We're quarantined." I paced the corridor outside the ICU. I finished describing the power struggle between the Secret Service and the CDC.

"If you're quarantined, the CDC won, didn't it?" Raney laughed. "I wish I could have seen it."

"Well, if you had, we'd have a lot of quality time together. You'd be stuck here with me." I looked down at my paper gown. I could think of more flattering outerwear.

"I can think of worse things." We rang off.

Johnny returned to Alex's room half an hour later with news that he had secured one room for us. He even brought coffee.

"It's not like we'll be sleeping together." He waggled his eyebrows like Groucho Marx. "One of us will always be with Alex."

I wished the situation were different, but I had to agree. Alex hadn't taken a major turn for the worse, but his breathing was labored even with the oxygen tube.

"If he has more difficulty, he'll be put on a ventilator with a tube inserted in his throat," Nurse Leena warned. "We don't want that to happen, because he won't be able to use the nebulizer.

I agree with Dr. Running Bear. It's important for him to have regular breathing treatments right now."

Five other children were in similar straits. One little girl who looked to be about six was now the sickest. Like Alex, she was on oxygen and being fed intravenously, but she was too ill to use the nebulizer to force steroids into her lungs. Her mother never left her room, not even to shower. Most of us made quick use of the bathroom reserved for family members, but this woman was too frightened for her daughter to be absent even for a few minutes. One of the other parents brought meals from the cafeteria and sat with her in hopes of calming her.

Johnny and I had given up our street clothes for scrubs since we had to "gown up" before entering the ICU anyway. Toby constantly whisked sheets and scrubs down to the laundry in the basement, where another orderly took charge of the soiled linens.

Johnny sat with me for a few minutes while we finished our coffee.

"I still can't believe what's happened since we came to New Mexico." I worked a kink out of my neck.

"By now, Alex should be taking care of his pony and riding all over the ranch with me. He shouldn't be holed up in a hospital room." Johnny's eyes glazed over. I wondered whether he was seeing the vast expanse of his cattle ranch or just tired. Tears moistened my eyes. *How often have I heard Alex or Emilie cry about life's lack of fairness? They're right. Life isn't fair.*

Johnny left to walk around the hospital, too wired on caffeine to sit still. "I'll be back later."

With eight children to monitor, Dr. Running Bear lived outside the ICU, on call around the clock. I wondered if he slept more than an hour or two at a stretch. Dr. Duval divided her time between the ICU and the surgical ward, where four more children, along with one adult showing similar symptoms, were being treated. Whenever I saw her, she had a phone to her ear.

Every inch of Alex's room, every piece of equipment was as familiar as my own Manhattan apartment. The nursing staff, the doctors on call, and the CDC personnel flowed around the periphery of my vision. A cap from a syringe lay on the blanket not far from Alex's hand. I stood, removed it, and tossed it into the trash before returning to my chair. I picked up my book.

I read the same paragraph a dozen times and had no idea what it said. Had anyone asked, I wouldn't have been able to tell them the name of the book, let alone the author. With little else to do, I prayed to that god I wasn't sure I believed in, the same way I did for Merry. "Can't hurt, I guess."

"What can't hurt?" Dr. Anderson entered and laid a hand on my shoulder.

"Prayer. I guess praying wouldn't hurt." I raised my face. "Time for us to meet officially. I'm Maxine Davies—Mad Max to Alex, Max to everyone else."

"Sharon." We shook hands. She pulled a chair into the room and joined my vigil. "How's your son doing?"

"My grandson. Everyone here makes the same mistake."

She nodded.

"He's not doing well at all. He was the first child showing symptoms, not long after he was admitted for surgery on his leg." I repeated the short version of Alex's fall, broken leg, and subsequent illness. I didn't expect her to remember. After all, when I first told her, we thought she was only here on a courtesy visit, with photo opportunities and a few brief remarks for the press.

"I don't know what to do. I feel so out of control. He looks so lost in that bed."

Sharon watched Alex take several noisy breaths. She didn't give me senseless palliatives, the old "He'll be all right, he's a fighter," or "You shouldn't worry." She didn't know if he'd be all right. She didn't know that this very sick boy was called *Captain Chaos* by his father and Johnny, and *holy-crap boy-child* by Emilie and by Charlie, his first crush. And she knew I had every damned right to worry, because without his typical animation— the impression of too much energy inside a skin designed to hold less—he looked diminished.

She simply said, "I'm no expert in infectious diseases. I trained as an orthopedic surgeon, and I haven't practiced medicine in a decade." As the wife of the vice president, Sharon's causes and public appearances prevented her from maintaining her medical practice. "I offered to help when I realized how ill-equipped San Felipe is to handle an outbreak like this."

"That was kind of you."

"It's also a physician's responsibility. I'm too much of a doer to sit idly by when I can be of some use," she said. She smiled at Alex when he snuffled.

"Me, too, although I seem to spend most of my time with Alex."

"It's enough for now. You should have seen the Secret Service's reaction when I gave up street clothes for scrubs. Keith, the leader of my detail, had the proverbial shit fit."

I raised an eyebrow. This mild-spoken woman never uttered a curse on camera.

"We have to watch our language when we're campaigning, but in the privacy of our home, both Milton and I swear up a storm," she explained. Milton Anderson, the vice president of the United States, presented a mild, soft-spoken yet firm public demeanor.

"When he ran his first campaign, I promised I'd tone down my dominant personality and my rather salty language. It's time for me to resurrect both. I told Dr. Duval and Dr. Running Bear they could call on me the same way they do with the staff doctors."

A small bit of humor returned to me. "I guess they waived the state medical licensing issues for the wife of the vice president."

"Ask forgiveness, never permission. We're staying silent about my legal status," Sharon smiled.

"Isn't your husband worried about your being trapped?"

"Of course he is, but he knows I do anything I want to. And he knows there's nothing he can do here." She leaned back in her chair, monitoring the screen behind Alex's bed. "Besides, he can't issue an order for me to be removed. He wouldn't violate protocol with the CDC or any other government entity. It's not his style."

"And he'd lose if he tried."

"*Keith* certainly lost. I can't remember the last time that happened." She cocked her head toward voices approaching from the nurses' station. "I sent Keith to help wherever he and the team could." Sharon winked. "He's not at all happy."

"At least he's not following you around like a Rottweiler ready to rip our throats out if we so much as glance at you." Alex moaned and coughed. My attention shifted back to the monitors, where his vital signs remained unchanged. "Dr. Running Bear needs all the extra hands he can get. I'm almost glad Alex is too sick to realize I clean him with the wipes."

Johnny and I had taken over Alex's personal hygiene, as had most of the other parents trapped with us.

"I've seen you helping not only with your boy, but also with a little girl when her mother was overwhelmed," Sharon said.

"Like you, I can't sit and do nothing. When Alex is asleep, I can always bathe or read to another sick child."

"Didn't I hear you reading to the little boy in room four in Spanish?"

"Yes, he doesn't speak English. My family has lived with a large number of Latinos in the past couple of years, so we've become proficient," I said.

More voices approached. Sharon scooted to the edge of her chair to leave. "I'll tell Keith you called him a Rottweiler. He'll be as flattered as he can be and still be inhumanly stiff."

"Being happy doesn't seem to be part of the Secret Service job description." I launched a real smile for the first time in two days.

Dr. Running Bear walked up. "I'm sorry to interrupt, Mrs. Davies—"

"Max."

"Max. I need Sharon. Can you monitor a baby?"

Sharon rose, fluid as a dancer. "What do you need me to do?"

The doctors moved off. News of two new patients drifted behind them like fumes from strong disinfectant. One baby, one old man. One case on Med-Surg was a man with an immune system compromised by emphysema from decades of heavy smoking. His primary symptoms, lung congestion and a deep cough, were similar to those Alex presented shortly after his operation.

Nurse Leena came for her routine check. She'd overheard Sharon and Dr. Running Bear talking about the old man. "Dr. Gupta thinks his illness is most likely a long-term complication from his life choices, and therefore not indicative of a change in pathology. She's fairly certain he doesn't have what infected the children."

"Do the new cases indicate potential spread in new directions?" I asked.

Nurse Leena shrugged, tapped her laptop, and moved on.

Johnny slid into Sharon's chair. "New cases, huh?"

"You heard?"

I rolled my shoulders again in a vain effort to relax my neck. Johnny turned me sideways and dug his thumbs into the muscles. I alternatively moaned in pleasure and grunted when he worked on a particularly stubborn knot.

"Dr. Running Bear has a penetrating voice. He and Dr. Anderson were talking about a baby that she's is going to watch." He stopped massaging my neck, and I realized I hadn't seen him in nearly an hour.

"Hey, where have you been anyway? Were you resting?"

"No. I've been down with Dr. Gupta. She stopped me after I met with Nurse Gilligan for our room assignment, because she wanted to go over my health form."

We'd all filled out detailed questionnaires that ran to several pages the day before.

"Why? Anyone can see you're healthy as a horse." I leaned over to let Johnny put his arm across my shoulders.

"I had dengue fever in Panama. I'm immune, but I wanted to be sure I couldn't be a carrier."

"And?"

"Can't."

CHAPTER SEVENTEEN

WITH RUMORS SWIRLING and medical personnel rushing around, our four o'clock briefing couldn't come soon enough. Johnny and I trooped into the cafeteria and took our seats with the rest of the parents. We all hoped we'd hear that the CDC had found the answer, but the doctors looked glum. All they gave us was more bad news. Two new patients. The sickest children were still receiving treatment for their symptoms, but little else.

"Why don't you give them antibiotics?" the father of another child in the ICU stood and demanded. "You have them. Use them."

Before Dr. Running Bear could respond, Dr. Gupta's soft voice floated over the assembled crowd of worried families and hospital staff. "That's a very good question, sir. As we explained, antibiotics have no effect on viruses. We found traces of the hantavirus in some patients' blood samples, but not in all samples."

The man remained on his feet. "So why not give these without hantavirus antibiotics?"

"Because some other organism could be causing the illness. We're keeping the children hydrated and waiting for their natural immune systems to take control."

"And what if they don't?" a woman I hadn't met asked. "Kids have died, and still you have no answers."

The man bore down. "Are we supposed to wait until our kids die, too?"

Murmurs and nods circulated the cafeteria. The doctors needed help winning the crowd over.

"I know where you're coming from," I said. "I'm as scared and frustrated as any of you. All we want is for this nightmare to end satisfactorily, but we need to stay calm and strong for our children's sakes."

Johnny squeezed my hand under the table, and Dr. Gupta's voice remained low in an attempt to mollify the parents. "We're testing everyone and everything, but this pathogen is tricky and sneaky. It may try to hide, but we will find it."

"You'd better find it soon before we lose any more children." The father took his seat and half-turned his back on the team leaders. His angry fear hovered like an ominous cloud.

"What's a pathogen?" a mother called out.

"It's what's causing your children to be ill," Dr. Duval said. "*Pathogen* is a generic term we're using because the organism could be a virus, a bacterium, or even a fungus."

"The good thing here is, if it is indeed hantavirus, you can't catch it from your children. It doesn't pass from human to human. It's only found in rodent droppings," Dr. Klein said. "We've triple-checked the hospital for infestations, but haven't found any signs of mice or rats. We don't think the pathogen originated here."

My phone buzzed with a text message from Emilie. *Partly true. It's inside the hospital itself, but mice didn't bring it in. Someone brought it inside on purpose.*

I tilted the phone so Johnny could see the message. He nodded ever so slightly, all the while looking confused as to how Emilie could know. Dr. Running Bear shot us both a glance.

"And this is supposed to be good news?" the angry man demanded, back on his feet. "I don't understand all the fancy words, but I understand this. If this whatever-it-is can't be passed between human beings, why can't I go home now?"

Other family members rose. Dr. Running Bear held up his hand. No one made a move toward the door. "As we've said, many of the symptoms are part of the hantavirus syndrome. Some symptoms aren't."

"It would help if we knew which symptoms aren't part of the hantavirus syndrome," Johnny said.

"Good point, Mr. Medina. The rashes and swollen lymph nodes don't belong to the normal block of hantavirus symptoms," Dr. Running Bear said. "We haven't positively identified the organism. In fact, it could be two different pathogens. Until we have a definitive answer, it's not safe for you to leave."

"But if I can't catch it from my daughter, how can I spread it?" The woman who asked this crossed her arms under ample breasts and glared from doctor to doctor, black eyes sparking.

"I'm running cultures to see if there is more than one pathogen. These organisms need time to grow," Dr. Gupta continued as if no one had interrupted.

"I put the samples through our centrifuge to separate the blood into all of its parts and looked at everything under the microscope." Dr. Klein ground knuckles into his eyes and shook his head. "I don't understand what I'm seeing."

"How can that be? I thought you were one of the best," the smoker threw at him. Nods from most of the other parents. Trilingual muttering filled the momentary silence.

Dr. Duval stood alongside Dr. Running Bear. "Dr. Klein is the best, but medicine is a science. Like all sciences, it likes to keep its own mysteries. What we are seeing under the microscope is a mystery, because we have never seen this combination of cells before in any outbreak I give you my promise we will solve it. Now, I need a promise from you. I ask you to stay patient and do as we ask." She looked into the eyes of each person, then to Johnny and me with a silent plea for help. "Do I have your promise? Mrs. Davies? Mr. Medina?"

Heads turned toward us. People looked at each other. We nodded. Other heads joined us, albeit reluctantly.

"Well, what Jerry said makes everything as clear as mud," Johnny murmured. I bobbed my head again.

Dr. Anderson's phone vibrated, and she slipped away as quietly as a cat on the hunt.

"Thank you all for your support," Dr. Running Bear said. "We're going to draw more blood today to see if any of you have changes in the number or kind of pathogens in your veins." His phone vibrated. He glanced at the screen and cursed. Before anyone could react, he bolted out of the room. No medical staff followed, so I didn't think it was a crisis in the ICU. I stared out the cafeteria windows facing the front entrance. A flurry of activity broke the isolated quiet of our quarantine. Three more black SUVs pulled up and stopped.

"Government vehicles," Johnny whispered. "Wonder which part of the cavalry is coming to the rescue."

"We'll find out soon enough." Six men and two women exited the vehicles and marched to the locked double doors. Because the entrance vestibule jutted out from the building, I could see Dr. Running Bear standing inside with arms crossed over his chest. Angry voices rose outside, but he didn't move. He held up one hand, palm outward in an age-old gesture. *Halt.*

Ignoring what was going on outside, Dr. Duval waved Toby to the front of the room. "In the next hour, Toby will be around to draw more blood."

Dr. Duval left to join the growing group of doctors at the front door. Johnny took my elbow and guided me toward the lobby. Dust motes danced a merry jig in the low sunlight slanting through the windows, swirling through air-conditioning currents and creating a sharp contrast to the dusty black vehicles hulking and snorting just outside the glass.

I wanted to be outside, to feel the sun on my skin, and to breathe the dry desert air. Living in air conditioning in a closed environment, especially one where the doctors didn't know the method of disease transmission, spooked me. The windows pressed down as if trying to suffocate me. Johnny wrapped his arms around me from behind, his chin resting on the top of my head. We watched the standoff. Doctors, including the team from the CDC, outnumbered the suits sweating in the late-day heat.

Dr. Running Bear answered his phone. From the sudden darkening of his skin, I assumed he wasn't pleased with what he heard. He listened for over two minutes without saying a word before barking an order: "Drive around back. I'll meet you at the loading dock."

We might as well have been will-o-the-wisps, invisible or ignored by Dr. Running Bear. Sharon slipped up behind me.

"FBI. They think our outbreak may be man-made."

It could be. I thought about Emilie's message. *It could very well be.*

Sharon gestured to Keith, her omnipresent Rottweiler. Together they headed to the loading dock. For once, Johnny and I didn't follow.

"Did you know there is a pretty good medical library here?" Johnny asked. "I've been doing some rather scary research."

"When have you had time?"

"Mostly when I should have been sleeping," he admitted.

What Johnny learned about the only named virus wasn't reassuring. We knew the symptoms because most of the children exhibited them, and that the virus was found in rodent droppings, but until today no one had told us it couldn't be transmitted through the air.

"We now know we probably can't get sick from Alex, but I'm far from reassured we're out of danger here. I don't feel safe, and I want to feel safe," I said.

Motes moved across my field of vision. *Are they carrying something that could sicken and kill Alex? Or Johnny? Or me?*

"The incubation period for hantavirus is all wrong. Alex fell about six days ago. True, he landed face down in the dirt. And true we'd both commented on the sound of mice and other small animals scurrying around the pine nuts."

"And?" I held my breath.

"I did the math. Initial symptoms show up between four and ten days after exposure, so if Alex really contracted hantavirus through natural means, he had to have been exposed before we reached the ranch. Hantavirus isn't endemic in Mississippi or Virginia, both places where he was within a week of our coming here."

"Could he have a super strain?" I didn't like where my mind was going, but I was powerless to stop it.

"I haven't found any articles describing such a thing, but some of the data is so dense you'd have to be a doctor to decipher it. The symptoms are clearly written for a layman like me to understand, however. It's perfectly clear that rashes are not part of hantavirus."

My entire body stiffened. I shivered again. "So, this isn't hantavirus?"

"I'm inclined to believe Dr. Gupta. She's the expert, and like her, I think something else is going on." He tightened his arms around me and kissed the top of my head.

My eyes glazed over as I stared through the glass. The sky was so crystal clear that it might ring like a bell if I flicked it. Movement behind me caught my attention. I refocused my gaze on two new reflections in the window as Dr. Gupta and Sharon walked up behind us.

"Thank you for believing me, Mrs. Davies. Not all the parents do," Dr. Gupta said.

"Please, call me Max."

"I'm Johnny."

"And I'm Meenu."

Sharon told us that the FBI had arrived from the Albuquerque field office. "You should have seen their faces when we stared them down."

I had to laugh, even though the situation was hardly funny.

"Why is the FBI involved?" Johnny asked.

"Because some cases originated outside the hospital. They want to treat this as a terror attack." Sharon rolled her eyes. "It isn't, of course."

I didn't find her composure reassuring. "If the pathogen could have been introduced deliberately by a person, I can understand why the FBI would construe this as terrorism and look into the outbreak."

"Unfortunately, as soon as someone mentions terrorism, the world turns upside down. People start believing the most outrageous rumors," Sharon said. She cautioned us to be circumspect in what we said, even to each other. Johnny looked at me. I looked back. We agreed. My pocket buzzed. So did Johnny's. Our watchdogs concurred.

"We don't know who or what is behind the outbreak," Sharon said. "Let's keep our conversations and speculations just among us, okay? If we speak out of turn, we could start a panic."

Johnny and I nodded. Until I was certain someone was maliciously infecting the children, I'd keep my thoughts closely guarded and my mouth shut.

"So, what can the FBI do?" Johnny looked again at the SUVs, most of which were pulling back onto the access road.

Dr. Gupta said, "Dr. Duval asked them to interview all the people in the community. We'll develop the questions. Tick wants to get out into the town, but she can't because of the quarantine. Until it is safe for her to leave, we'll let the FBI be our eyes and ears."

"Boy, the agent in charge was not amused when he learned his role would be subservient to Dr. Duval. Not any happier than the Rottweiler is," Sharon said.

Dr. Gupta changed the subject. "We need your support."

"How can we help?" Johnny asked before I could. I was momentarily distracted by two agents, who appeared to be in violent disagreement near the last Suburban. I wondered what it was about.

Sharon laid a hand on my goose-fleshed arm. "Help the families stay calm. You already set a terrific example through your actions and demeanor. And what you said at the meeting diffused a potentially unpleasant situation."

"It's not like we don't have an equal amount at stake," I said. I freed myself from Johnny's comforting embrace and stood more upright than I thought possible. I wanted to collapse into a puddle of self-pity and fear, but that would have to wait.

"I don't want the families to know just how much this isn't behaving like a normal hantavirus outbreak, if there is any such thing," Dr. Gupta said. "It would upset them too much. I'm concerned that most don't trust us to find the solution."

"How so?" Johnny asked.

"Why don't we go back to the cafeteria for a cup of coffee?" Sharon stepped to my other side and steered Johnny and me away from the window. Dr. Gupta followed. *Is there something she doesn't want us to see, or does she not want to risk being overheard?* "I know it's late in the day, but none of us are getting much sleep. Another jolt of caffeine isn't likely to change things."

My phone buzzed with a text message: *She really needs you to intercede with the families. They are so close to panicking.* Emilie, once again using her expanding special gift to put my mind at ease.

I showed the message to Johnny, who squeezed my arm before he batted at his face as if he could stop Ducks from touching him from a distance. I grinned in spite of the gravity of the situation.

"Who is it? Your granddaughter or her friend?" Sharon asked after Johnny's reaction. "Dr. Running Bear and one of the nurses, Leena I think her name is, mentioned you have 'spooky watchdogs' helping."

"I do. My granddaughter with a text, her friend Ducks with a tap on Johnny's cheek."

"I wish he'd stop doing that," Johnny grouched, still not comfortable with any physical manifestation from either watchdog. "He could just as easily text."

Johnny's phone buzzed. *Roger that* was the message.

Once we were settled in with fresh coffee, Sharon turned to me. "I know one of your friends."

I had a lot of friends, but none had mentioned knowing the wife of the vice president. Enough moved in the same political and social circles, though, so I hazarded a guess. "You must mean Hank Scott."

Johnny and I met him and his wife Valerie Bysbane when they were volunteering at a Habitat village after Hurricane Katrina. Hank was the former secretary of the treasury and a Nobel Prize-winning economist; his wife was a syndicated columnist for the *Washington Post*. They'd giggled about hiding in plain sight, since few people recognized either of them. Johnny and I enjoyed Friday night potlucks with them for more than six months.

"That makes three friends we have in common, since I assume you know Val, too," Sharon smiled. "I was referring to Eleanor Stephans."

That fit. Eleanor, my closest friend, mentor, and the alpha Great Dame, knew everyone worth knowing, both inside the government and out. An economist with expertise in rebuilding nations after wars, she was in near-constant demand to speak around the world.

"I guess I don't need to ask how you know her."

"We've been friends for a couple of decades. She's an amazing woman. Time enough for sharing stories later. Right now, we need to present a united front."

Johnny rubbed his forehead. Fatigue magnified his worry lines. "What aren't you telling us?"

As it turned out, a lot. Hantavirus was indeed confirmed in several of the children, including Alex, but it wasn't the only pathogen Dr. Klein found.

"He's found pieces of at least four other organisms that he can't identify."

"Pieces?" If Johnny's frown deepened any further, he'd need Botox to smooth it out.

"As he said at the meeting today, he's working day and night to solve the problem," Dr. Gupta said.

"So, Alex has hantavirus, but he also has other symptoms that don't fit that diagnosis," Johnny said, putting some of his research to good use.

"Yes and yes. Symptoms vary among the children." Dr. Gupta rocked her tea cup on the tabletop. "Tick is mapping the outbreak to determine where the clusters of cases are. She wants to know where each set of symptoms started in order to understand the method of transmission, the timing, and the potential origin."

Most of the sickest children went to a single school on the reservation, but summer vacation was in full force. The school couldn't be where they were all infected.

"Their classmates are being monitored, as are the teachers, but Tick hasn't found a pattern, much less the initial case. If this were a typical outbreak and the school were the reservoir, we'd see more cluster cases there."

I pointed out the obvious. "Well, Alex doesn't go to school here. Okay. If Alex has hantavirus plus another pathogen, how did he get it? We've been to Johnny's ranch, a ride up into the foothills, and here. The only thing all of the sick children seem to have in common is the hospital."

"Alex has something else, too." Dr. Gupta looked grave. "Jerry doesn't know what it is, but whatever it is, it doesn't occur here naturally."

"That's true. Other children were brought in after they got sick. So far, only Alex seems to have arrived in a healthy state," Sharon said.

"What about the baby? How did it get infected?" Johnny asked.

"I have no idea," Meenu said. "He's about six months old. We sent CDC inspectors from Albuquerque to his house, but they haven't found any sign of rodents. The house is clean, but he's gravely ill."

"Will the FBI do a thorough assessment?" Logic told me that the FBI was the agency best suited to eliminate all extraneous information.

"It will."

"Go on, Meenu," Sharon said. "Tell them everything."

"We have new symptoms."

Some children had signs of rash on their faces and torsos and complained of pain in their lymph nodes like Alex did. Others had worsening coughs and presented pneumonia-like symptoms, one with pulmonary edema, or swelling in the lungs. Again, like Alex, these children were on oxygen. The child with edema was on a ventilator and not expected to survive.

"Which child is it?" The parents would need our support managing the reality of their loss.

"The girl two doors up from Alex."

The room where the mother never left her daughter's bedside.

"You said this combination of symptoms doesn't occur in nature." I knew I didn't like where this was heading. No way, no how could this be good news. "Why is someone targeting children in the hospital and in the community at large?"

Ducks buzzed in with a text on Johnny's phone. *Don't ask why; ask who.* Johnny held it out to the two doctors.

"Can he read minds now?" Johnny asked.

"It would seem that both he and Em can eavesdrop move closely than I've ever seen. It could also be that we are transmitting our feelings very strongly," I said.

Sharon lowered her voice so that it didn't carry beyond the edges of our table. "We think these pathogens have been purposefully released into the community. It's as if someone is using this hospital as a giant Petri dish."

Silence hovered over our coffee cups. Reaching hands froze in mid-air. No one moved as each of us processed the information.

Before I could respond, Toby chirped his way into the cafeteria. "There you are. Time for Toby Vampire to take more blood." He pointed to Johnny and me. "You two stay. The doctors can leave."

CHAPTER EIGHTEEN

TOBY STABBED A needle into my vein and filled two syringes with blood. He'd done this so many times daily that I barely paid attention—his incessant chatter made me want to throttle him.

"Now, don't you worry. We'll find out what's going on soon." He removed the needle and bent my arm over a cotton pad. My arm ached slightly. He turned to Johnny. "Your turn, big guy."

My mind tossed like an unruly ocean current. The phrase, *a giant Petri dish*, gnawed at my brain like a nest of fire ants.

Could it be that someone released this whatever-it-is on purpose? Why is someone trying to kill the children? And what about the few adults who've fallen ill? Are they of a similar ethnic background? Of the same socio-economic level? From the same physical location? In the wrong place at the wrong time, like Alex? How much of the release was targeted at specific people, if someone is acting intentionally? How are they transmitting the pathogen? And who the hell has access to it?

I pressed my lips together, afraid I'd blurt out a question that should be kept secret. Toby finished with Johnny and dashed away.

"He should count himself lucky I didn't strangle him," I growled.

"He won't shut up, will he?"

Johnny and I left the cafeteria, fresh Band-Aids in the crooks of our elbows. I squeezed Johnny's hand. We needed to talk alone. I wanted his advice on the thousand questions elbowing for room in my mind.

"Did you notice how he said he was helping find out what was going on?" I picked at the edge of the Band-Aid. "Is he giving himself a role he wishes he had? Something doesn't feel right. Did you see him break the seal on the needle before he stuck you?"

"I don't know. I wasn't watching him."

Just like me, I had to admit.

Before we reached the stairs to the second floor, my phone rang.

"You're right," my special granddaughter said. "Someone in the hospital is behind this."

I flinched and looked over my shoulder. Johnny and I were alone in the corridor. No ghosts or solid human beings hovered, yet the hair on my nape stirred.

"I won't ask how you know this," I said after a startled pause.

"It's something Mr. Ducks and I have been working on. I can't explain it."

"Do you have any idea who it is?" I asked, turning back to the matter at hand.

Johnny's phone buzzed. Ducks. We listened to our respective callers for a few minutes. Both sensed an evil presence loose in the hospital and in the community at large. Both felt it might be a man, but they weren't yet certain. It might be two people. Ducks felt a weak female presence.

Johnny slowly turned in a full circle to be certain we were alone. "We need to figure out who wants people to die," Johnny said.

"And why," I added, covering the speaker on my phone to add a comment to Johnny's side of the conversation.

"I've been doing a lot of thinking. What if someone wants to make people sick and then ride to the rescue with a cure?" Ducks asked. "Like that condition, um, what's it called?"

"Munchausen by proxy," Johnny said.

My eyebrows rose. "How do you know about that?"

"What? I read about it in a thriller where child abuse was suspected," he said.

"Right. Munchausen." Ducks went silent for a few moments. "Could it be something like that, or hero syndrome, except the dead children are a miscalculation?"

"I don't see how," Johnny said. "The person or persons would not only have to have a stash of the pathogens in the hospital itself, but wouldn't he also need a similar stockpile of the cure? So far, if he thinks he has the miraculous cure, it's been a dismal failure."

I was frustrated with Ducks and Emilie. I wasn't being fair, but I'd grown accustomed to them having all the answers. Now, in the middle of a crisis, they only had vague feelings. I didn't know who to turn to—Ducks and Emilie, who weren't here, or Johnny and the doctors, who were.

"You'll have to be extra careful. Let me add Mr. Ducks on a conference call. He's over in the school bus," Emilie told me. Whip, Emilie, and Ducks had returned to Mississippi, our sailing vacation postponed until further notice.

"Do you think this person will use anything else? Like a gun?" I'd had enough of being stalked by armed strangers to last the rest of my life. I owned a gun and had a license to carry it. I'd used it once in my life, taking the life of a madman. I never wanted to point it at a human being again.

Ducks' voice came on the line. "Not guns. I don't sense a shooting situation, but if you tell me you have your trusty .38, Max, I'll feel a little better."

"I do." My revolver was upstairs in the room Johnny and I shared, in my over-large Jimmy Choo handbag, one of two bags Merry bought on the last day of her normal life. I'd liberated them for my personal use.

"I have my Sig, as well," Johnny said.

"I'm glad, but it won't be effective against the pathogens," Emilie said.

"It would be effective against the person spreading the illnesses," Johnny said.

"We'll keep working on it. We'll find out who it is, even though we haven't been able to yet. He hasn't shown his hand." Ducks tried to sound confident.

"Or he's blocking you," I said, the thought flashing without warning.

Ducks clicked off, leaving Emilie, Johnny, and me on the line. I gave her an update on Alex and promised to call her later that evening. I'd call her father, too, after he got back from the job site. We closed with air kisses.

"I don't like the fact that neither she nor Ducks have a clear feeling about what's happening." Johnny said.

"Yea. All they get is that it's centered in and around the hospital."

"That much is obvious," he said. Exactly what I was thinking.

We checked Alex's room, only to be told by a nurse that he was down in X-ray. Again. With nothing to do in the ICU, we followed the corridor to the physicians' offices. Dr. White had commandeered an empty one for her workspace, and we needed to find it.

A door on the second floor was ajar; we looked inside. The walls were lined with what had to be every white board in the building, boards divided by symptoms, each patient diagrammed with background information, the date the illness began, where the patient was when he fell ill. Even a local map with push pins in it. Flip-chart paper covered the walls themselves, holding the overflow of data the white boards couldn't handle.

"'Welcome to my parlor,' said the spider to the fly." Dr. White stood in front of a puzzling graph of incomprehensible scribbles. "This is where I crunch data, although I'd be better off crunching Wheaties for all the success I'm having. I'm trying to find the disease vector to see where this mess started, but I'm not having the success I'd hoped."

"Remind me what a disease vector is? Dr. Duval talked about it, but I forget."

"Sorry. It means I'm looking for what infected these patients. A disease vector is generally some kind of organism that transmits viruses or bacteria into a human."

"You mean like mosquitoes transmitting malaria in tropical climates?" Johnny said. "In Panama we had to take anti-malarial drugs all the time. Didn't do a damned thing to keep the mosquitoes from dining on my blood."

"That's a good example. Did you have malaria?" Dr. White asked.

"I did. And dengue fever, too."

"You've told Meenu?"

"Of course. She's up to date on my somewhat colorful medical history." Johnny rolled his head, vertebrae in his neck complaining with each rotation.

"Watch out for odd symptoms. If you had malaria once, you could get it again," Dr. White said.

"No mosquitoes here."

"You could have a relapse without a new bite. That would compromise your immune system." She studied a board and tapped an equation I didn't understand. "If this illness is transmitted by an insect bite, whether a mosquito, a tick, or something else, I need to find the original bite on the body."

"I haven't noticed any on Alex. About the only holes he has, other than the surgery on his fractured leg, come from IVs and blood work," I said. I couldn't remember if Alex had complained about mosquito bites or not. I didn't think so—if he had any, I'd have noticed by now during his daily swabbing.

"He had a few old ones he got in Richmond, but they've cleared up."

"How long ago was he bitten?" Dr. White asked.

"Probably three, maybe four weeks," I said, studying the board with Alex's name at the top. Johnny followed suit, and together we read everything Dr. White had on him.

"This isn't right." Johnny pointed to a notation about origin of the illness. "We went horseback riding up a trail near Navajo Springs. Alex climbed onto an outcropping and fell, breaking his leg. When we flew him into the hospital, he had no pulmonary symptoms."

"Did he get dirt on his face?"

"Sure. He fell face down in the dust. I remember brushing him off when we turned him over to look at his leg," I said.

She corrected her original entry. "And you're sure he didn't have a cough before?"

"Positive. His cough developed after he came into the hospital. Before that, nothing." I finished reading the list. "Wait a minute.

Dr. Running Bear said he had some breathing issues during surgery, but he thought it was from the dust he'd inhaled. He kept Alex to monitor his lungs in case he developed pneumonia."

Dr. White made a cryptic notation on Alex's board. Like most doctors, her handwriting was barely legible, although much of what I could read I still couldn't understand. I pointed to a section on his board.

"Back to his chart. You also have him showing signs of cough, fever, and malaise two days after he first complained of body aches. All three symptoms showed up at the same time on his second day in the hospital," I said.

"When he complained that his body hurt, I thought it was because of the fall," Johnny said. "Although we didn't see the actual plunge, he thinks he bounced off rocks from about twenty feet up. He cracked a couple of ribs."

If she's wrong about Alex's symptoms, could she be wrong about the other patients as well?

"Where did you get this information?" I asked.

"Mostly from his charts and talking with the nurses and Dr. Running Bear." Dr. White looked at me. "I should have spoken with you. Broken ribs complicate matters. They could have masked the onset of the virus."

"What about his rash?" Johnny asked. There was no mention of it on the board.

"Tell me more about that."

I filled her in on when Alex's rash started, since I'd been the one to notice it first—how it had spread, what it looked like, and how the lymph nodes were swollen. "When he's awake, he complains that it's painful," I finished.

The epidemiologist made several new notations on Alex's board. She moved from column to column, patient to patient, to see if any others presented similar symptoms. Three children did, including the boy who died. Each had come to the emergency room already sick.

"I need to see these kids. Jerry and Meenu have examined them, but I have to see the rash for myself. I can't leave anything to chance. Jerry took scrapings and studied them under his super-duper microscope. He's still searching." She continued circumnavigating the room.

"No answers?" I asked.

"Nothing definitive."

"What are you looking for?" Johnny walked with her.

"Anything that ties these cases together. Like I said, I crunch data. I've got everything on my PC, but I'm an old-school, visual kind of gal. I need white boards, markers, and patients." She rubbed the back of her neck. "Just when I think I'm getting close, I receive new data that doesn't fit, like the rash and swollen lymph nodes. It's like a jigsaw where multiple puzzles have been dumped together. With no picture, I can't tell what's important and what's not."

"Oh my. Square pegs and round holes, huh?" I didn't envy her the task ahead.

"If you want to interview the other parents, either Max or I can translate for those who are more comfortable speaking Spanish," Johnny offered.

"I'll take you up on it. In fact, I'd like one of you to be with me at all the interviews. The parents are more likely to open up when they see someone they trust and who is in the same predicament."

I'd do anything to help her find the disease vector so the doctors could heal Alex. I wouldn't admit it, but I didn't care all that much about the others. My grandson came first.

My phone buzzed. *It's okay. Worry about Alex. Let the doctors take care of the rest. Ducks.* This new normal of eavesdropping watchdogs still unnerved me. I held it out for Johnny to read. He turned from the boards. "Did you perform an autopsy on the child?"

"The first child?" Dr. White asked.

"What? Has another child died?" I put a hand to my throat. No one on any ward mentioned more deaths. Of its own free will, my hand moved to my mouth, the easier to bite a knuckle.

"I shouldn't have said anything. We have three bodies downstairs. Only one died here. The others were brought in by their families as we requested. We put all outside doctors, clinics, and funeral homes on alert. Any corpse has to be brought here immediately. We also issued a warning that precaution be taken when handling the bodies," she said.

"Why?" I asked.

"Until we identify the pathogen, we have to assume the worst. If the disease spreads through bodily fluids, handling a dead body could be a transmission point. It could be every bit as deadly as coming into contact with sprayed droplets from a live person."

"Like Ebola?" Johnny asked.

"Exactly, except we aren't dealing with Ebola. I'm going down to the makeshift morgue and see if Jerry has any new information." Dr. White headed toward the door. "Sharon and Meenu suggested we keep everything under need-to-know protocols."

"You can count on us," I said. Too bad Alex wasn't his old self. He'd have loved to be involved in such a mystery.

Johnny cast a final look at the boards before we left Dr. White's workspace. She closed and locked the door behind her and headed down to the morgue. Johnny turned me to the right toward the ICU and Alex; Toby rushed past us toward the ICU. I was about to call out when Johnny put a restraining hand on my arm.

"His lab is in the basement of the main building. Why would he be in the wing with the physician offices?" Johnny had a strange look on his face.

CHAPTER NINETEEN

DR. WHITE OUTGREW her office space by the third day and commandeered the largest conference room in the hospital. A sign next to the door read "Classroom." Three walls were now lined with the portable white boards. The fourth wall was a ceiling-to-floor, permanent white board covered with flip-chart paper. Tick constantly changed the data as she added new symptoms or crossed out others as unimportant.

"Isn't this equipped with Wi-Fi and smart boards? You'd think they'd have them in a state-of-the-art hospital," I said.

"You would. Looks like an oversight when they built the facility. It would help if it had what I needed, but I make do. Have you heard we admitted our first healthcare worker overnight?" She glared at the boards, hands clasped behind her back, as if demanding they divulge their secrets. "He's in critical condition. I don't think he'll live."

"I hadn't heard. Someone who works in the hospital or a community worker?" I asked.

"He's an orderly whose been on duty since the outbreak began."

"Did he work in the ICU?" A couple of orderlies rotated in and out, most of them cleaning, disinfecting, and removing the used protective gear and bedding in the burn and laundry barrels.

"And everywhere else. Anyway, he said he's felt sick for a few days, but didn't say anything because we are so short on staff. When he woke up this morning with pustules all over his torso, he knew he was in trouble." Dr. White erased and corrected a note on a board, her already tiny handwriting even smaller. Some boards were nearly solid black from her cryptic notations.

"That little girl next to Alex has pustules, too." I didn't remember anyone else with them. Rashes like Alex's, yes, but large pus-filled blisters, no. "Can whatever is causing them be treated?"

She nodded. "If caught soon enough, it doesn't have to be a death sentence. There's an outside chance for the orderly."

I grew as warm as a menopausal hot flash when a memory nudged at me.

"You might ask if he has any healing cuts. Look on his hands," I suggested.

"Why?"

"I just remember a tray of spilled and broken syringes. I don't know if any had been used already. That could be the cause of the orderly's illness if the needles were already infected," I said.

"Will do."

The lockdown continued, with no end in sight to new cases and the multiplication of symptoms. I returned to Alex to relieve Johnny for a couple of hours. He updated me on Alex's condition.

"Alex's breathing is stable. He had inhalation therapy about an hour ago. He's still congested, but the nurse said he shows no signs of pneumonia."

"That's good news. You look beat. Why don't you go lie down?" I said.

Johnny stood and stretched. Before he left the ICU, he kissed me and gave me a big hug. I suspected he'd head over to the medical library. He and Ducks were in continual communication by phone and text about what each was learning.

Alex started panting as if trapped in a nightmare. I shook his shoulder, and Leena slipped in to take his vitals. Alex's eyes flew open. He screamed.

"What's wrong?" I sat on the bed and drew the boy into my arms.

Alex's words emerged between pants. "A—a dragon. A—a white dragon. It leaned over me and breathed on me." His body shook.

"A dragon?" I asked. Alex had never been interested in dragons, other than *Dungeons & Dragons* on his computer. He nodded against my chest.

I stared up at Leena, who shrugged before she pushed a syringe into his IV port. "It's a light sedative to calm him down. Is this the first time he's had nightmares?"

"I think so."

"In all other ways, he's holding his own. Dr. Running Bear scheduled daily CT scans to be sure his lungs stay healthy."

"Will you tell Dr. Running Bear about this nightmare?" I asked. *Could it be a hallucination, or did Alex remember someone bending over him?*

"Don't worry, I will," Leena assured me.

"I heard four more cases came in overnight. Three from the surrounding community."

"Yes. It's spreading outward from San Felipe."

Alex relaxed in my arms, and I eased him back onto the bed. "How soon do you think the FBI's investigation will give us some solid leads as to how this is expanding?" I asked.

"Not soon enough." Nurse Leena made a couple of entries on her laptop.

"By the way, when I reviewed Alex's medical history with Dr. White, several entries on his board were incorrect." The variance in when Alex's symptoms began continued to worry me. I couldn't imagine how Dr. White's information could be so wrong.

"Like what?" Nurse Leena looked at me. I gave her a rundown. She frowned and searched Alex's health record. "That's weird. I don't see some of the information I entered right after he came into the ICU. I'll check with the other nurses. I could swear we didn't take anything out."

"Could someone have changed it later?"

The nurse shot me a look of utter confusion. She moved the cursor over the record. She didn't answer, so I pressed further.

"Shouldn't there be a history in each record of who made actual changes?"

"What do you mean?" she asked.

"Aren't all entries time-stamped with some notation as to who entered the data?" Surely a state-of-the-art hospital had at least that amount of accountability.

Nurse Leena looked troubled. "Let me get someone more technical than I am to dig into this."

My watchdogs had added Nurse Leena to their network. Although she wasn't quite as in tune with them as I was, she was in close touch with similar spiritual leaders in her own community.

"I wish I knew what to make of this outbreak. Too many symptoms, too many contradictions for it to be occurring without help," she murmured.

"What do you mean?"

"I'm certain the outbreak is caused by human intervention." Leena closed the laptop and walked to the door.

"Like someone introducing something into the hospital?" I asked, relieved that my watchdogs weren't the only ones operating with that suspicion.

"Yes." She told me a couple of shamans were going to perform another healing ceremony on the hospital grounds in a day or so. They were currently purifying themselves in a sweat lodge. "They'll try to drive the demons out."

"And what if the demon is human?" I asked. Ducks tapped my cheek encouragingly. "How do we drive him out?"

Leena looked at me, dark eyes impenetrable. "I have no idea."

Two and a half hours later, Toby took Alex downstairs for his CT scan. I went to find Johnny, who wasn't in our room or in the cafeteria. I grabbed a bottle of water and dropped into the medical library. No Johnny. He had to be in the conference-room-cum-diagnosis-lab.

Floor tiles stretched in front of me. Not bothering to resist the urge, I played hopscotch down the length of the corridor. I was glad no one saw me. It felt good to act goofy for a minute or two.

I found Johnny standing near Dr. Duval, who was in deep

conversation with Sharon. They didn't notice Dr. White let me in. I walked over to Alex's board. New entries in red screamed at me. Johnny pointed at one word underlined in red on three boards—*pox*. My breath caught in my throat, leaving me light-headed.

"Oh my God. Does that say what I think it says?"

Dr. Duval turned. "Yes, Mrs. Davies. Alex has some form of pox. His rash has formed small blisters in the last few hours. It is not the pustules we expect to see, not like the girl has."

"Or the orderly," I added, but I couldn't shake the chill that ran across my shoulders.

"That is correct. It is not smallpox, so do not jump to that conclusion. That was eradicated back in the seventies," she assured me.

"But smallpox still exists in some labs, doesn't it?" Johnny and his damned research again.

"Yes, Mr. Medina. We have frozen samples, and so does Russia. Both are officially locked in the most secure areas in the world. I repeat, this is not smallpox," Dr. Duval said.

I struggled to stay calm. "Other than chickenpox and smallpox, what other kind of poxes are there?"

"Has Alex had chickenpox?" Sharon deflected my question with one of her own. She hadn't been present when Dr. Gupta took our health histories. With the change in some data on Dr. White's boards, all the information had to be validated anew.

"He did when he was four. His mother said he was the most miserable little boy she'd ever seen. He spiked a 105 fever and was hours away from being admitted to a hospital when the fever broke."

I thought back on Merry's frantic phone calls. She wouldn't let me come down to help, so I comforted her as much as she would allow from a distance. "He should be immune, shouldn't he?"

"This is not chickenpox. Neither is it shingles." Dr. Duval's eyes never stopped moving from board to board.

"Isn't shingles something only older people get?" I asked. My friend Grace once had an attack and was in dreadful pain for weeks until the last of the blisters disappeared.

"We rarely see it in a child. Besides, the blood work shows no sign of *varicella-zoster,* the virus that causes chickenpox and shingles. Rule that out." Dr. Duval's island intonation, so lilting, so gentle, should have calmed me, but it didn't.

"What do we rule in, then?" Sharon pointed to three additional boards where pox also appeared in red. One was the little girl next to Alex. One was the first child who died. And the newest was was an older child recently admitted.

"Did that first child die from pox?" I asked.

"We do not know. We know he had a form of pox when he died. If it was the cause of his death, we are not sure."

"Didn't the autopsy tell you?" Again, Johnny with a question designed to drag more information from the doctors. I wished for a moment he hadn't done so much research, taking away my ability to retreat into comforting ignorance. He was right, though.

"Is Johnny on the right track? What did the autopsy show?"

A new voice joined the discussion. "It showed us too much."

Dr. Klein, the pathologist, walked in with a fistful of paper. I hadn't heard his knock or noticed Dr. White open the door, so deep was I into the enormity of what the doctors faced.

"I've run a dozen different tests on his blood and other tissues, as well as on the samples taken from all the patients. So far, what I have is a viral and possibly bacterial stew."

That didn't sound very professional, but I got the gist. "Back to that spilled jigsaw puzzle, huh?"

Dr. Duval, Sharon, and Dr. Klein were lost. I explained the metaphor Dr. White and I had used.

"Every time I think I have the answer, all I have is another question," Dr. Klein said, staring at reports in his hand. He shook his head and focused on the floor. My gut said he was looking for clues that either didn't exist or were confusingly plentiful. I doubted he'd find the answers in tile patterns. *Maybe he should play hopscotch with me to clear his mind.*

Dr. Duval pointed to the word that terrified me. *Pox.* "We must focus on this first. Have you isolated the virus that is causing Alex's symptoms?"

"Yes and no," Dr. Klein said.

Johnny put his arm around my shoulders.

"What I have looks like a virus smoothie, if you'll forgive the metaphor. It's as if a bunch of viruses were tossed in a blender. Some are such tiny fragments that most likely can't infect anyone, while others appear whole but damaged. And still others are larger than normal. I can't figure out which are active and which ones are dormant."

Dr. Klein sounded and looked exhausted. I doubted he'd slept much since the CDC got here.

"I'm running cultures on everything," he finished.

"It is time for the daily briefing. We will keep this among the five of us for now. I will speak with Dr. Running Bear in private. There is no need to panic the parents. Jerry, brief Tick, will you?" Dr. Duval asked before leading us toward the cafeteria.

"And *I'm* not panicked?" I whispered to Johnny. He squeezed my shoulder. Halfway down the corridor, I realized Dr. Duval never answered my question: What other types of pox were there?

Instead of a brief meeting with medical updates, Dr. Running Bear stood beside Keith the Rottweiler, whose face was purple with fury. A revolver lay on the table in front of him.

Uh oh. I looked at it quickly. "Whew. Not mine," I whispered to Johnny. "Mine's in my handbag back in our room."

"My Sig's in my kit," Johnny whispered back.

"We were searching the hospital with Dr. Running Bear this morning, when we found this in an unlocked file drawer in a nurses' station on the second floor." Keith's body language dared someone to claim the gun. He held it up. "Whose is this?"

A mousy nurse raised her hand. "It's mine."

"Take her away." Two agents levered themselves from the wall and took a step and a half toward the terrified nurse.

"Wait," Dr. Running Bear said, his voice low but authoritative. He held up a hand. "Don't jump to conclusions."

"What conclusion should I draw, Dr. Running Bear?" the Rottweiler sneered. "Our advance team warned the staff that guns would not be allowed on the premises when the vice president's wife was visiting. This nurse is in clear violation of our safety protocols."

"I don't remember any such warning," Dr. Running Bear said.

"Whether you remember or not is irrelevant. We always secure a facility. No guns of any kind. This breach won't be tolerated.

"Where did you get this?" Keith demanded. He turned toward the nurse, who was doing her best not to quake. The two agents moved closer.

"I brought it to work. I have a license to carry it." Her voice quivered, and a tear trickled down her cheek. "I always lock it in my desk or in a cabinet. I must have forgotten with the scramble to care for all the sick children. I'm sorry."

"Sorry?" Keith's face turned an even darker shade.

"You may have noticed, agent, that the territory around the hospital is damned empty."

Dr. Running Bear glanced around the room, nodding to the assembled staff and parents. He gestured to the vista outside. "I encourage my nurses and doctors to arm themselves, particularly when many of us work nights. It's for our own safety."

Keith looked at the crowd in front of him. "How the hell many of you have guns?"

Every nurse and doctor raised a hand. So did several of the parents. I raised mine, as did Johnny.

"How the hell many of you brought your guns into the hospital?"

The same hands stayed up.

"Jesus." He scanned every face.

"The guns wouldn't be much good if they were at home or in our cars, would they?" Dr. Running Bear gestured for his nurse to take her seat.

Sharon broke the tension by laughing. "As my kids would say, get over it, Keith. Let's let this little 'oversight' not bother us any longer."

"Welcome to Wild West, agent," Dr. Running Bear joined in the laughter. "If you want mine, you'll find it locked in the upper-left hand desk drawer in my office. I can give you my keys if you like. I fired it a couple of weeks ago, but cleaned it before putting it away."

"Why did you fire your gun?" asked the agent-in-charge, who was not in charge.

"Six-foot rattler in the parking lot right next to my front

car door. I didn't want to have to treat anyone for snakebite."
Dr. Running Bear turned away from the agent, dismissing his
concerns. "Now, can we move on to fighting the pathogens? I
guarantee guns won't be of use in this fight."

With that, he provided a brief medical update, after which
Johnny and I returned to the ICU. We put on our gear and
entered Alex's room. Toby the vampire was drawing another
blood sample.

"Oh, good. I was getting ready to hunt you down. I need your
blood, too. Still checking to see if the virus is spreading."

CHAPTER TWENTY

JOHNNY AND I followed Toby to the central nurses' station. We shed our gowns, rolled up our sleeves, and exposed our lower arms.

"You're the last ones on this floor. I've bled everyone else," he said, setting his supplies on the counter.

Toby's persistent vampire joke had grown a long gray beard by the third time I heard it. Now, my nerves were raw, and all I wanted was for him to take the sample and get the hell away from me.

Johnny went first. Toby tied a rubber tourniquet around his upper arm, swabbed his inner elbow, picked up a syringe, and slowly inserted the needle into a vein. Blood filled the plastic tube. Toby pulled the original tube away and inserted another one. When that one was full, he released the tourniquet, extracted the needle, and told Johnny to hold a cotton ball tight against the puncture. A Band-Aid followed. When my turn came, I scarcely paid attention. The routine had become so, well, routine.

Toby exited with the tray of blood samples.

"I'm going to the head," Johnny said, heading out of Alex's room, only to catch a face-full of spray from a bottle Toby was using.

"What the hell? Watch where you're spraying that shit," Johnny snapped at Toby. He stalked off to the bathroom, wiping moisture from his eyes and mask.

"What's in the bottle?" I demanded an answer.

"Disinfectant," he said shortly. Then he was gone. I lowered my mask and took a tentative sniff. Whatever it was didn't smell like anything. Not disinfectant. Not cleaning materials. It hung in the air, however, like a greasy film. I pulled my mask back over my nose and mouth.

Once Johnny returned and we were alone again in Alex's room, he absentmindedly rubbed his arm and stared at the beeping machines. "What's the matter?" I'd been so focused on Alex that subtle changes in Johnny's behavior evaporated like fog at dawn. I stared hard at him and didn't like what I saw.

"Don't you feel all right?"

Something in the way he stood put me on alert. Usually so erect and square shouldered, now he leaned his head against the wall, his right hand holding his left arm. He shook himself before turning to me.

"I'm all right. I was thinking about Toby."

His hand went back to his left arm, probably still sore from the needle. He glanced at a sleeping Alex. We kept our voices low.

"What's wrong?" I asked, my radar locked onto his arm.

"Something about the way Toby took our blood. Not to mention recklessly spraying whatever that was. I can't quite figure out what was different, but something was." He pushed his mask aside and rubbed his nose. When he coughed, we both stiffened at the sound of congestion. "Guess I'd better not touch Alex, huh?"

I shook my head.

We needed to talk about the blood extraction with Dr. Running Bear. Now that I thought about it, Toby had changed the way he extracted blood several times. Today, he selected a needle from the far end of the row instead of picking up the nearest needle as he had in the past.

"The protective sleeve of the needle he used on you lay beside it, but he placed the needle in the sleeve after he drew your blood. My syringe was sealed when he picked it up."

"Could he have removed the sleeve to save time? After all, he's been taking blood daily. Maybe he wants to speed things up." Johnny rubbed the back of his neck.

"That doesn't make sense. Why change his style for one of us and not for the other?"

Johnny winced.

"Do you have a headache?" I asked.

"I think we'd better find Dr. White."

CHAPTER TWENTY-ONE

WE TRACKED THE epidemiologist down in her locked diagnosis room. She answered our knock and stepped aside to let us in. If she thought we looked silly and out of place in our protective gowns, masks, and gloves, her face didn't give her away.

"What's the matter?" Dr. White shoved a couple of stools our way. "Take off your gear, and tell me what's going on."

Johnny stripped to his light blue scrubs, and told her what we'd experienced with our blood work.

"So, Toby didn't follow protocol?"

"I don't think so. It's not the first time something seemed off, either," I said. "I'd be more comfortable if you'd call Dr. Klein and take a fresh sample. Can he test it without anyone but you and him knowing about it? I particularly don't want any of the hospital staff to know."

Dr. White called Dr. Klein on her cell. He promised to be up as soon as he finished an autopsy.

"Who died this time?" I asked. With death surrounding us, I tried to sound sanguine but failed.

"The orderly who came in last night," she sighed.

My mouth dropped open. "But he was just admitted."

Apparently, he'd lost consciousness a few hours earlier and died of what Dr. Klein thought was congestive heart failure brought on by pulmonary edema.

"These symptoms don't go with any kind of pox, do they?" Johnny asked, growing pale. Sweat peppered his forehead.

"Not usually. We'll wait for Dr. Klein's autopsy results before we list his cause of death."

Ten minutes later, Dr. White let Dr. Klein in. She updated him quickly with a few spare sentences. Dr. Klein reached for a tourniquet and went through the steps to extract blood from our left arms.

"I'll run the tests tonight. If I find anything odd, I'll let you know." He put the vials in his pocket and left.

"You did the right thing. Can't be too careful in all this chaos, though I doubt there's anything to worry about," Dr. White said.

I mustered up a weak smile. "I'm probably seeing bogeymen where there aren't any. I've been known to do that in the past."

"And you've seen evil when the rest of us missed it," Johnny said. "Don't forget you recognized the look of that endangered child in Mississippi."

I gave Tick a quick recap of my daughter's death and the girl who had been trapped in a dangerous situation. I concluded, "I don't really think we have a bogeyman on the loose. I think we have a flesh-and-blood human on the loose. I don't know who it is, though."

I mentioned my unnerving conversation with Nurse Leena about Alex's electronic record and my suspicions that it might have been changed.

Dr. White stared thoughtfully at her boards. "I'll check this out. If someone tampered with or confused the records, we need to know who. We can't let things fall apart here just because of extenuating circumstances. Too bad we don't have a forensic IT tech on hand." She paced the room.

"The FBI should have one to spare, shouldn't it?" I asked.

Johnny and I headed for the cafeteria for an afternoon snack. We sat in deep, silent thought for a long while. Johnny picked at his slice of apple pie. I tried to write off his diminished appetite—I wasn't all the hungry either. The cafeteria food lost whatever allure it had when we first arrived eight days earlier. At least the coffee remained strong and hot.

"Something is so wrong here. Like Dr. White, I don't know who's involved, but someone who works in or has access to this hospital is behind the outbreak," Johnny said. Melting vanilla ice cream surrounded the remainder of his pie.

"And how do you know this?"

"My gut." Johnny rubbed his temple with the heel of one hand.

"Not you, too."

"Hey, Ducks and Em don't use their guts. They have avenues that I don't. So, gut it is until I learn otherwise," he said, trying to smile.

"How does your gut factor into your research? What's really bothering you? Tell me." I took a large sip of coffee and looked Johnny square in the eyes before reaching for his hand. I was surprised at how cold it was, but no way was I releasing it until he told me everything.

"On the day of Alex's accident, he was as healthy as the pony he was riding. And now he's the sickest boy I've ever seen."

"Alex and a lot of other kids," I said. I squeezed his hand.

"None of this should be happening," he said. A shaft of sunlight crept across our table and stabbed us in the eyes. Johnny flinched and blinked. I looked closer at him. Bloodshot eyes, an apparent headache because he frequently rubbed his temples and the back of his neck, although not at the same time. He hadn't been getting any more sleep than me, but even so, he lacked the spark I expected. "First of all, not everyone who is exposed falls sick. And hantavirus is endemic in the region, but it hasn't been active for many years."

"True. Many local residents have probably been exposed, shown cold-like symptoms, and recovered. No harm, no foul. But others get sick. And some died. And why Alex? Why so many now? Why here in this hospital?" I asked, picking up the thread.

It didn't make sense. Alex, for all his clumsiness, had to constitution of an ox, like Johnny. Neither was ever sick. The speed with which Alex's illness exploded in his body couldn't be explained.

I told Johnny about Alex's nightmare. Johnny shook his head. "A white dragon breathed on him? I was there all the time. I didn't see any white dragon."

Once we'd given up on our snacks, Johnny went to lie down for an hour. He needed rest for the night shift. I took short daytime naps. The bed in our room had an uncomfortable mattress, which made me long for my king-sized bed at home or even the queen in my RV.

Truth be known, I longed to be any place but where I was— where I could go outside at will, where I wasn't an actual prisoner. Wearing my protective clothing, I stared at my reflection in the walls of Alex's room. I felt a little like Gort, the alien in *The Day the Earth Stood Still*—the original, with Michael Rennie and Patricia Neal, not the remake with someone and someone else.

Half an hour later, turmoil in the ICU woke Alex. His eyes cracked open, fear replacing sleep.

"What's happening, Mad Max?" he wrote on a tablet in wobbly letters, his throat sore from the oxygen tube. "Is the dragon back?"

"No dragon is going to get you while I'm here." I stroked his sweaty hair. "I don't know what's happening, though. A new child came in yesterday. A lot of doctors are working on her."

A swarm of doctors and nurses buzzed around the nurses' station and filled every square inch of the new child's room. Emilie surrounded me like a warm blanket, but something had changed in the ICU. The atmosphere was as charged as a thunderstorm. A growing sense of dread washed over me as if someone, the evil someone, were near.

Dr. Duval and Dr. Running Bear stepped out of the room, heads together in consultation. Their masks muffled their whispers, so I couldn't hear what they said. I could see several nurses, along with Dr. White and Dr. Klein, inside with the child. Sharon came up beside me and jerked her head toward the outer door. I returned to Alex, patted his hand, and told him I'd be right outside.

"That child came in yesterday. She has similar but worse symptoms than Alex, yet she tested negative for hantavirus," Sharon said.

I rubbed my eyes and wiped an oily smear from my forehead.

I had to stay strong. Emilie and Ducks were with me, but they couldn't shoulder my burdens, lessen my stress, or alleviate the worry I lived with daily.

"Her family thought she had a cold. She sneezed and coughed. They thought it was nothing to worry about, but they kept her home, away from her brothers and sisters for a couple of days."

The public's lack of cooperation wasn't helping the professionals corral this outbreak.

"How many times do you have to remind families that every illness should be checked out right now? No matter how slight," I asked, exasperated.

"Many locals take care of their own family. Or they turn to traditional healers, Max. It might be too much to expect them to change their ways and run to modern medicine when plants and chants have healed in the past." Sharon put her hand on my arm. "Modern medicine won out yesterday when she spiked a fever and began coughing heavily. When she brought up bloody sputum, her family brought her in."

I knew of only one disease with that symptom. "TB?"

Sharon shook her head, eyes unfocused. She retreated into her head much like Emilie did when she went to her special place. Sharon's special place seemed unlike Emilie's, though. My pocket buzzed. *She's not one of us. But she's close,* Emilie said. I put the cell back in my pocket. Sharon turned to look at me.

"My granddaughter says you have ESP, but you don't know how to use it," I said.

"And how would she know?"

"Because she does. That's why she's so spooky."

My phone buzzed with a smiley face text. I held it out to Sharon.

"I hope she can help. We need all the watching she can give us." Sharon turned back toward the ICU, but didn't move forward. Emilie buzzed me again. *She's keeping all her channels open.*

Sharon pushed through the door, and we re-entered the ICU.

"Who's doing the analysis?" I asked.

"Dr. Klein will. He'll use the samples Toby Vampire took." Sharon gave a twisted smile.

"Ask Dr. White to test a second sample. She'll know why."

I left Sharon at Alex's door. A curious expression crossed her face, and she moved toward the swarming room. Alex moaned in his sleep, but he didn't thrash. The nightmare hadn't returned. I sat in the recliner and tried to read. *I might as well try to fly.*

I closed my eyes and let my mind drift. Well, not exactly drift. Like a stone in a typhoon, nothing was calm. Nothing was clear. Nothing drifted.

Hours later, when the new child appeared to be stable, Sharon and I joined Dr. Duval for a late dinner. I'd barely snacked with Johnny, and a light meal might hold me over until breakfast. Food helped me keep a clear head. Dr. Duval gave me a few new details beyond the growing number of patients admitted and the rising death toll. Six so far, including the orderly. I nibbled on limp lettuce and speared a cherry tomato, which tasted like red nothing. Again, I shoved my food aside.

Sharon and Dr. Duval's talk was over my head. I was close to smacking the table with my palm, my frustration peaking just below *out-of-control.*

"I know it's easier for you speak in medical shorthand, but I'll be much happier if I knew what all this means. How can I cope if I don't understand? How can I help anyone?" I demanded.

"I am sorry, Mrs. Davies," Dr. Duval said. She pushed her empty plate aside, folded her hands, and nodded. "You have been most helpful. You and your friend, Mr. Medina."

Dr. Duval walked us once again through the history of this outbreak, from the earliest patients like Alex, who had definitely been diagnosed with hantavirus. Three of the original group had died. Alex was doing better, but was still in critical condition.

I said, "And I've seen your diagnosis boards, you know. Have you added any other possibilities beyond pox and hantavirus?"

Sharon and Dr. Duval stared at each other. A long moment passed.

"The new child—"

"The one in room five?" I clarified.

"That's the one."

"When you come to the diagnosis room again, you will see another terrifying word on the boards." Sharon reached across the table, unfolded my fingers, which I'd clenched into fists, and held my hands.

What could be more terrifying than pox? I mean, I knew diseases like Ebola were death sentences for the most part, but about the only way for Ebola to spread in the States was through a sick passenger bringing it in on a Boeing jet. Neither endemic nor contagious, it wasn't likely to arrive from Africa and spread. "What's the new frightening disease?"

Dr. Duval rose, moved to the coffee machine, and returned with fresh cups. "The child has pneumonia. We are positive about that. She also has a form of plague."

The blood must have drained from my face, because Sharon gripped my icy hand in both of hers. I gulped a couple of times before I shook my head. *Plague?* That was right out of the Dark Ages.

"Plague?" I squeaked.

"It is more common than you think. The Western United States has had a handful of cases over the past decade." Dr. Duval explained the methods of transmission. Bubonic plague, the original Black Death, was transmitted by a flea bite from an infected animal. It hit the lymphatic system. Pneumonic plague, much less common that bubonic, passed from human to human through droplets in the air, much like the flu was transmitted. It hit the lungs. The last form of plague was septicemia, which infected the blood stream.

"It's a good thing," Sharon said.

I was having none of this. I had a sudden image of sinister figures spreading plague throughout the hospital, only in the Dark Ages the dark figures were rats. Now they were humans.

"How can plague be good?" I demanded.

"All forms of plague are caused by a bacterium, which is readily treated with common antibiotics," Dr. Duval said. She shifted in her chair and glanced at her watch.

"Do we have enough in the hospital?"

"The CDC is flying in more from Los Angeles. We will be resupplied tomorrow. Now, if you do not mind, I want to get back to our diagnosis room. Perhaps Dr. Klein and Dr. White will have some news." Dr. Duval stood.

Sharon and I bid her goodbye, and Sharon gently squeezed my hand. "I'd worry less about plague than hantavirus or pox. We successfully treat plague all over the world all the time."

"And what about pox? What kind of pox do we have here?"

Sharon's blue eyes darkened. "We still don't know for sure."

"Is that why Alex has a rash?" I knew Sharon could feel the pulse jump in my wrist.

"Don't panic. We're testing to see if it's human monkeypox, which is a virus, but we haven't seen human monkeypox virus in the States since 2003."

"But how is it transmitted if we don't have monkeys to spread it?"

"The last outbreak was thought to be the result of prairie dogs infected by Gambian rats, which had been dumped into the wild. The rats were smuggled in because they were cute, and people wanted them as pets. When pet owners realized that these rats could grow to nearly three feet in length, they turned them loose. The disease all but wiped out wild prairie dog colonies."

"Oh my God. I'm ever amazed at how much damage humans can do to upset the balance of nature," I marveled.

"Don't get me started. We could be lamenting for days. We need to stay focused. So, if we have human monkeypox, there are treatments." She paused. "Have you had a recent smallpox vaccination by any chance?"

"Actually, I did about a dozen years ago. My second one. My last husband and I were going to Tanzania on vacation. He was super cautious, so we got every vaccination and its brother." I had laughed at how worried Reggie was about my health. I wasn't pleased to be poked and prodded, because my arm ached for weeks with the aftereffects.

"What about Alex? Has he been vaccinated?"

"No. He was a baby when I went to Africa. I wouldn't have taken him anyway—my daughter would have had forty conniption fits."

"Yeah, sounds like my mother. When I told her I was trapped here for the duration, she absolutely lost it. She went so far as to call the head of the Secret Service and demand, actually demand, they whisk me out of here. She's on her ear with anxiety."

Sharon's mother sounded like me. When it came to the kids, I could go from normal to raging tiger mom in three point two seconds flat.

"I'd give anything to have seen that. Imagine the mother of

a vice president's wife going nose to nose, figuratively of course, with the head of the Secret Service. I'd pay money," I laughed. I squeezed Sharon's hands before releasing them. I returned to an even keel.

"Oh, she wouldn't hesitate to go at him face to face. She'd evoke her ancestors and threaten to do something unusually cruel and permanent to him," Sharon smiled.

"Her ancestors?"

"My grandmother was full-blooded Choctaw. She passed her coloring to me. Through my mother, she also passed along a sense of right and wrong, the strongest spine ever, and a tongue that refuses to be held."

I could picture her. I expressed the desire to meet Sharon's mother, and grandmother, too, if she still lived.

"Both are very much alive. In due time, I hope you'll meet. Now, what about Johnny? Do you know if he had his vaccination?"

At that moment, I realized Johnny hadn't shown up when he said he would. Emilie's voice fairly screamed in my head. *Uncle Johnny's sick!*

Ducks texted a similar message. *Oh my God. Johnny!* I stood so quickly that I knocked my chair over. I flew out of the cafeteria, took the stairs two at a time, and rushed to the room Johnny and I shared. I steadied myself on the doorjamb, my breath ragged.

"Johnny!"

He didn't respond. His breathing was so labored that I heard it from the doorway. Sharon panted up behind me.

"We need to get him into isolation, STAT."

CHAPTER TWENTY-TWO

I GRABBED THE door jamb to steady myself, my breath ragged from running up the stairs. My legs buckled so that I nearly fell. I don't remember walking into the room or anything. When I became aware of my surroundings, I was standing beside his bed and staring down at his flushed face, wet with the sweat of fever. He croaked a phlegm-y cough. I bent to touch his forehead.

"Don't." Dr. Running Bear grabbed my arm to pull me away. I hadn't heard him come in. Right behind him was a gloved, gowned, and masked orderly, and Sharon a few feet behind.

"I called him," Sharon said, shrugging into her own gown. I took two steps backward before bumping against Dr. Running Bear's strong body. I shook with a violent chill, teeth chattering.

"Max, are you ill?" Sharon asked.

I shook my head and clamped my jaws shut, managing to say, "He can't be sick. He was just fine." Terror locked my vision onto Johnny's face. "What's wrong, Johnny? Can you talk?"

Please don't let anything happen to Johnny.

"Leave the room, Max." Dr. Running Bear pushed me toward the corridor so that the orderly could wheel the bed from our room to the ICU.

I raised terrified eyes. "Do you know what's wrong with him? Is he going to be all right?"

"I have a good idea. If I'm right, he'll be pretty sick for a while, but will recover."

Dr. Running Bear draped his arm over my shoulders. He looked deeply into my eyes as if assessing both my mental and physical states. He kept his arm around me as we followed the bed. I couldn't help but remember following Merry's casket out of the funeral, the church filled with friends and flowers. Since that day, the cloying scent of lilies made me queasy. The sharp disinfectant used in this hospital also made me queasy. Like then, tears flowed unchecked. Like then, I didn't give a shit.

I ignored the phone buzzing in my pocket, the warmth trying to suppress the chill, the feather battering my cheek. For the first time, no watchdogs could help. I was alone again in the midst of a crisis.

Just before the doors to the ICU swung open, a sudden thought stopped me in mid-stride. "Aren't all the beds full?"

Dr. Running Bear turned sad eyes down at me.

"The girl in room five and the baby died. Johnny will be across from Alex."

"Oh my God." I must have looked even more terrified, because Dr. Running Bear reassured me that the room had been disinfected by two of the orderlies.

Sharon stepped forward with a gown. "Let me help you." She dressed me like I was a baby.

The orderly maneuvered the bed into room five. As soon as Johnny's bed went through the door, I fled the ICU for the false safety of the room we had shared. I shut myself in the bathroom, vomited, and stood there shaking. I rinsed my mouth and scrubbed my face and hands thoroughly at the sink. I went back into the empty room. I didn't know where else to go, what to do. Fear bounced from Johnny to Alex to Johnny. Alone with my terror, I sank to the floor and curled into a fetal position, sobbing.

I became aware of minute, inane details: dust on the floor, an old stain from a spill, something blue and round in a corner. It reminded me of a blue M&M. I hated blue M&M's. I refused to eat them when they first were introduced. I took a principled stand, exactly as I had when Crayola removed "flesh" from its color palette. Sometimes, you don't mess with tradition.

Everything around me faded to black.

I had no idea how long I lay there. When I became aware of my surroundings, Sharon and Dr. Duval were bending over me, and Sharon had her fingers on my neck.

"Strong and steady," she said.

Dr. Duval felt my forehead. "She doesn't have a fever."

A nurse delivered a small flashlight. Dr. Duval shined it in my eyes, and Sharon helped me sit up. "Do you feel dizzy? We can get you into a bed."

"I'm all right. I didn't fall." I pulled away and struggled to stand. My legs trembled, and I had to hold on to Sharon or return to the floor. Sharon brushed off my clothes and steadied me. An odd expression crossed her face, vanishing as quickly as it came. Both Dr. Duval and I noticed it. I was too shaken to respond, but Dr. Duval nodded.

"You need some juice." Sharon sent the nurse to fetch a cold beverage.

"You need to be with Johnny now," Dr. Duval said. I was vaguely aware of Emilie's presence. The doctors walked me to the ICU.

Johnny was hooked to the same rack of monitors that beeped and swooshed as were in Alex's room. Every blip on a screen screamed at me, reminding me of how little I knew about what was keeping Johnny and Alex alive. Even more, the noises fed my terror because I was completely without the ability to help them. I grabbed the end of the bed and let it hold me upright.

Nurse Leena entered, tall and reassuring. She nodded to the doctors before proceeding to Johnny's bedside. Sharon and Dr. Duval withdrew. The nurse clipped a blood oxygen monitor to a finger, made sure the blood pressure cuff was securely fastened on his right bicep, and hung a bag on the IV stand.

"Intravenous antibiotics and fluids." She inserted a needle into the back of Johnny's hand, the one I'd held only a few hours before, and taped it to the skin. "We can administer his medications and fluids through this, just like we do with Alex."

"Why is he on antibiotics? Does Dr. Running Bear know what made Johnny sick?" My voice was hoarse, barely above a whisper.

"His orders."

"Then he has a strong suspicion about the pathogen," I said, trying to be logical.

Nurse Leena nodded. She pulled the sheet and blanket up to the middle of Johnny's chest, adjusted the bed so that his head was raised, and set one monitor to take readings every fifteen minutes.

"He does. He didn't order a sedative because Johnny hasn't roused since we took charge of him. He's in good hands."

"Yours."

"I meant Dr. Running Bear's, but yes, mine too."

We moved a chair so that I could sit in Johnny's room and still see into Alex's. My boy was awake and sitting up, his eyes the size of hubcaps. I walked across the ICU and stood inside his doorway. I knew without having to be told not to touch either of them without changing my gloves. I didn't want to transmit what Johnny had to my grandson.

The onset of Johnny's illness in no way paralleled Alex's. To be sure, both had coughs and fevers, but Johnny was ill in a different way. I struggled to remember what Dr. Gupta told me about the different pathogens—which were bacterial, which weren't. I tried to reassure Alex they'd both be all right. Alex's voice was marginally stronger, although his words continued to rasp between chapped lips.

"But what happens if both Uncle Johnny and I don't get well?" From the unfiltered mouth of a boy came the question I couldn't voice.

"I promise you, Captain Chaos, you'll be riding with Uncle Johnny soon enough."

"Can I have a real cowboy hat?"

Ah yes, back to the hat. "I promise."

"One just like Uncle Johnny's?" he pressed.

"Only cleaner."

The chuckle that followed brought on a wrenching coughing spell followed by a groan.

"My chest hurts." It had become a mantra.

"Well, you did crack a couple of ribs when you did your face plant. Is your chest hurting any less?" If I'd been nearer, I'd have hugged him and ruffled his hair, which would have resulted in one of his looks.

"I guess." Alex collapsed back against his pillows.

I spent the night sitting just inside Johnny's room. I popped over hourly to visit Alex, a spider skittering along a web stretched between the two patients.

I prayed and wept, wept and prayed, until exhausted. Then, I slept.

CHAPTER TWENTY-THREE

NURSE LEENA JOSTLED my shoulder a little before dawn the next morning—not that dawn penetrated the ICU. The glow from the overhead lights created a disorienting sense of timelessness. I blinked and checked the readings, first on Johnny's and then on Alex's monitors. No perceptible change. She beckoned me to follow her.

"They'll be all right for a while. We're needed downstairs."

We left the ICU, changed, and walked toward Dr. White's stronghold. Leena knocked on the door.

At first glance, the room seemed unchanged from the day before, but my initial impression soon proved wrong. The white boards and flip charts were still there, but the data was different. Dr. White had erased the earlier chaos and created three discrete sections. Headings in red screamed across the room at me.

Hantavirus. Pox. Plague. Under each heading were patient names, histories, and symptoms. On separate boards and flip charts were timelines, locations, and situations where patients fell ill. Her map had more colored pins pushed into several locations.

Johnny's name was under *Plague.*

I stepped back and drew in a sharp breath. Leena gripped my elbow to steady me. Together we moved into the room. The entire CDC team, Dr. Running Bear, Leena, and I stared first at each other and then at the boards.

"As I suspected, Johnny's pathogen is plague," Dr. Running Bear said. "I started him on antibiotics because I was sure as soon as I saw him. Plague responds well to most of the common antibiotics. We're giving him massive doses through his IV. Think of it as Agent Orange, only friendlier."

"All indicators are for pneumonic, not bubonic, plague," Dr. Duval said, laying her hand on my arm. Her touch reassured me slightly. I put a hand on top of hers, mine small and palsied, hers larger and stronger.

"We'll monitor you closely for signs of infection too, since I'm certain you and Johnny have, how shall I say this delicately, been close," Dr. Running Bear said.

"You mean it's sexually transmitted?" I didn't know whether to laugh or cry.

He reddened and looked away. "That's not what I meant. Pneumonic plague passes through droplets like shared saliva or being coughed or sneezed on."

"Well, we've definitely shared bodily fluids."

On the plague board, Johnny was next to the child from room five, who died just before Johnny fell ill. The baby was listed with Alex under *Hantavirus*.

"I don't understand. How can three completely different pathogens be infecting and killing people here?" None of this made sense. I needed Johnny to translate, but he was lying in bed a floor away struggling to breathe.

"That's the million-dollar question," Dr. Klein said. "I've run every test I can, sent more samples back to headquarters in Atlanta, and done a voodoo dance to break the enigma."

Dr. Duval smiled at him. "Perhaps you should dispense with voodoo. It may work in my homeland, but I doubt it will be effective here. Maybe you should encourage that Native American shaman to return."

"Two will be here tonight," Leena said.

Dr. Duval nodded. "It could not hurt, and it might help keep the parents calmer."

Dr. White stood in her thinking pose, hands clasped behind her back. I stuffed my hands into my scrub pockets to keep them from shaking, and rocked back and forth on my sneakers. I didn't know what pattern the epidemiologist saw. What I saw was a veritable crazy quilt of symptoms. Nothing stitched together. Strips of colored yarn connected symptoms. The more I studied the white boards and charts, the less comfortable I felt. We were in a maelstrom.

"You got that right," Dr. White unlaced her fingers. I must have muttered out loud—I had no sense that she was sentient in the same way Emilie and Ducks were. My phone chirped.

You spoke out loud. You're broadcasting really loud, but she can't understand you, Emilie texted. *She has too much science in her brain to trust her gut.*

I texted a response and apologized for breaking Dr. White's concentration.

"No problem." She stared at a string of numbers on a chart. "This makes no frigging sense. It's all wrong."

I moved next to her. Three columns made up the chart. First column, three medical codes. Second column, a series of numbers. Third column, more words and numbers I didn't comprehend. None of the columns had headers because the doctor didn't need them. To me, the numbers were nothing but numbers.

"What am I supposed to see?" I asked.

Tick walked me through the chart. First column contained a series of codes for the three probable diseases. Second column was the normal rate from initial exposure to the appearance of symptoms. The third column was what was out of whack. The actual timeline from exposure to symptoms was acutely accelerated.

"No way are these natural rates of infection. Someone or something has modified the viruses and bacteria. Something or someone has enhanced the pathogens' potency."

"What kind of scientist does research to modify pathogens?" Curiosity overcame terror. I had to know what and who we were dealing with. "Other than someone who is mad, that is."

"Microbiologists and molecular geneticists are the most likely, although others might be interested in modifying genes," Dr. Gupta answered.

Dr. Klein waved a sheaf of papers, indicating that he had new or additional data to add to the boards.

"It's even more fucked up than you think." With that preamble, he added information from three more autopsies.

The child across from Alex died from pneumonic plague, that oh-so-rare disease that was both endemic and quiescent in Western America. This strain, though, was unusually virulent. The child came in with pneumonia, which responded to antibiotics, indicating that it was bacterial. Two days after she was admitted, she developed plague. Two days after that, she was dead.

"If plague isn't prevalent in her community, she had to have been infected after she arrived," Dr. White said.

"What kind of treatment did you use?" I asked.

"Inhalation, antibiotics. The usual stuff."

"I agree with Mrs. Davies' concern about the accelerated timelines," Dr. Duval said. "Pneumonic plague usually appears between one and six days after infection. Two days puts the origin of the infection inside this hospital."

"But everyone who works here has been in quarantine since you guys swept in." I wasn't liking any of this. Not one bit. "And now Johnny has plague. He didn't have pneumonia before he got sick and hasn't been outside in eight days."

Before I could ask another question, we heard a knock at the door. Dr. Klein was closest.

"Who is it?" he asked.

We made a point of never leaving the room unattended. Only the CDC staff, select members of the hospital staff, Sharon, Johnny, and I were admitted. Dr. White and Dr. Duval had keys.

"Sharon."

Jerry unlocked the door. Sharon slipped in, followed immediately by her Rottweiler, who had special dispensation to go anywhere in the hospital.

Toby glided along the hall just behind them before heading out of sight. *What's he doing here?* An incoming text showed a warning face from Emilie. *Watch the vampire.* Suited me fine. I promised myself I'd speak to the Rottweiler about my suspicions.

Tick picked up a skein of red yarn and strung it between boards to link illness with locations where people fell ill. "I don't know where to go next. I can't find the common denominator."

Sharon walked among the boards, stroking the strands of yarn. She stopped. Turning on her heel, she went to a clean flip chart. She drew three circles which overlapped at a central point. Venn diagrams. She labeled each circle with the pathogens, then filled in names of the patients. When she added locations, a complex set of data points became clear. The nexus of the infection was indeed the hospital itself. She turned to Dr. Running Bear and Dr. Duval.

"Shit. It *is* us. We're ground zero."

"Ground zero?" Keith studied the diagrams. No one spoke. "I see. Most of the illnesses started inside here, but not all of them."

"You do community outreach, don't you?" Dr. Duval asked. She walked from board to board, from flip chart to flip chart, with Dr. Running Bear alongside. The two tall doctors, one black with a shaved head, one bronze with long black hair, stood side by side. Their hands moved in a syncopated dance, one pointing to a bit of data, the other touching an answering piece of information.

"Did you stop them when you suspected hantavirus?"

Dr. Running Bear shook his head. "We had no reason to, because hantavirus doesn't spread from human to human."

"What do you routinely do?"

"We have a vaccination outreach program. If we go out onto the Rez with free shots, we prevent more routine childhood diseases."

"That's one of the reasons the Indian Health Service was established," Sharon added.

Shortly after her husband was elected vice president, Sharon had become a champion of the Indian Health Service partly because of its outreach efforts, partly because of her heritage. Several of the nurses did home visits, educated people on good nutrition, and identified potential future health problems.

"Lord knows most reservations have high incidences of alcoholism, diabetes, heart disease, obesity, and other societal diseases and conditions that are preventable or at least could be managed by lifestyle changes." Leena walked over, another tall person staring at the charts. "Dr. Anderson, we've made a lot of progress with some of the families," she assured Sharon.

"Just because we can't save them all immediately doesn't mean we stop trying," Dr. Running Bear smiled. "We've paused for the time being, though."

"I've missed several routine visits since we were quarantined. I worry about how three of my families are handling my departure," Leena said. Each nurse regularly saw the same series of families, the better to identify health changes when they began and not after bad habits became entrenched. Nurse Leena saw two alcoholic fathers who beat their children when they "got liquored up," which was as soon as they got their disability checks. Another family was headed by an elderly woman crippled by arthritis and diabetes.

Dr. White put her hand next the circle marked *Pox*. She pointed to three names. "Were any of these children vaccinated recently?"

The nurse checked her laptop. "The two-year-old and the six-year-old were scheduled for Pertussis inoculations this month. I don't see any notation that they had them."

"Alex doesn't fit into that equation at all. He's current on everything. Heck, he was even current on tetanus. Besides, he wouldn't have had any vaccinations since he broke his leg," I reminded them.

"We need to send the FBI to interview the families again, especially the extended relatives of the baby." Dr. White shot a look at Dr. Klein, who edged toward the door. "Also have them ask if any of the pox and plague victims had home visits and when. I want to know if anyone remotely linked to the hospital has had any contact with anyone in the families since we went into quarantine."

"Leena, did you find out who changed Alex's chart?" I blurted.

Dr. Running Bear's head snapped around, and his hooded eyes bored into mine. "Someone changed a chart?"

The nurse nodded, as did Dr. White. "A forensic IT tech from the FBI is examining our records to see who accessed Alex's. The tech seemed pleased that an underlying database controls the health records. He'll find the trail," Leena answered.

Keith snarled at this latest revelation. Sharon called across the room. "He's done."

"Who's done?" Dr. Running Bear asked.

"The FBI technician." Sharon held up a piece of paper. "Do you have anyone on staff named Milton Greene?"

"That's the orderly who died. Why?" Dr. Running Bear's shoulders tightened.

"Because that FBI tech says he modified the charts," she reported.

"Not possible. Orderlies don't have access to the records." Leena's normally smooth brow wrinkled.

Sharon held out the piece of paper. "Here are his ID and password."

"I repeat, that's not possible. Only someone with administrative rights can set up a new ID. I sure didn't do it." Dr. Running Bear looked lost.

"Who else has these rights?" Keith asked.

Leena answered, "The head nurse and the emergency room doctor. No one else. Even I don't have privileges. Neither would give Milt access. He had no need."

"Well, someone did," Keith said. I heard his teeth grinding from ten feet away.

"If someone in the hospital is behind the outbreak and is tampering with our health records, our top priority beyond keeping the patients alive is to identify whoever is infecting the community before we have a full-blown epidemic. Find the person with unauthorized access, and we will find the source," Dr. Running Bear said.

Dr. Duval let herself out into an empty corridor, cell phone already at her ear.

"I've wondered about the staff, Dr. Running Bear," Sharon said. "I asked Keith to work with the Secret Service and the FBI to run background checks on everyone to rule out as many as possible."

"They're underway." Keith's posture was as rigid as his jawline. A muscle tic danced in one cheek.

Dr. Running Bear tensed. He was silent for several seconds. "Much as I don't want to think someone on my staff could be involved, you made the right call. Let me know how I can help."

"Do you have everyone's fingerprints on file?" Keith asked. Dr. Running Bear shook his head.

"No reason to. We're a hospital. Our normal security is managed though our ID badges. We swipe in when we come to work and out when we leave. Other than that, we've never needed more stringent security."

"Until now," Sharon said.

"Let's see what the FBI turns up. If it doesn't find anything, we'll fingerprint everyone in the hospital and run the prints through IAFIS," Keith said, explaining that IAFIS was the FBI's master fingerprint system. "Anyone who served in the Armed Forces should show up."

"That's a lot of us," Leena said.

"Johnny as well, but back to the question at hand," I said. "Why would anyone want to do this? Sicken children, I mean?" My phone vibrated with an incoming call. I stepped to a corner of the diagnosis room, far from the door. "Hello, Ducks."

"I've been doing a lot of research on how these pathogens are transmitted. Johnny and I thought we should be asking why it's happening. It's not why. It's how. Later, it's who."

My brain buzzed on this shift in emphasis. Ducks asked several questions, none of which I could answer.

"Ask Dr. White." He hung up.

Five faces stared at me, two with knowing expressions, three without.

"That was Ducks, my home-school teacher. He and my granddaughter—"

"The special child?" Dr. Running Bear asked.

"The special child." I held up my hands. "I'll explain later. He said we're asking the wrong question. We should be asking *how*. The *how* will lead us to the *who* and *why* later." I repeated the gist of the short conversation. "Ducks suggested we focus on how someone could get his hands on the pathogens. How hard would it be to set up what in essence would be a home laboratory? What skills would be needed?"

Dr. Gupta sorted through the stack of printouts Dr. Klein had left on the table, extracting a series of images. She opened her laptop and ran quick searches for the three specific pathogens loose in the hospital.

We gathered around the small screen. *If this room is used for education, it needs a computer hook-up to the Internet and a big-screen television.* I filed the idea away for later execution.

Dr. Gupta started with hantavirus. She found a site with images of the virus, along with captions with size measurements. After sorting through Dr. Klein's printouts again, she stopped when she came to his research. "The virus in Alex's bloodstream, for example, is half-again as large as the one I'll call the control sample." She tapped the screen.

She did the same for pneumonic plague and monkeypox, which was the only form of pox that could be infecting the children. Each time the pathogen in the blood of the local patients was not the same as the control bacteria. Each was larger.

"We have odd fragments in the samples, which complicate our ability to draw conclusions. Their very presence throws more confusing data into the mix. Are the fragments damaged, or are they immature organisms?"

"How have they been modified?" Sharon asked.

"A couple of days ago, Johnny and I wondered if it was possible to artificially engineer a super form of hantavirus. Is that really what's happening here? Is someone creating superbugs?" I ran my fingers through my hair, making it stand on end.

"Perhaps. If that's the case, it could completely change our understanding of the outbreak. I still don't know what the fragments are or if they are capable of infecting anyone, but they definitely aren't anything I've ever seen or researched." Dr. Gupta frowned at the laptop.

Dr. Duval unlocked the door and entered.

"You don't think they're new strains of what we know is here, do you?" Sharon twisted a lock of hair around her finger.

"I don't know. That's why I sent messages with images to my virology colleagues around the world. Their verdict: nothing they've seen before. These fragments are completely unknown," Dr. White said, rocking on her heels, hands linked behind her back.

"Let's hope they can't infect anyone," I said.

"Hope is for the uninformed, Mrs. Davies," Dr. Duval said. "We will find the scientific answer."

Dr. Gupta clicked to other sites while we thought about what Dr. Duval said. Each time, the virologist came away with the same non-answer—the pathogens, whether virus or bacteria, were not behaving as they should.

"Not only are the pathogens significantly larger, the incubation period is too tightly compressed," she said.

"Johnny said something about the incubation period when we were walking the dates of Alex's infection back to the date we arrived." I said. Heads turned my way. "What? We know how to use the Internet."

Sharon and Dr. White laughed. "There's much more to medicine than being an Internet doctor," Sharon said.

"I know that, but I don't see how it could hurt to be better educated, do you? I'm not a scientist, but I don't have to be one of Dr. Duval's uninformed. I do want more than hope. Hope is not a strategy, and hope alone won't cure Johnny and Alex." I looked from doctor to doctor. "So, I have a question. Could these pathogens have been grown and modified in a private lab somewhere?"

"The CDC grows pathogens all the time. Besides, setting up a lab is relatively easy," Dr. White said. "I have one in my home where I play with all sorts of bacteria. Most of them I find in dirt outdoors or on my skin. Setting up a home lab can be pretty cheap, too."

"What if someone wanted to produce ultra-deadly pathogens? Since pneumonic plague spreads through the air, could someone grow a bacterium twice the normal size, spray it, and cause wide-spread illness and death?" My mind raced ahead of my mouth. I stopped and stared into the distance.

"What? What do you remember?" Sharon asked.

"Toby sprayed something in the ICU a couple of days ago, right after he took blood samples from Johnny and me, and right before Johnny got sick. Toby said it was disinfectant, but I couldn't smell anything, even after I pulled down my mask. Whatever was in the bottle left oily residue on my skin. Johnny took a full blast in the face before he went to wash it off. I wonder if there is any trace on the wall."

"Sounds like a conspiracy theory run amok," Dr. White said.

"Maybe not." Sharon turned toward Keith. "Sic 'em."

Keith grabbed a couple of vials and some swabs, and then he was gone, but not without shooting a look in my direction. I couldn't tell what he was thinking.

I'd never had any reason to think about how easy it was to set up a home lab. Now, it was all I could think about.

"Can you tell me what I'd need to set up a home lab? I assume it's a bit more complicated that the home chemistry set my brothers had in elementary school."

"It is, but not as hard as you think. Much of the equipment can easily be purchased at medical supply stores, with some components even coming from Home Depot," Sharon said. "The point is, no one tracks who buys Petri dishes or various solutions. Not even high-powered microscopes and desktop centrifuges are routinely monitored, although they all have manufacturers' serial numbers. You don't need a license to buy what you need."

The more the doctors talked, the more spooked I became. If anyone could set up a home lab and grow these viruses, it could be anyone who worked in or near the hospital.

Dr. Gupta, Dr. White, and Dr. Running Bear tossed around more theories. Sharon and I stood on the sidelines, listening intently but contributing nothing of value.

I distilled some of what I understood. Point one: It was easy and relatively affordable to equip a home lab. Point two: Viruses and bacteria could be grown in cultures. Point three: Someone with decent knowledge of virology might be able manipulate the pathogens to make them more or less infectious.

"So, I could go to several stores and online catalogs, order up a bunch of equipment, install a lab in my home, and no one would be the wiser. That right?" I was onto something.

"Right. A few thousand dollars would do the trick—less if you bought used or last year's equipment," Dr. Gupta answered distractedly.

"Next question. Can I go on the Internet and order a sample set of pox and plague bacteria?"

Four heads turned in my direction as if choreographed.

"No," Dr. White answered for them all. "You have to be a licensed lab with a reason to use such pathogens. Not every lab can call Pizza Hut for a delivery of pneumonic plague with a side of monkeypox."

"What kind of labs could have these bacteria?" I asked.

"Research universities with BSL-3 or BSL-4 labs," Dr. Gupta said.

"And that means what?"

"I'm sorry. BSL stands for biosafety levels. Three and four are the top levels of security," she said. "Depending on the university, plague and pox could be researched in either a level-three or level-four facility."

"How many are working with these pathogens?" I had to get an answer which would satisfy Johnny were he here and healthy. I was certain I'd need this information when I talked with Emilie and Ducks shortly.

"I'll get a list from headquarters," Dr. White said. "We may find clues there."

"The next question, Max, is whether any labs have reported any samples missing," Sharon said.

CHAPTER TWENTY-FOUR

SHARON AND I left the doctors in the diagnosis room. We tried to unravel the answer to the unthinkable question: *Who in the hospital is infecting people deliberately?* Sharon turned to me.

"Keith has turned into the Rottweiler again. Maybe he can find out if anyone working at San Felipe had access to at least two potentially deadly pathogens in a previous job. Have any employees ever worked in a BSL-4 lab?" Sharon mused aloud. "He'll sniff out the perps if anyone can."

"Oh great. I'm not going to be able to look at anyone who has been here since Alex was admitted without wondering if I'm looking at a mad scientist," I said.

"Let's see what Keith's swabs of the ICU turn up."

"I'm in denial." Nurse Leena was on her way back to the diagnosis room when she caught up with us in the middle of the corridor. "I've worked with these people for years. They're my friends, and I trust them."

"Well, whoever this is can't be trusted." Sharon hooked her arm through mine.

"How do we identify him?" I wondered.

"Are we sure it's a man? Or even if it's a single person?" Leena moved slowly toward the corridor leading away from us.

"My granddaughter thinks it's a man, but she's not yet sure." I stared down the hall, hoping to see a big sign—*Mad Scientist!*—hovering over someone's head. "She thinks it might be two people. That would explain why she can't get a clear reading."

"Two people?" A possibility Sharon clearly hadn't considered.

"Maybe a man and a woman," I said.

"Why would a woman knowingly infect random people for no discernible reason? It goes against our nurturing nature," Leena said, shaking her head.

"No matter what, we need to broaden our thinking." Sharon picked up the pace and dragged me away from the diagnosis room. "Time for equal-opportunity suspicion."

Before I could say anything more, my phone vibrated. Ducks.

"What's happening? Does anyone have any firm proof of how whoever is doing this got his hands of the pathogens?" he asked.

"Not really." I gave him a quick update on the most recent conversation concerning sources of the bugs. Emilie's flow of warmth and Ducks' feather told me that they were there to help. For the moment, I stopped feeling isolated in the midst of the crisis.

"It's definitely someone in the hospital. I feel a female presence but don't think it's a woman acting alone. You'll feel better if you rule out the nurses," Ducks said. I could hear Emilie in the background. I was glad they were together. At least for half of my family, life had returned to normal. "Em says to look for someone who is sneaking out at night."

"But we're under quarantine. No one can sneak out." I must have spoken louder than I realized, because my words caused a stir. Sharon shot me a look.

"Look for someone who smokes." Ducks said goodbye and rang off.

"Who was that, and what did you mean, *no one can sneak out*? How the heck would someone who's not here guess that anyone who is here could sneak out of the hospital?"

"They don't eavesdrop in any traditional sense, so don't worry about them compromising national security," I feebly joked. "Both can read my feelings. Em can cast a broader net and feel how people around me are feeling. Until now, she focused on Alex, but with Johnny falling ill and a possible whoever-it-is on the loose, she's expanding outward in ever-widening, concentric circles."

"So your granddaughter uses ESP to watch over you?"

"In a sense, yes. She and Ducks both have it, with Em's being much stronger. No matter what other people think, I know they help keep me safe."

We rounded a corner, heads down, communicating in whispers. Every corner, every doorway could harbor a sick killer. I wanted to glance over my shoulder to be sure we weren't being followed, but I didn't. That would have been too paranoid. Instead, I kept my focus on what lay ahead, in the empty corridor and beyond.

"I'd rely on Em to help us sort out what's happening. More than once, I've trusted that child with my life. She's never failed me. No matter that they aren't here physically, she and Ducks will do what they can. For now, we need to find out who the smokers are," I said.

The stately Haitian doctor caught up with us in time to hear my last statement. "And your sentient granddaughter suspects someone is sneaking out of the hospital, does she?" Dr. Duval's face was impassive. "Someone who has something to hide?"

"She does," I said.

"And you believe her?" Again, the unflinching, molded face.

"I do."

"I do, too." Dr. Duval stopped and retreated into deep thought. We waited until she nodded. "The new cases from the community could be from someone infecting unsuspecting citizens, someone who has violated our quarantine, and who will do so again until he is identified."

"Or she," I said.

"Yes. It could be someone the families are used to seeing. The community knows the hospital is quarantined, but the full impact may not have soaked in. If a family sees someone familiar from San Felipe, they wouldn't question why that person was there," Sharon said. She jumped slightly and glanced over her shoulder. She found nothing and frowned. Probably Ducks letting her know she was on the right track.

"How can anyone leave? I mean, you and Dr. Running Bear issued orders that we had to remain here." My head was muzzy, with too many thoughts crashing into each other. Fully half of my brain remained in Johnny's room, and yet the doctors needed me and my watchdogs to help solve the mystery. Not for the first time, I wished I could leave well enough alone and concentrate only on Johnny and Alex.

No chance of that, Ducks texted.

"Orders don't mean anything if one is determined to violate them. I need to talk with Dr. Running Bear." Dr. Duval turned back toward the diagnosis room.

I caught a thoughtful look on Leena's face. "What?"

"There's one place where people might pass through our perimeter without anyone being seen or seeming to be out of place." Leena patted her shoulder where her nicotine patch kept her cravings under control, and Ducks' puzzle-piece statement clicked into place. "People smoke on the loading dock where we have no security cameras. We never needed to install them."

"Until now," I said.

I looked at Leena, who looked at Sharon, who looked at me. The loading dock was a weak link no one had considered. Dr. Running Bear had reluctantly given in to requests to let people smoke. Those who refused the patch were allowed to go outside on the honor system not to leave the premises or have close contact with anyone outside the quarantine perimeter.

"We don't stand watch over them. Keith sent an agent to monitor everyone who leaves or reenters through the dock door. Delivery people, smokers, and those who want a breath of fresh air must sign in and out. He sits at a table just inside the door," Sharon said.

"Is someone on duty twenty-four hours a day?"

"No. We lock the doors at night, though," Leena said as she led the way upstairs toward the ICU.

"Anyone with a key could get back in, couldn't he? I mean, the doors open outward by pushing the lever, but don't you need a key to return?" I stopped at the door to the ICU to put on my gown.

"Is it a smart lock?" Nurse Leena and I stared at Sharon. "Does it register all activities like a hotel room key does?"

The nurse shook her head. "No. It's a standard brass key. Think of your house key."

Sharon dropped the gown she was about to put on. She spun around and walked away.

"She and Keith have a lot to talk about," Leena concluded. She pressed the pad to let us into the ICU.

My thriller-filled brain jumped to the obvious. "You know, some family members could have slipped out to see how their children were doing. Or families could have brought children to see their parents who are quarantined. Or someone could have paid a home visit with vials of pathogens."

Leena's practical brain took a slightly different track. "I first want to know who left the premises. Then why."

I found Alex sitting up in bed. He'd improved enough to eat solid food for the first time since he became ill. I looked closely at his tray. Gruel-like Cream o' Wheat, a piece of dry toast, and apple juice. I expected a complaint.

"Hi, Mad Max. They brought me something to eat." He picked up a spoonful of cereal and let it plop back in the bowl. "It's great, but I wish I had some brown sugar."

"You haven't been on real food for many days, so your diet is going to be boring for a while. I'll ask one of the nurses if she can find brown sugar or honey. How does that sound?" I sat on the edge of his bed and watched Alex take slow bites of whatever meal this was. I doubted if he knew if he was eating breakfast or lunch. At least he was eating. "How are you feeling?"

"Better. Can I my cell phone?"

"*May* I?" He may have just been at death's door, but he wasn't going to get away with bad grammar.

"May I. I want to text Em, Dad, and Charlie."

"Not Mr. Ducks?"

"Nah. He'd just give me a pile of homework."

"Brat."

After he finished eating, his eyes fluttered, and he dozed off. I slipped his phone into the charger and left him to his nap.

I repositioned the chair near the doorway of Alex's room to

be able to look into Johnny's. His curtains were half-drawn, but I could see him lying in bed. I tiptoed across the hall. He slept deeply, rousing to cough before lapsing back into a deep sleep. He hadn't awakened since before he was admitted to the ICU. When I turned to search for a nurse to see about sweetener for Alex's future meals, I bumped into Toby.

"I want his blood sample before he wakes up," he said without a *hello*. He replaced one pair of gloves with a fresh set.

"What do you mean? Johnny hasn't been awake since he came in here."

Toby pushed past me into Johnny's room and pulled the curtains across the windows, effectively dismissing me. I would not be dismissed. I pulled the curtains aside and followed Toby in time to see him push a syringe into the IV port.

"What the hell are you doing?"

"Don't question me." Toby's cheerful façade slipped once again. "If it's any of your business, I'm cleaning his port with saline."

Since when does Toby have anything to do with an IV port? I'd never seen him touch them before. I left the room and was at the nurses' station in five quick strides. I told the nurse in charge about my conversation. She walked to Johnny's room and entered. I hovered just inside Alex's, straining to hear anything going on across the hall.

"She must be mistaken," I heard Toby say. "I didn't do anything wrong."

"Bullshit!" I muttered.

Moments later, the curtain twitched aside and Toby left. No longer our friendly Toby the vampire, his scowl was a warning for me to stop interfering. The nurse assured me that Johnny was in good hands.

"Toby might have overstepped his bounds a bit, but he was only trying to help because we're stretched thin," she said.

I stared at Johnny, trying to see if there was any change in the way he looked or breathed. If anything, his breathing seemed less labored. Perhaps the antibiotics were winning the battle.

Alex roused, saw me standing in front of Johnny's room, and demanded my attention. "Do you think I can have my Game Boy?"

I raised a finger and walked out to the room I no longer shared with Johnny. The Game Boy and some new games Johnny brought had been there since *Q-Day*—quarantine day. I'd kept the hand-held unit charged. I knew Alex would want it as soon as he felt better, and I would do anything to keep him from getting bored and restless.

"Oh wow! New games," he exclaimed when I returned.

CHAPTER TWENTY-FIVE

WITH JOHNNY SLEEPING and Alex occupied with his Game Boy, nothing in the ICU required my immediate attention. I stumbled back to our room with napping on my mind, only to rediscover that I had no bed. The blue M&M, or whatever it was, was gone. Poking my nose into every open door, I found an empty room down the hall, pulled the door half closed, and stretched out fully clothed on the bare mattress. I punched a pancake-thin pillow into submission, wiggling around until my head rested between lumps.

Time to leave the monitoring of my sick family to the hospital staff, and the guarding against further intrusions to Emilie and Ducks. I set a mental alarm for two hours.

I woke more refreshed than when I lay down but by no means at ease. The crick in my neck was a persistent annoyance. I made a quick circuit of the ICU, which showed both of my patients asleep. After I grabbed what seemed like my thousandth cup of coffee for the day, I discovered Dr. Running Bear, Dr. Duval, Keith, and Sharon in the diagnosis room, on a conference call with the head of the Secret Service detail that hadn't been quarantined.

"I'll set up an observation perimeter at the back of the hospital," Keith said. "I want eyes out there around the clock."

"What do you want us to do if someone sneaks out? Apprehend or follow? Our job is Dr. Anderson's protection, not undercover police work," the outside agent said.

"Do neither," Dr. Running Bear said. "We're looking for a name and photos of anyone exiting the hospital or anyone coming to the loading dock. Since the delivery people are CDC or FBI employees, we shouldn't have anyone from town hanging around."

"So, are you asking a couple of the local FBI agents for help?" I butted in. I wanted every possible law enforcement officer on duty. "They're trained in police work."

"Already on it. They'll work twelve-hour shifts patrolling the perimeter of the hospital," said the outside agent.

"What about the local sheriff or the reservation police?" Sharon asked.

"I'm sure they'll help as well," said Leena, who'd entered on my heels.

"Let's not get too many people out there. Remember, we need to act as if everything is normal. We don't want to alert anyone who may be watching either inside or outside the hospital," Dr. Duval cautioned.

"Most of the people who live on the reservation are hunters, right?" I asked. I had the semblance of an idea.

"Hey, we don't want armed civilians patrolling the hospital grounds." Keith hadn't forgotten about the number of guns in the hospital. "Leave the police work to professionals."

I raised my right forefinger before folding my hand into a clam shape. Sharon elbowed her Rottweiler. "She wants you to be quiet and listen."

Keith growled.

"What I mean is, do any of you hunters have motion-detection cameras?"

"It's illegal to use them, Max. But I see where you're heading," Dr. Running Bear said. His eyes may have been bloodshot, but his mind was alert. "Some of the biologists over at the University of New Mexico in Albuquerque probably have a couple to monitor migrating animals."

"If we could get them on loan, you could set them around at likely exit paths. That would extend the reach of your security measures, wouldn't it, Keith?"

"Interesting idea, Max," said Sharon. Keith nodded.

"Several environmentalists have these cameras, too. They watch for poachers, illegal hunters, and tourists out picking rare plant specimens. There's no flash, so no one would know he was being photographed. I'll make some calls. Who should they contact?" Dr. Running Bear asked.

Keith gave him the name and number of the agent outside.

In the four o'clock briefing, no one mentioned new surveillance protocols. We didn't want the unidentified culprit to know that we were actively hunting him. Dr. Duval reported on patient status and the new admissions.

"We admitted two more children overnight from the same family on the reservation. They have rashes, fever, and body aches. More cousins who live in the same house have similar, though more minor, symptoms."

The children's father was assigned a room at "the inn," our darkly humorous name for the unused wards. Maybe "Hotel California" would have been more appropriate—we all checked in and couldn't check out.

"We will move the rest of the family into quarantine to monitor them for signs of infection. With these new cases, we have overflowed the ICU and need to expand the Med-Surg ward as an isolation ward," Dr. Duval finished.

Dr. Running Bear pointed to Nurse Gilligan, who held up a handful of papers. "If you have been sleeping on that ward, please see the nurse for your new room assignments. Several of you will be moved to the maternity wing."

"Really?" one of the fathers snorted with contempt.

"We aren't admitting any mothers about to deliver, so we might as well use the beds." Dr. Running Bear smiled to reassure parents. "If you want a place to sleep, that will be better than a plastic chair in one of the lounges."

As for the outside world, Dr. Duval reported that the media had latched onto the story about a cluster of unknown illnesses felling children on the San Felipe Reservation. She read from a story in the local paper: "Doctors are tight lipped, but we have reliable sources who tell us the children all have bubonic plague. The CDC has placed San Felipe Hospital under quarantine. We're following this closely and will bring you updates as they happen."

Bubonic plague? The media makes it sound like we're about to experience the return of the Black Death from the 14th Century.

"It's good no one in the media knows about the pox," I whispered to Sharon, "or we'd have panic over misreporting a smallpox outbreak."

"You got that right, girlfriend." Sharon's eyes never left the front of the room, but she reached over and squeezed my hand.

Dr. Duval stepped forward, her eyes dark with anger.

"Someone inside the hospital has been talking to the press. I do not know who it is, and I do not need to know, but it stops now. I cannot keep you from confiding in your families. I can only ask that you not do so. Anyone you talk with might be the reliable sources mentioned on the local television station."

"Misinformation can lead to panic, which is the last thing we need," Keith said. "I don't want to confiscate your cell phones, but I will if you don't give me your word you won't talk to the press again."

Dr. Duval continued, "It is natural to want to answer questions in times like these, but we have enough to manage without an army of reporters trying to get inside and pushing their microphones into our faces."

The father of the baby who died jerked his head toward the window. "Too late. They're here."

Outside, satellite trucks filled the circular drive, where the CDC trucks and vans had parked just over a week before. Sharon's limousine, the black Suburbans, and the CDC vehicles were around back. The local FBI also parked in the rear when any of its agents were on the premises.

News crews staked out monitoring stations all around the front. Vans with local and network news logos jockeyed for positions, raised transmission masts, and swung dishes toward satellite locations to broadcast live. We could see wild gesticulations from cameramen, but we couldn't hear anything.

Reporters smoothed their hair and checked to see that their blouses were tucked in, or straightened their ties, before recording stand-up comments.

Dr. Running Bear held up his hand to quiet the murmurs seeping from every crevice in the cafeteria. He nodded to Keith, who moved to the windows.

"Sorry, folks. From now on, the blinds remain closed."

Again, the contemptuous father questioned Dr. Running Bear. "Are you afraid we might write messages on napkins and hold them up?"

"It could happen, although I think you understand the gravity of our situation and won't do anything like that," Sharon said. "Please note that some of these outlets use parabolic microphones to eavesdrop through windows, so please be careful what you say in the cafeteria or in the lobby in particular."

"We'll do everything we can to protect your privacy and that of your families while you're here. To that end, I know some of you won't like this, but there can be no more smoke breaks on the loading dock," Dr. Running Bear continued.

General muttering signaled dismay at the revocation of this last, small freedom.

Dr. Duval seconded his pronouncement. "It has been my experience that reporters are remarkably inattentive to health precautions if they can break a story. In Indonesia after the tsunami wiped out a large part of Ache Province, reporters climbed over bloated bodies of the dead to get a good photo. Many contracted cholera after contact with contaminated water, even though they were properly warned."

"We'll lock down this hospital even tighter than it is. No one is to speak to the press under any circumstances." Keith peered around the crowd. "Do I make myself clear?"

Heads nodded.

"Nurse Gilligan has plenty of nicotine patches. Please see her as soon as possible," Dr. Running Bear said.

I felt even more claustrophobic. I couldn't step outside; now I couldn't look outside, either.

Dr. Duval looked at the father of the girl who had died from plague, and then at two other families whose children were in nearby rooms. I sure as hell hadn't talked to anyone outside of

Ducks, Whip, and Emilie. Oh, and Eleanor and Raney, but none of them would talk to the press.

"Did any of you talk to the local paper?" The doctor's words seemed mild enough on the surface, but her tone was anything but.

Parents shook their heads—all but one mother, whose child was infected with hantavirus. She shriveled into herself, shoulders hunched, head pulled in. Dr. Running Bear saw the movement. He went to her and laid a hand on her shoulder.

"Look at me, Mrs. Nakai."

She raised teary eyes.

"Who did you tell?"

"Only my son," her voice quavered.

"And your son works for the *New Mexican* over in Santa Fe, if I remember?"

"He does. I only wanted him to know what was happening to his baby brother."

"Did you tell him his brother has hantavirus?" Dr. Duval asked.

Mrs. Nakai's voice shrank into her body. "I did. I told him he wasn't as bad as the children with plague."

"I understand." Dr. Running Bear turned back to the rest of the room. "Mrs. Nakai meant no harm, but you can see how easily harm was done. Not only are the media here, but the reporters have the wrong information. You can expect calls from worried family members who hear we have bubonic plague. We do not, I repeat, we do not have bubonic plague here in the hospital."

"The media latched onto one word, *plague,* and misreported the story. The more they repeat *bubonic plague*, the more likely we are to have a panic. From now on, Dr. Running Bear and I will brief the press daily at ten in the morning," Dr. Duval said.

"You said my daughter died from plague," said the father, standing in protest. "If it's not bubonic plague, what killed her?"

Dr. Duval stood next to Dr. Running Bear, the two of them a formidable wall against ignorance. "We have pneumonic plague. It is a cousin of bubonic plague, and, like its cousin, it responds well to antibiotics."

"But if antibiotics work, why did my daughter die?" asked the man. Arms crossed over his chest screamed that he was believing none of the explanations.

"Your daughter came in with pneumonia and pneumonic plague. She was too sick to be saved," Dr. Running Bear said.

Dr. Duval nodded. "Please, when your family asks, tell them we do not have bubonic plague. Please also tell them we are treating the disease with antibiotics. Dr. Running Bear and I will handle the press." What she didn't say was that pneumonic plague spread ten times faster than the Black Death.

The meeting broke up; I checked in on Johnny and Alex before an early dinner, which I ate alone by choice. I wanted some me-time to sort out my thoughts. I was no closer to an answer than I had been earlier in the day. After an insipid grilled cheese sandwich and a halfway tasty cup of potato-leek soup, I settled back with a coffee. With the cafeteria blinds closed, this had become yet another place where the difference between day and night didn't exist.

Emilie called. "I can't get any feelings right now. Do you think he left the hospital?"

"Boy, do I wish that were true." I stared at the covered windows, behind which were beautiful vistas of wild desert. "No, dear child. Keith had his men surreptitiously conduct body counts. Whoever is behind the outbreak is still inside. No one is missing."

"He's gone silent, then. He'll have make a move sooner rather than later. When he does, Mr. Ducks and I will follow him."

"I'm glad you can from a distance. I'd have no worry to spare if you two were close by."

"We're never far away. Love you, Mad Max."

"Love you, too, my dear."

Answers played hide-and-seek and fears chased each other through my mind—I'd about run out of childhood metaphors when Dr. Gupta entered the cafeteria. She paused, until I waved her over. After she selected her food, I scrutinized her face, hoping to see good news writ large. I didn't see anything, small or large, good or bad. I saw a short, weary woman.

"How's Johnny?" Dr. Gupta stirred sugar into hot tea after wrapping the bag around her spoon to extract the last drops.

"Sleeping when I left. Leena says that's what he needs, but his condition remains unchanged. He still hasn't woken up." I stared into my cup and wondered where the coffee had gone. Surely, I'd fetched it less than ten minutes earlier. A quick glance at the wall clock showed I'd been sitting lost in thought for close to an hour. I excused myself and returned with yet another refill.

"She'll call me if there's any change," I continued. "I thought the antibiotics would have started to work by now."

Dr. Gupta frowned. "His constitution may be resisting the treatment. I'll speak to Dr. Running Bear about changing his medication. We have more than one in our arsenal."

To take our minds off of the crisis, we chatted about her children—she had four—and Emilie. We both missed our families. At least I was here with Alex and Johnny. The thought gave me a tiny bit of solace, even though one of my men was on the mend and the other was closer to death than I wanted to admit.

At last one of the hidden answers could be found. "May I ask a question? What do nurses use when they clean out an IV port?"

The virologist chewed and swallowed.

"Generally, we use saline solution. If we don't have that, we might use distilled water."

I lapsed into silence while my brain replayed what Toby had done that morning. I explained my concerns.

"That's standard procedure, Max. We flush the port before injecting medications unless we are pushing the meds through a solution bag on a stand."

"Do lab techs normally handle medications or do procedures like cleaning IV ports?" I pushed.

"Not usually, but these aren't normal times. Anyone with basic training can push medications through an IV port. All it takes is a bit of guidance, the right drugs in an injectable solution, and a doctor's order to release the medication. That said, having a technician dispense medications would be a serious breach of protocol. Not that too many of us are standing strictly on protocol right now." Dr. Gupta glanced at the drawn shades.

I bobbed my head, as much indicating that I wasn't done thinking about this as agreeing with her assessment of the situation.

"I thought Johnny was getting his antibiotics through the solution bag, not by direct injection," I said. Something still wasn't sitting right, and it had nothing to do with too much caffeine, which turned my stomach into an acid pit.

"You'd better check when you get back upstairs."

"Oh, I will. To change the subject, will you tell me more about these BSLs? I may have heard of them, but I'm sorry to say I paid no attention. Now, I want to know everything I can."

Dr. Gupta talked between bites of dinner. "I can't tell you as much as you'd like to know, because the actual research in these facilities is highly classified. But there are four levels, each tied to a different level of security."

The numbers referred to the amount of security needed to work with the pathogens. Not all pathogens were created equal, so the CDC used different protocols for containment based on the relative danger to the community should the pathogens escape the lab environment. In Level-1 labs, the organisms might include *E. coli* and cell cultures for other bacteria that weren't particularly dangerous. No special decontamination or containment measures were in force. At Level-2, the organisms held moderate danger to humans, including Lyme disease, measles, and MRSA. Maybe cholera.

"Level-2 labs have restrictions on who can enter, higher standards for decontamination, and more extreme precautions when using sharp instruments. Things get exciting in Level-3 and Level-4." Dr. Gupta's face glowed, more from warming to a favorite topic than from her hot tea. "By Level-3 you begin working with what Dr. Klein would call 'the bad boys.' We have very strict protocols for protective clothing, filtered air, and double-door access, although the older Level-3 labs don't necessarily have the double-door access."

"What kind of bad boys would be there?"

"Things like plague, SARS, West Nile, rabies." She conducted much of her research in one such lab.

"And Level-4?"

"Serious research only. All pathogens undergoing Level-4 research are lethal. Many have no known treatment or prevention other than avoidance of contamination. We conduct most of our drug research on vaccines for the worst pathogens in Level-3 or -4 labs."

"But I wouldn't think plague could be in a Level-3 lab."

I struggled to comprehend the differences. "I'd consider it potentially lethal."

"Plague is, but it can be cured when caught early. Pathogens in Level-4 include the hemorrhagic viruses like Ebola, because patients who contract such diseases have very little chance of survival. For some of the hemorrhagic viruses, fatality rates are over 90 percent. AIDS was there until we found a treatment protocol that worked. Were we to do research on smallpox, it would be restricted to this level," Dr. Gupta explained.

"But we aren't doing research on smallpox, are we?"

"If we were, it would be under highly controlled conditions, and I wouldn't be able to disclose where. Double-door access, air and water filtration, space suits with their own air supplies, and other decontamination procedures would have to be followed to the letter."

My coffee cup was empty again, but I didn't want any more. I'd be awake most of the night as it was. I'd moved the recliner from Alex's room to Johnny's, rousing at any change in his breathing, his shifting in bed, or a nurse checking his vital signs or changing an IV bag.

I knew we'd been over this before, but my shopworn brain needed a refresher course. "Assuming money wasn't a problem, you said I could set up one of the Level-3 or -4 labs, didn't you?"

"You wouldn't need all that much money, Max," Sharon interjected, inviting herself to the table. "And as we talked about earlier, some of what you'd need you could get at Home Depot."

"Not the space suits, but you could build a small cabinet with secure air filters. You'd put your arms through holes and use heavy lab gloves to protect yourself if you worked inside of one."

I felt worse the more she talked. I held up a hand. "Okay, let me see if I get this. I can order a lot of the lab equipment, new or used, from supply houses using the Internet. I can buy and build filtration systems with parts I buy at a big box store. Assuming I want to do something like this, it looks like I'd be set to conduct research."

"You would still need access to the pathogens themselves. As I said, we don't sell them on eBay," Sharon smiled. Pathogens were even more strictly controlled than narcotics.

"And remember, you have to be a licensed lab with sufficient protocols in place. You must have trained researchers, usually microbiologists, virologists, and pathologists—all sorts of -*ologists* before you can get your hands on the bad boys. Most of all, you'd have to have a reason for the research, usually a government grant. Idle curiosity wouldn't gain you access," Dr. Gupta said, shaking her head.

"Unauthorized personnel do not handle these pathogens," Sharon added.

"So, where would I find the Level-3 and -4 labs?" I asked.

"Scattered around the world. The CDC, Fort Detrick in Maryland, some universities, NIH, and other government facilities." Dr. Gupta stopped counting them on her fingers. Her eyes met mine. "I never thought about how many labs there are just in the States."

"Just in the States? Does the US government have these labs in other countries?"

"Yes and no. We set up temporary labs when we have viral outbreaks. Think Ebola or AIDS in several African countries," she said.

"Or plague here," Sharon added.

"I assume somewhere is a list of which pathogens are in which labs." I wasn't too happy with where my brain was leading.

"Of course. We maintain strict control of our inventories."

"When Dr. Duval talked about smallpox the other day, she said the samples in Russia and in the U.S. were frozen in *officially secured* labs."

"That's right. As I understand it, smallpox is locked away in a freezer somewhere deep inside the CDC." Sharon stared at a dish of melting soft-serve vanilla before pushing it aside. Sprinkles stained the remainder a cheery pink and green. We felt anything but cheery.

"And you're positive no one can access the samples without you knowing it?" I'd turned into a Rottweiler myself. I couldn't let the idea rest.

"Absolutely. Those of us in biomedical research stay sane by believing smallpox is locked away forever," Dr. Gupta said.

Sharon asked more questions while I tuned out to form others.

"What if a lab was destroyed?" I finally asked. "Would we know?"

"*We* would, but you, as part of the public, wouldn't," said the virologist. "We guard news of such incidents very closely. You might hear about a fire in a warehouse or office building, or of structures blown apart by weather phenomena, but little else. More than likely, these would be local stories and wouldn't register in the wider world."

"You mean, the building where my engineering company is located in Manhattan could also house research labs?"

"Technically, yes, but it's highly unlikely. We don't usually locate them in large cities, for obvious reasons. We need to verify their security. Should leaks happen, we don't want them happening in large population centers. They might be in a strip mall outside of Topeka, for example. Or near a major university like Virginia Tech."

"Have any labs burned down or been destroyed by some other means? Earthquake? Tornado?"

No matter how uncomfortable Dr. Gupta was, she nodded. Sharon slipped out of the cafeteria, cell pressed to her ear. Dr. Gupta and I turned to each other.

"Was it something we said?" I asked.

"I certainly hope so." She picked up her tray. "I'm going to grab a nap in the diagnosis room. Why don't you get some rest, too?"

I went upstairs to settle in for the night. Nurses came and went, taking readings from the monitors, changing soiled bed linens. I talked with Alex until he was too sleepy to speak with anything resembling his normal degree of Alex-centric chatter. I sat inside Johnny's room, held his hand, and lost myself in a book I'd borrowed from one of the nurses: *Prey* by Michael Crichton.

Johnny seemed to be holding steady right up until the middle of the night, when suddenly he wasn't.

CHAPTER TWENTY-SIX

ALARMS JERKED ME awake. I leaped from my chair and whirled to see lines that should be stable spiking all over Johnny's monitors. Someone shoved me out of the way. Light codes and cell phone alerts brought doctors and nurses running.

I felt the door at the end of the ICU whoosh open before my brain registered people entering. Nurses from Med-Surg joined the ICU night staff in Johnny's room. Last came Dr. Running Bear, living up to his name once again. He tied his mask as he shoved to the front of the room. He cast a look at me over his mask. I knew what it meant: Time for me to get the hell out of Dodge.

I retreated across the hall to Alex's room, changed my gloves, and tried to control my trembling hands. Lucky for him and lucky for me, Alex was fast asleep even with all the tumult. I stroked his head to assure myself that he was getting better. His forehead was cool and dry. I assumed he had grown used to alarms going off. All the monitors in his room registered reassuring normal lines and blips. I pulled a chair into the doorway.

Seconds turned into minutes. Another doctor arrived across the hall. All the night nurses were in the ICU. Fragments of words drifted out of Johnny's room, twisted and unintelligible.

I heard "coded" several times. A nurse squirted out of the hive, walked with quick strides to the medical cabinet behind the nurses' station, unlocked the door, and extracted a tray. I strained my neck to see what was on it, but all I could see was a shrink-wrapped kit.

I closed my eyes and turned to the mantra I used when Merry lay near death. I whispered, "Please, don't let Johnny die."

No one answered. No feather. No spreading warmth. No call from Whip asking how Alex was. Nothing. I'd lost Merry; I wouldn't survive losing Johnny, too, no matter who else needed me.

I curled into a ball in the chair, arms locked around my knees, and rocked. And rocked. And rocked. I laid my head on my knees and wept, silent sobs wracking my body.

Please, dear God, not again. Please don't take someone else I love. Please don't let Johnny die. I barely registered Dr. White's arrival, Dr. Klein in her wake. I raised my head when Dr. Klein ran back out of the room. I replaced my head on my knees, salt tracks on my face drying in the air conditioning.

"Charging."

"Stand back."

"Push [mumble] of epi."

Each phrase slammed against my skull. The pattern repeated itself.

"Charging."

"Stand back."

"Push [mumble] of epi."

I closed my eyes.

Sometime later, a hand squeezed my shoulder.

"Johnny?" I peered blurry-eyed into Sharon's face.

"He's going to be all right." She sat on the arm of my chair and held me while I sobbed.

"I can't lose him," I whispered against her paper gown.

"You won't." Dr. Running Bear helped me stand and led me toward the door of the ICU. I tried to pull away; I wanted to stay. The doctor's grip, gentle but firm, refused to release me. He steered me to an empty room, the one where I'd napped earlier, sat me on the edge of the bed, and took both hands in his.

"Johnny went into cardiac arrest."

That set off the alarms. His respiration stopped when his heart did. They'd used the defibrillator several times, because as soon as he seemed to stabilize, he crashed again.

"One of our night nurses, who usually works in the emergency room, guessed he OD'd from a narcotic overdose."

"How can that be? He wasn't on pain killers," I asked.

"That's right. There was no reason to administer narcotics of any kind. All I've given him is the antibiotic, which was working until a few hours ago."

Dr. Running Bear released one of my hands. Sharon sat on my other side and picked it up.

"He didn't take the drug, Max. Someone gave it to him," she explained. She removed my gloves and gown and wadded them up to be thrown in the burn barrel.

"Someone entered his room while you were sleeping and injected him with an overdose of morphine." Dr. Running Bear's face tightened. Crazed as I was, I didn't want to be around when he found the perpetrator.

Leena entered with a pill and a glass of water, which I swallowed without thinking. I jerked upright and spilled the remainder of the water. *I just swallowed a pill without asking what it was.*

"What did I take?" My eyes flared wide in sudden understanding of how easy it would be to give a patient the wrong medication without the patient knowing what he took.

"It's a very mild sedative, Max," Dr. Running Bear explained. He stood and motioned Leena to leave. "You need some rest."

"But Johnny. I need to be with him." I tried to stand, only to be pushed gently back by Sharon.

"You stay here. He's in Leena's good hands."

"How did someone give Johnny narcotics? I was sitting with him the entire time. Who would do that?" I was clear-headed enough to get the question out.

Sharon took my hand again. "We don't know."

"Rest assured. I will find him." Dr. Running Bear's face was smooth again, his expression impassive—all but his eyes, which flashed with rage. "I will not let this hospital be compromised more than it already is."

"Would you like me to stay with you?" Sharon asked.

I nodded. Whatever I'd swallowed worked, because I floated above the surface of a pond, lighter than air. I closed my eyes.

I was in a landscape devoid of color, alone. No matter which direction I looked, I couldn't see any landmark, person, or building. Unbroken grayness hid the demarcation between sky and land. I searched for something or someone just beyond the horizon. I called out, but couldn't hear the sound of my own voice.

A cool hand smoothed the hair from my forehead.

I fell into a deep sleep.

CHAPTER TWENTY-SEVEN

NO SUNLIGHT PENETRATED my blind-darkened room, but my internal clock suggested I'd slept until late morning. I stretched my arms over my head and opened my eyes to see Sharon sitting on the edge of my bed. She held up a hand and smiled.

"I thought you'd want to come say hello to Johnny. Shower first and get yourself prettied up. He's awake, sort of." She rose and stepped aside.

Showering faster than I thought possible, I did as she directed. When I was clean, I suited up and entered the ICU. Nurses moved in syncopated rhythms; no one rushed to an emergency. Dr. Running Bear and Dr. White met me outside Johnny's room. Like Sharon, their eyes were bright.

"Don't stay too long. He's pretty weak. Come down to the diagnosis room when you can." Dr. Running Bear led Dr. White and Sharon toward the swinging doors. I took a deep breath and pushed aside the curtains obscuring Johnny's room.

"Hey, funny man."

"Hey, yourself, pretty lady," Johnny said, his voice weak. "Heard you were playing sleeping beauty."

I swallowed a lump the size of Nebraska. "Yes. I took a nap

after you stopped coding. Dr. Running Bear ordered me to leave once he had you stabilized." I swallowed hard again and wiped away a tear. Before I could stop myself, I climbed into bed and buried my face in the notch in Johnny's neck.

Johnny touched my face with a trembling hand. "I'm going to be all right. No need to worry. I'm not leaving you."

"I was so scared." I didn't try to hold back my tears. I let them soak Johnny's hospital gown.

"If I'd have been conscious, I'd have been scared myself," he said. He stroked my cheek, wiping away tears with a thumb.

"I wanted to stay, but Sharon is a force unto herself. So was the sedative Dr. Running Bear gave me." I pulled down my mask and kissed his forehead; I clung to his hand, reluctant to release it. We were silent, overcome with emotion and fatigue. Johnny's eyelids fluttered as he struggled to keep them open. I squeezed his hand. "Sleep. I'll be back later."

He nodded, eyes closed. By the time I was out of the room, his breathing was deep and regular. I shut my eyes against more tears. I wasn't going to lose Johnny. I stuck my head in Alex's room. He was lost in his Game Boy. I pulled an ear bud free to interrupt him with the good news about Johnny.

"I know. I knew before you did," Alex said, glancing at me before returning to his game, thumbs working overtime to move the arrows around Grand Theft Auto.

Leena stepped up beside me and pulled Alex's door partially closed. "Are you coming to the diagnosis room?" she asked.

While I was all but passed out, the CDC team had been busy. The nurse gave me a few hints while we walked together but left the detailed discussion for the team.

No sooner had I entered the locked room than I blurted out the question most pressing. "What the hell happened to Johnny? Forget the rest. Forget the growing mystery. Tell me why he crashed."

At the height of Johnny's crisis, Nurse Leena had shone a light into his pupils. Pinpoint and non-responsive. Depressed breathing. Dr. White had drawn a vial of blood for Dr. Klein to test. I vaguely remember him bolting for the door. "Someone on staff directly injected Johnny with the morphine," Dr. Running Bear said.

"We don't know who," Sharon said. She glanced at Leena and Dr. Running Bear. "God, I'm getting damned sick of saying we don't know."

"Rest assured, I will find him." Dr. Running Bear walked over and did a quick visual assessment of my physical condition. He must have approved of what he saw, because he smiled and patted my back.

"With Johnny having plague, we would never order morphine. It slowed his heart rate and made his breathing shallow."

"So, someone walked past me and injected morphine. I don't remember anyone coming in.

"You could have been asleep, Max."

Possible, because I often dozed in Alex's or Johnny's rooms.

"You'd think I'd notice." I stared off into nothing.

"Not if it was someone who routinely was in the room," Sharon said.

"Or if it was the white dragon Alex saw." I told the group about his nightmare. "Do any nurses routinely wear white scrubs?"

Dr. Running Bear nodded. "Some do."

"We believe he was injected through the port, so we changed it and sent it to an off-site lab for analysis," the nurse said.

Muzzy-headed or not, I had a vivid image of someone pushing a needle into the port on the back of Johnny's hand. I turned to Leena. "I saw Toby doing something to the port earlier. He said he was cleaning it with saline. Could he have been injecting Johnny with morphine at that time?" I asked as I paced the diagnosis room. Pacing had become my favorite activity when I was thinking through a problem. I had picked up one of Whip's habits.

"No. That was too long before Johnny coded. The amount of morphine in his system put him into near-instant cardiac arrest," Dr. Running Bear said.

"I've asked everyone on duty last night to tell me who came into the ICU. No one saw anyone who wasn't supposed to be there," Leena said, putting her arm around my shoulders.

I shook my head. "Then we should be looking for someone who was supposed to be there, shouldn't we?"

"None of the ICU patients is on morphine," Dr. Running Bear confirmed.

Dr. Duval interjected, "We are also looking for the syringe used to inject the morphine, if that was going to be your next question. It has not left the hospital. All our waste is separated and stored until it is safe to be destroyed."

"It wasn't the next, but that would have come up sooner or later." I paused mid-stride. "Could someone have tampered with a saline syringe? Drained it and replaced the liquid with morphine? Or dropped a morphine syringe on a tray that normally holds only saline?"

"It's possible, although the labels are different colors. Both liquids are colorless. Operating as quickly as we have since the crisis began, mistakes can happen, although it's highly unlikely," Dr. Running Bear said.

"Mistakes? Or deliberate?" Dr. White planted her fists on her hips, daring anyone to tell her she was imagining bogeymen. Even though she'd suggested as much when I mentioned Toby's spraying something in the ICU, it was impossible to completely dismiss anything as conspiracy theory run amok now.

"It could be either, Tick. We shouldn't jump to conclusions or name someone without provocation, but I, too, lean toward a deliberate, inappropriate use of an opioid," Sharon said.

I took a lap around the room, hands clasped behind my back in imitation of Dr. White. Each board held a clue that I was this close to deciphering.

I froze in front of the plague board. "What if Johnny wasn't targeted? What if the person with the pathogens doesn't care who gets sick? What if he doesn't care who dies as long as someone does?"

"That would be one sick puppy," Dr. Klein said. "It's not unheard for medical professionals to accidentally administer an overdose. And others have acted as angels of death to end a patient's suffering."

"I dismiss all ideas of an angel of death here. Whoever this is, he's infecting healthy people, not trying to kill sick ones," Dr. Running Bear said.

"Not only is San Felipe ground zero for the outbreak, it's also a laboratory experiment." Sharon closed her eyes. "But what does he hope to gain?"

"If it were a single pathogen, I'd suggest he is testing delivery mechanisms to see if it could be weaponized to infect masses of people," said Dr. Duval.

Dr. White added, "With three pathogens, that makes no sense."

"He isn't testing a new super-pathogen, because we've been able to treat most of the cases." Dr. Klein again studied a wad of papers in his hands.

My bitterness flared. "All except Johnny."

Dr. Running Bear was direct.

"Johnny's case is different. I think the person, whoever it is, is afraid you and Johnny were getting too close to an answer. I think he or she saw you as a threat and acted to stop you through the attack on Johnny. And if that's the case, no way should either of you be alone without one of us with you. I know it's an imposition, but it's for your own sake."

I agreed.

"We cannot follow the money like they do in movies, so we must follow the origin of the pathogens," Dr. Duval said. "When we find that out, we find who had access to them."

"Do they have DNA?" I asked.

"Yes."

"Might these pathogens have some signature that would identify who was conducting research? Or where they came from?" I'd hung around Alex and Ducks too long. I felt a rush of warmth, like an answered prayer. *Welcome back, Em.*

"Yes and no," Dr. White said. "Indicators would point us to the strain we're facing, except these pathogens have been manipulated. I've been talking with several of my contacts at headquarters. I sicced a whole passel of them on the mystery."

Sharon had a sly look in her eye. "I sicced someone else on the problem. What you may not remember is that my husband, Milt, used to sit on several intelligence committees when he was a senator, and still has dinner with the current leadership at least twice a month. He has resources even I don't know about. I asked him to sniff around."

Well, now. This should be interesting. I pulled up a stool and perched on its edge. Dr. White leaned against the unmade hospital bed she slept on nightly.

Dr. Klein picked up a pen and opened a fresh page in his

notebook. "Let's hear what you have."

"Okay, first, my husband's warning. This is all highly classified. We aren't officially *read in* to the situation, so you can't talk about it to anyone outside our circle of trusted co-conspirators."

She looked at each of us. We nodded, and she continued.

Ten years earlier, teams of doctors in several undisclosed locations conducted government-sponsored research on some of the worst diseases in history. Their charter was to determine what would happen if they could be weaponized, become part of a biological warfare inventory, and possibly be used to attack the U.S. All work was conducted in BSL-4 labs.

"These buildings have every safety procedure, from space suits to special, pressurized entrances, to air scrubbers and much more." Dr. White said. "It's a pain in the ass to get in and out. No one—but no one—without a specific clearance and a demonstrable need to know even knows these exist."

"How do you get a clearance?" I asked.

"It's a long process. Let's keep it to if you don't have a need to know, you won't have to go through vetting by the FBI and other government agencies," Dr. Klein said.

"Milt says even *he* doesn't know where they all are. I choose to believe him. It makes for a happier marriage if he gets to keep some of his secrets," Sharon grinned. "The general population wouldn't know if they were working next door to such a lab."

"That's right. Most of the buildings are nondescript. You don't want neon signs saying 'Warning. Bad bugs inside!' They'd be a magnet for all terrorist groups, foreign and domestic," Dr. Klein said.

I laughed. "I remember the hysteria when Ebola was on the loose in a monkey lab somewhere in Virginia years ago."

"In Reston in Northern Virginia. No matter how hard the scientists tried to contain news of the outbreak, it slipped out. If it had not been handled so quickly, if the virus had not been restricted to the lab itself, and if it had been a strain that easily infects humans, we could have had a total panic," Dr. Duval said. "I was just entering medical school at Emory University when it happened. I studied the outbreak through to resolution. That is when I decided to apply to the CDC."

"Years later I read a book about this subject. Fascinating as much as it was frightening." I said. I resumed pacing. "Do you think this could be terrorist related?"

"I don't know, but I doubt it. So does Milt. He's keeping his options open, though," Sharon said.

Since 9/11, our collective consciousness had been focused on foreign terrorists, primarily those who infiltrated from safe havens in the Middle East or South Asia. How soon we forgot that one of the worst terrorist attacks on our own soil was Timothy McVeigh's bombing of the Murrah Federal Building in Oklahoma City. Though the attack occurred early in the modern terrorist narrative, news reports claimed that the police were looking for a Middle Eastern man. Turned out to be a home-grown terrorist with blue eyes and light brown hair.

No one at San Felipe appeared to have Middle Eastern origins. I dismissed the possibility of a foreign terrorist. If we had a terrorist, it had to be someone born in the good old U.S. of A.

Sharon referred to her notes. "So, according to my husband, somewhere in the Midwest a BSL-4 lab reported a protocol breach. An unauthorized individual without the proper clearance penetrated the interior of the facility. My husband says these labs all have panic buttons. The protocol is to hit the button and get out through the decontamination chambers."

"*Beat cheeks* is the official term for such evacuation procedures," Dr. Klein said. "Was that protocol followed?"

Sharon consulted her notes and confirmed it.

Dr. White said, "We'd either escape if any pathogens were released or arrest an intruder if he was unauthorized. I was in our main lab when a power outage shut down the air locks. Scary time until the generators kicked in. I was happy I didn't have to evacuate."

"Anyway, no one at the time knew who the intruder was or where he was in the building. Some of the doctors and scientists fled through back exits into decontamination chambers. The intruder, the lab itself, and presumably the pathogens were likely destroyed when the building exploded. Everything and everyone inside were incinerated within minutes," Sharon said.

"Are you suggesting our own government blew up the building?" I tried not to look shocked.

"I mean the building exploded. No one reported seeing anything other than the building explode. The official report stated a buildup of natural gas was the cause," Sharon said.

"You said the *official* cause was a gas leak and a spark. What was it really?" Dr. Klein stopped making notes on various boards and pages.

Sharon shrugged. "Whatever it was, it did a damned thorough job."

We chewed on this news silently. If a BSL-4 lab had been destroyed, hadn't all the dangerous agents inside been destroyed too?

"Could the government have destroyed its own lab?" I had great difficulty accepting what Sharon said. "Isn't it more likely that someone inside purposefully or accidentally set off an incendiary device?"

Dr. Klein stared off in space. "Is there any way of knowing if any samples were stolen prior to the fire?"

Another lengthy period of silence followed the question.

"That's the part of the classified report that was redacted. My husband used political leverage to see the original. No one knows for certain if all the biological agents were destroyed. What was never made public was that two bodies were found in the ashes. The government identified one as the intruder. He'd been a construction guy working on one of the rooftop scrubbers. His buddy thought he went to the porta-potty. Seems he went through the front in search of a cleaner toilet. He may have brought Armageddon down on the lab." Sharon rubbed her hand across her eyes. We women had long since dispensed with makeup.

"And the second body?" A dead body was something I could understand.

"Incinerated beyond recognition, but one of the research doctors is unaccounted for. He may be dead. He hasn't been seen since. Nothing in the report identified the second victim," Sharon said.

"Wouldn't forensic scientists be able to extract DNA to identify the second victim?" I asked.

Dr. Klein wasn't buying it either. "So, the report said a John Doe died, huh? Bunk."

"And how do we get from a bombed-out lab somewhere in the Midwest to an Indian Health Service hospital on the San Felipe Reservation outside of Santa Fe?" I asked.

Dr. Klein added more information from his autopsies on various charts.

"I have no idea," Sharon said.

"Well, if one of the doctors or scientists stole some of the agents before the fire or when he fled through the decontamination room, that would explain why we have multiple diseases in this outbreak," Dr. White said, springing from the bed to one of the white boards that listed diseases.

"It also explains why I have fragments of bacteria and viruses in the same samples. My guess is the agents weren't kept frozen. If the person who stole them didn't have a freezer handy, they would have begun to degrade," Dr. Klein said.

"That makes sense," Dr. White said. "We have this soup of diseases bubbling away. Who was it? Who was the doctor who escaped the fire?"

"He has to be someone who is now in this hospital or in the community at large." Dr. Klein finished adding his data points.

"Or she. Don't we have to keep an open mind? It could be anyone," I said. Once more, I didn't like where this was heading.

Dr. Duval moved toward Sharon. "The CDC has not lost any labs. It might have been subcontracted from Fort Detrick in Maryland. Can you ask the vice president to find out whose lab it was and what pathogens they were researching?"

"I can, but I can't guarantee he can or will tell me." She pulled out her phone.

"Well, if he can't, ask him to find out if the three pathogens we're fighting were sent to that lab," Dr. Running Bear said. Sharon left the room, phone at her ear.

"When was the fire?" I asked. Again, the people in the room stared at me. "What?"

Dr. Duval looked puzzled at first but then turned to Nurse Leena. "As soon as we know the date, Leena, can you look at personnel records to see who was hired after that time?"

Nurse Leena looked troubled, but nodded.

"Remember, we cannot talk to anyone else about this," Dr. Duval said.

My phone vibrated with a text: *Too late.* Ducks.

How do I tell these people that the number of people not *read in on highly classified data has increased by two?*

Sharon returned to the diagnosis room, glanced at her phone, and sent a text. "I need Keith's help, even if he's not read in."

"What would they do to you if they found out? Fire you?" I laughed.

"Not likely, although Milt can get really angry when he feels he's been crossed," Sharon shrugged. "Anyway, I sent Keith a head's-up that I need to talk with him. He's watching the door to the loading dock. Time for a stroll over there."

"It's nice to have connections, isn't it?" Dr. White continued scrutinizing the boards. *If she looks long and hard enough, will the answer appear like a specter in front of her?*

"Sure is." Dr. Klein left for his lab.

Dr. Running Bear and Dr. Duval stayed, as did I. I had no idea where Dr. Gupta was, and Leena left to care for patients before investigating the personnel records.

"We haven't had any new patients in two days, have we?" I asked, fairly certain of the answer.

Dr. Running Bear shook his head. No new patients was good news, but if the person responsible for the infections worked in the hospital, no one inside was safe. I thought about what happened to Johnny—if the person was sneaking out, the public wasn't safe either. I bet he was lying low to lure us into a state of false security.

I looked up in time to see a strange look cross Dr. Running Bear's face. He glanced over his shoulder, but no one was close to him. He stared at me. I shrugged. I didn't know if one of my watchdogs had reached out or not. The spooks were silent on my side.

CHAPTER TWENTY-EIGHT

SPLITTING MY TIME between the diagnosis room and the ICU, I gradually spent more time away than in. Alex was healing well, both his lungs and the incision in his leg. He'd be well enough to leave for Johnny's ranch in a day or two, were it not for the quarantine. Johnny grew stronger and itched to get "back on the case," as he called it.

"Whip, Alex is doing fine," I said on my daily call.

"I know. He's been texting non-stop," Whip laughed. "What's this about a hat?"

I explained Alex's obsession with the Stetson. "We need to think through when you can come out. It should coincide with Alex leaving for the ranch, but we have to wait until the CDC says it's safe to lift the quarantine."

We chatted a while longer before ringing off with a plan. Whip would fly out with Emilie on my private jet as soon as we knew Alex's transfer date. I called the leasing company to have one prepped and waiting at the general aviation airport outside of Biloxi. Once we were free to leave, the family could be here in a few hours.

Dr. Running Bear couldn't send Alex and any other healing patients home. Not yet anyway. He advised the ICU nurses that no one was to be moved from the unit unless another critical case arrived. I overheard his discussion with the parents.

"We can watch for setbacks if they are here," Dr. Running Bear told them.

What he didn't say was that a trusted individual was deliberately contaminating the hospital—until we identified and stopped whoever was turning the hospital into a giant test lab, no one was really safe. The restless father of the dead baby would have gone ballistic, literally.

"Once the crisis is over, the hospital out of quarantine, and you are all released, the CDC will send in a special cleaning crew to sanitize the entire hospital from ceiling to floor."

He assured the parents that it would be safe to bring their families back to San Felipe in the near future.

Alex made excellent progress with his crutches. He was once again the terror of the ICU. When he was done for what I hoped was his final CT scan, I received a call from Johnny's sister-in-law

"I have something for Alex. Can you come to the loading dock and pick it up?"

I had no idea what she meant, but I made my way to the dock. She stood at the end with a hat in her hand. "Johnny ordered it. It was supposed to be a surprise for Alex when he came home."

She put the hat on the ramp and climbed back into her truck to leave. When she was gone, I fetched the hat, went back upstairs, and hung it in Alex's room before returning to Johnny's. An hour later, Alex returned and went back to bed. Before he could disappear into his Game Boy, he spotted the addition.

"Oh wow! My Stetson."

"I'm glad you did this, funny man," I told Johnny. "He needed that."

"And I need you to make me feel better, pretty lady."

I leaned over and kissed him.

Johnny responded well to the change in antibiotics. His plague symptoms diminished hourly, or so it seemed to him.

Whatever the doctors used to neutralize his morphine overdose left him with no apparent permanent damage. The only side effect was his growing restlessness to get out of bed.

Dr. Running Bear allowed him to sit on the edge, feet hanging over for ten minutes at a time, as long as a nurse or an orderly was present. The first time made him so dizzy that he lasted two minutes before lying back in a cold sweat.

We were barely finished with Johnny's first standing session when I answered a buzz on my phone, a text from Sharon asking me to come to the diagnosis room as soon as possible. I helped Johnny back to bed and waved to Alex before leaving the ward. A new addition stood outside the door—a Secret Service agent was stationed where he could block entry into the ICU, if necessary. The thirty-something nodded when I walked past.

"Ma'am." The agent's eyes were never still, regardless of the empty corridor. His erect posture said he was going to stay that way until he was replaced by another agent.

In the diagnosis room, all the CDC doctors, Leena, Dr. Running Bear, and Sharon watched Dr. White redo her boards once again. Flip chart pages littered the floor, face up and reordered to present a story whose plot only she could decipher. Silence shrouded the room. I perched on a squeaky stool and tried not to fidget while I watched Dr. White's hands fly along a board wiped clean of earlier data. In the center of the board she'd drawn a crude image of a person with a large question mark on its torso.

"Since we assume the hospital is ground zero, we also have to assume the question mark works here."

"Nothing new with that," Dr. Klein said.

"Alex is patient zero for hantavirus, Max. He was the first and was infected here," Dr. White continued.

"Even though he fell in dirt near Navajo Springs?" I asked.

Dr. White jerked her head at a timeline lying on the floor. "Yes. He'd have needed at least eight days after his fall to start showing symptoms under natural circumstances. He was intentionally exposed to a heavy viral load that infected him remarkably quickly."

Dr. Duval turned to Sharon. "Do we know anything more about the two people who died in that lab explosion?"

Time for a little levity. "You mean the one that never happened?" I asked. I shot a look at Dr. Duval, who smiled.

"Yes, that one."

Sharon told Keith that identifying the people who died was top priority. So far, the outside worker's name and background were not in question. He had worked for the HVAC company for several years and was known in the local community. His body had been positively identified and released to his family for burial. Besides, the body was found in the downstairs men's room.

"Wait a minute. Was that men's room behind a security door?" I wasn't sure why I asked, but the answer seemed important.

Sharon flipped through the redacted report. "No. It was off the lobby, but not in any secure area." Sharon looked at Dr. Duval and said, "His presence couldn't have triggered the alarm."

"Didn't you say the authorities found charred remains in the lab?" I asked.

"The victim was male, and like I said earlier, one employee was not accounted for when all the personnel were counted," Sharon said.

"Do you know his name yet?" I asked, impatient. *Who the hell died?*

"I don't." Sharon stared at the figure with the question mark emblazoned on its chest. "But he was a biochemist."

I pounced. "So, you do know who he was. Sorry, but I never believed the *authorities* didn't know."

"Milt *said* the authorities had no idea. He also said no name appeared anywhere in the official or redacted report," Sharon said in defense of her husband.

"If he was a biochemist, his identity has to be recorded somewhere," Dr. Duval said.

Nothing made sense. "Why was that so classified?" Dr. White asked.

"I have no idea. More important, Milt can't seem to break the wall to find out. No matter what, someone high up won't talk." Sharon took a brief stroll around the room.

"I wonder why." I chewed on the question and spat out some seeds but found nothing I could swallow.

"No fingerprints?' Dr. Klein asked.

"Apparently not," Sharon said.

"No dental records?"

"None that matched anything on file."

"DNA?" Dr. White asked in exasperation.

"If I had to guess," Dr. Duval said, "there is no *official* record of this person anywhere. He does not exist, because he is not supposed to exist."

Sharon confirmed Dr. Duval's guess. No one would go on the record having identified the corpse. The charred remains were never claimed. "It's literally a dead end."

"None of this makes sense. That report is full of contradictions and obfuscations." I stared at Sharon, looking for her to confirm that the report was a lie.

"I agree. I do not think the reality of what happened in the destroyed lab ended with the official report. I asked for a list of certified doctors and researchers in that facility as well as our list of CDC-approved personnel conducting research on our three pathogens in other labs around the country. I should have it in a few hours, if not sooner," Dr. Duval said.

What will that tell us? That there are multiple people authorized to conduct research in the lab? That perhaps hundreds of others might have had access to the pathogens in other labs? So what? Unless we know who the dead man was—

"Did you find out when the fire was?" I asked

"Six years ago."

"And how many people were hired after that date?" I continued.

"Three," Leena said. "One doctor who stayed three years before moving on, a nurse whose been working around the clock in the ICU, and Toby the vampire."

Click. Another bit of the puzzle fit. Warmth enveloped me at the same time the feather stroked my cheek.

"Toby? He's a lab technician, isn't he? He wouldn't have access to the pathogens, right?" I asked. "And since he's here, he's not the dead biologist, obviously."

"No, he wouldn't. What about the pathogens themselves? Did we ship them?" Dr. Klein asked, busily filling in details around Dr. White's drawing.

Dr. Duval said, "Now that is odd. We have records showing we shipped hantavirus and monkeypox to several labs, but we have no records of anyone conducting active research on plague. Of course, we have all three pathogens in the CDC, but my associates have no indication the plague bacterium came from us."

"Where else could plague come from? I thought all BSL-3 and -4 pathogens were under government control," I said.

"The government is large and highly complex, Max. We all learned the hard way on 9/11 how little one section of the government shares with another. It's all about compartmentalization." Sharon looked at the phone in her hand as if the blank screen held the answer. "Milt says the military has stockpiles, probably as much as the CDC does, if not more."

More?

Dr. Duval confirmed what the vice president told his wife. "Several DoD facilities continually conduct research on pathogens that could be weaponized to use against large population centers. DARPA researches delivery mechanisms. Fort Detrick works on biological defense."

"Does DARPA have biotechnology facilities doing genetic research?" I asked.

"It might, and what do you know about DARPA? The average citizen has never heard of it," said Sharon, staring at me with renewed respect.

"Well, I'm not an average citizen." I explained that DARPA was interested in the engine my third husband Reggie was testing when he crashed. He'd hired a couple of top engineers away from the government to work on design and development.

"So, you have a revolutionary engine?" Dr. Klein asked.

"We do, although the basic premise isn't all that new. We haven't put it into production because it's still at the experimental stage. When we do, it could change how people in the Third World travel," I said.

Dr. Klein unleashed his inner geek gene. "What does it run on? Not nuclear energy—our government would never allow miniature reactors on the freeways."

"Don't I wish. Not nuclear. Water."

"Shit." Dr. Klein stepped over and clapped me on the back.

"Back to the crisis at hand. I remember the anthrax scare after 9/11. All fingers pointed to Fort Detrick, but nothing was ever proved," I said. Stories appeared in the press daily about envelopes filled with white powder being shipped to government officials. I laughed at one reported police response to a powdery substance found in Beth Israel Hospital: "Be advised. The powdery substance has been identified as a crushed peppermint candy."

"I can neither confirm nor deny," Dr. White said, grinning despite the gravity, "that several military research centers may or may not have the plague bacterium."

Confession time. "I consume thrillers like I consume coffee, so my idea may be far-fetched and colored by the stuff between the pages of my favorite novelists. But my friend Ducks has been poking around the Internet for several days. What he's found about the destroyed lab is available on respected news sites as well as on conspiracy sites."

Ducks found several old reports from newspapers in Missouri. The St. Louis *Post-Dispatch* headlined three days with reports of a six-story building in a suburban business park exploding. Other local papers reran the story, but the national papers gave it scant coverage. Ditto the large broadcast networks. The fire remained a local story with a very short shelf life.

"The *Post-Dispatch* reported witnesses seeing a flash of light heading directly into the building before it exploded." Conspiracy websites propagated a drumbeat of theories charging the U.S. government with destroying the lab with a missile.

"That's too crazy for words," Dr. White said.

"You'd think all major outlets would have published screaming headlines and interrupted network programming with breaking news reports if that were true," Dr. Klein reasoned. "Wouldn't it have been major news had a missile been confirmed hitting the building? Unless, of course, this never happened, because the lab didn't exist."

"Rats. No government conspiracy, huh? How disappointing." I thrust my lower lip.

"Like Tick, I can't confirm this was the location of the lab," Sharon said, checking the redacted report she carried with her at all times. She refused to leave it in the diagnosis room—if it fell into the wrong hands, either the unknown perpetrator would be tipped off or a parent would call the Santa Fe *New Mexican.*

Either way, all hell would break loose.

"Let's assume, for the sake of playing devil's advocate, the place was destroyed. Can we estimate how fast the pathogens would degrade?"

Dr. Klein parsed his words with caution. "For laboratory pathogens to remain viable outside the controlled environment, they would have to be frozen using liquid nitrogen."

"So, the idea that the smallpox virus is kept in a standard household freezer deep in the recesses of the CDC is the stuff of vivid imagination?" I was getting closer to an answer, but I wasn't sure I'd recognize it when I saw it.

"Hold onto that image, Max. It is as good as any." Dr. Duval picked up where Dr. Klein stopped. "If someone stole pathogens from a laboratory, we would expect to see degraded fragments as well as whole organisms."

Dr. Klein had been bothered by the fragments since he first identified them after the autopsy on the first child. And when he lined up whole organisms and compared them with what he knew to happen in nature, he concluded his pathogens were man-made. Or at least man-enhanced. He nodded.

"So where does this take us?" I was willing to accept any of the ideas we'd discussed as potentially true, but we were no closer to the identity of the person who tried to kill Johnny than we were when Alex first became ill.

"We need the name of the dead man in the lab." Sharon speed dialed her husband, only to reach his voicemail. She left a message.

"Maybe Keith can pull more strings," Dr. Duval said.

My time in the diagnosis room was up. I was antsy about leaving Alex and Johnny alone for too long. Just before I left the room, I had another thought. "Does anyone know where Toby and the ICU nurse came from?"

Loving grand exits as I did, I swept out of the room. Those remaining behind had yet one more riddle to solve.

Between the diagnosis room and the ICU, I called Emilie and Ducks. I found both in the school bus working on calculus problems. Emilie put her phone on speaker.

"You guys are on the right track with links to that lab. Sharon Anderson is pulling in as many favors as she can to identify the body found in the office park fire. Did you guys pick up any more hints in your research?"

"Not really." Emilie fussed. "I can't figure out why I can't get a clearer feeling."

"I suspect the culprit is Toby the vampire, but I have no proof. I hope it's not just because I don't like him." I must have sounded as frustrated as I felt, because Ducks' voice penetrated my roiling thoughts to offer a solution to my helplessness.

"Can Dr. Running Bear send someone to his house to see what's there?"

Well, duh, Max. "No, but the Secret Service can dispatch the local FBI. We need to stop Toby, if it is him, before he hurts anyone else."

"Stick close to Dr. White, Sharon, and Uncle Johnny," Emilie warned. "We'll do some more research. Call if you learn anything new."

I thumbed my phone off and immediately speed-dialed Keith, who had given me his number. In seconds, I learned we were on the same wavelength. He'd sent an outside nurse practitioner to visit all the families of the sick children under the guise of checking their health. If Toby had visited any of them in the past ten days, Keith would know. He expected an answer later in the day.

Leena sidled up to me and spoke quietly.

"My cousin is a cop with the Bureau of Indian Affairs. I asked him to pay an unofficial visit to Toby's house. He has no qualms about picking locks. He laughed when I told him what I needed. He said he'd deal with the fallout if he gets caught," she said.

I relaxed as I made my way back up to the ICU, but couldn't help tensing when I passed Toby on the stairs.

CHAPTER TWENTY-NINE

SHARON AND I met for breakfast the following morning, as had become our habit, health crises and fatigue permitting. Circles under our eyes ratted us out.

"I got to thinking about what Leena said. She talked about three people coming to work here after the lab-that-didn't-exist burned. Two are still here," Sharon mused.

I ate a spoonful of instant oatmeal and made a face. Like Alex, I missed brown sugar and raisins. I missed breakfasts with something other than cereal, hot or cold.

"Toby and one nurse, she said. I don't know which one it is," I said.

"Leena never mentioned her name to the group, but Keith and Dr. Running Bear know who she is. Keith asked the FBI to check their backgrounds," Sharon said.

"How can we be certain the nurse is female?"

"No male nurses in the hospital. I know your money is on Toby, but it could as easily be the nurse." Sharon slathered marmalade from a plastic packet onto half of an English muffin.

"Or both," I said, sipping coffee.

"Or both." Sharon stared at the muffin, which, though toasted and dressed with jam, looked dry and unappetizing. "The thing is, we need motive and proof before we can talk to either one. We don't want them to bolt."

"We know the fire was in 1999, but has anyone confirmed the pathogens were at the lab?" I asked.

"Not yet. Dr. Duval should have the answer later today." Sharon pushed her plate aside, half of the muffin untouched. She must have been as sick of the food as I was. She cradled a mug between her palms, eyes focused on something I couldn't see. "The *why* of this mess escapes me, not that we seem to be getting closer to the *who*."

"And the *how*. You're right. It's time to turn to the how and why. I can't grasp how a nurse chartered with caring for desperately ill patients could be involved in making them sick."

"It eludes me, too," Sharon said.

"Do you know that Leena asked her cousin to search Toby's house? He's a reservation cop of some kind."

"I don't think I want to know about anything illegal, but has he found anything?" Sharon winked.

"I'll check to see if there is any progress," I said. I carried my empty dish and mug to the rubber conveyor belt, which whisked them into the bowels of the kitchen.

Sharon left me outside the cafeteria. "I'm going hunting for Keith to see if he's learned anything new about either of our two suspects."

"I'm going hunting for Leena." I made a tour of the ICU, spoke with the nurses, and laughed at Alex, who was wreaking havoc on his crutches. I tried not to look at each nurse through a lens of suspicion. *Which one is involved with Toby, if any? If it is him.* I hated myself for harboring these thoughts despite all the work they'd collectively done to help Johnny and Alex.

I counted the nurses and put names to all but one. I'd stood next to her when eavesdropping on the lobby one day, but she melted away before I could introduce myself. I took a step toward her, but she walked into a patient's room.

I huddled quietly with Johnny, bringing him up to date on what he missed while ill.

"You've been busy," he said, gripping my hand, thumb rubbing circles on the back. "I wish I could have helped."

"You're helping by getting well," I assured him.

Johnny snorted.

We discussed my continuing dislike for Toby. "I'm positive he's involved, but we have no evidence. I don't know for sure which nurse is under, um, observation as well."

Now that Johnny knew about the potential of a second person, an ounce of responsibility shifted from my shoulders to his still-weak ones. I felt a rush of warmth, almost a warning not to put too much on him all at once. *Don't worry, Em, I won't.*

"Alex doesn't know anything about any of this." I held up a raised finger before folding my hand like a clam. "We can't let on that someone may be intentionally hurting people, because he has no filter on his mouth. He's liable to blurt out a question to Toby and inadvertently warn him that the FBI has him under surveillance."

A whoop in the hall warned nurses that Alex was galloping along on his crutches. "Avast, matey!" I poked my head out of Johnny's room and saw he had a handkerchief over his head and a black eye patch covering one eye.

"Look what Nurse Paula made for me, Mad Max."

I didn't know who Nurse Paula was. I caught the eye of a mousy woman taking inventory of the locked drug cabinet, the same mousy woman who'd stood next to me. I mouthed "Thank you" and winked.

I watched her count syringes for a moment or two. I closed my eyes and rewound mental tapes of the people I'd met. She was the kind of woman who faded into the background, who didn't initiate conversations like the other nurses. I took a step in her direction to thank her for making Alex's pirate costume. Once again, she turned her back and disappeared, this time into a linen closet.

I wanted to follow her, but Johnny's cough called me back to his side. Before I returned to the co-conspirators in the diagnosis room, I checked the monitors, which I had finally learned to read nearly as well as the nurses could. Nothing out of normal. I kissed him and told him where I was going.

"Go. I think I'll nap a little." Johnny's eyes half closed to underscore how weak he was.

I turned back at his door. "Have you seen Toby around lately?"

Johnny shook his head.

Odd. Toby had been omnipresent during the run-up to and at the height of the multiple outbreaks. "Is he even still in the hospital?" I asked the empty air. Johnny was asleep.

Nurse Paula, Alex's new pirate buddy, entered with a tray of syringes. She didn't introduce herself or make eye contact. "I'll draw his blood today."

She was as mute as a stuffed rabbit and about as scared looking. I stepped aside to let her work, but I didn't leave Johnny's side. I fussed with his pillows, all the while watching to be sure the nurse followed all protocols.

Leena met Paula outside the room. "Thanks. I'll take the samples when you're finished. I'm going down to the lab."

A few minutes later, Leena and I walked toward the diagnosis room, the vials of blood safely resting in her pocket.

"I don't remember seeing Paula—that's her name, isn't it?— in the ICU."

Leena slowed and stopped. "She wasn't on duty when the CDC quarantined the hospital. She came in after we put out the call for additional help. She usually works on the maternity ward, but with no babies being born and all deliveries diverted to other hospitals, we pushed her onto Med-Surg. She's helping wherever we need her."

"If she's usually in the maternity ward, I'd expect a bit more positive interaction with the patients and their families. She seems so cold and distant," I said.

"Now that you mention it, she's all about TLC with the new mothers and babies. Not here, though. She's really timid," Leena mused before leading the way forward once again. "Maybe she's terrified of contagion."

A feather tapped my cheek. I stepped in front of her. "What's troubling you? Paula arrived after the lab fire, didn't she?"

"Yes," she whispered. I stared into her eyes before stepping aside so we could walk on in silence, each working out our own individual plot twists.

###

"We have a bit more intelligence on that fire," Dr. Duval said as soon as the group reassembled. Because of the critical nature of our situation, she'd been able to unlock the name of the dead man on the BSL-4 floor. "Stephen Robert Byers, a post-doctoral research assistant, was killed."

We looked at each other, but the name meant nothing. He was apparently well-regarded as a virologist—just like Dr. White—but wasn't a medical doctor. Dr. Duval continued. "His degree was in microbiology. From what I learned through a few discreet inquiries, he was a rising star. A terrible loss to the research community."

Dr. Gupta frowned. "I worked with a Robby Byers, a grad student doing research for his doctorate out of the University of Washington. He was brilliant . . . I haven't thought about him in years."

"Byers had a twin who at one time had been an equally rising star, until he was fired from a lab conducting research for the military. He left his lab unsecured overnight once. He apparently had a crisis of conscience, because he protested in front of the facility and proselytized against biological weapons research." Dr. Duval looked at a couple of printouts in her hand.

"Did he try to sabotage the lab or project?" Dr. Klein asked, now fully buying into conspiracy theories.

"I have seen no evidence that what he did in the lab was designed to destroy the research," Dr. Duval said.

"Robby never mentioned a brother," Dr. Gupta said.

"He lost his security clearance and was blackballed by most of the research community. Given what his colleagues remember about him, he hated that the government was conducting highly classified research on weaponizing some of our most lethal pathogens. Our public position was that we were conducting no research of biological agents," Dr. Duval continued.

Click. Another piece fell into place.

"But we are, evidently." I began doing more laps around the room.

"Max, don't speculate on what we may or may not be doing," Sharon said.

"Could it be possible, although unlikely, that the good brother brought the black sheep into the lab-that-wasn't for reasons we haven't yet unraveled?" I pressed.

"I can't see that happening. I can't imagine anyone being so irresponsible as to bring in an unauthorized person, even his brother," Dr. White said.

"Stupid, too," Dr. Klein spat. "Dr. Byers would have lost his security clearance quicker than a hummingbird's heartbeat."

"Do we have the brother's name?" Dr. White flexed her fingers. *Does she see herself taking down the brother in a fight to the finish in the main lobby?* I couldn't see her doing anything of the kind, but she was passionate about research.

"Tobias Ogden Byers."

"Toby," Dr. Gupta breathed.

"Now we have to prove he's behind the attacks," Sharon said. "And why the hell he's doing it."

We froze for several long seconds to absorb Sharon's information. Silence filled the room; we would normally be talking over each other. My thoughts bounced around like pachinko balls, never still, never finding the slot where I would score a point or find an answer.

Concentration shattered as first one cell then another rang or buzzed. Sharon, Leena, and Dr. Running Bear snatched at their pockets. I started for the door but stopped mid-step when my phone buzzed with two text messages. *Not Uncle Johnny,* texted Emilie. *Not Alex,* texted Ducks.

Sharon listened to the speaker and nodded. "Damn it!"

Dr. Running Bear barked a few orders, while Leena said, "You're sure. Nothing in the house?"

"What the hell is going on?" I fumed.

Doctors Gupta and White huddled in a corner, Dr. White gesticulating, Dr. Gupta murmuring under her breath, both staring at messages on their phones.

Dr. Running Bear hung up first, his face revealing a rare display of raw anger. "Stay here, everyone. Leena, come with me."

"I may have to stay, but I'm going to get some damned answers." Sharon punched a number on her phone so savagely she broke her nail. "Shit!" She listened, punctuating the speaker's words with encouraging "uh huh," "okay," and "thanks." She thumbed the phone off and fell back in her chair.

Questions flew at her like bees from an upended hive.

"Who was that?' I asked.

"What happened?" Dr. Gupta moved closer to us.

"Keith," Sharon said. "Someone sneaked up and attacked him from behind." She ran her hands across her eyes.

"Is he all right?" I asked. Keith, our symbol of strength and safety. I couldn't imagine how I'd feel if he were seriously injured.

"He says he is, but Dr. Running Bear and Leena are going to check him out."

"Does he know who hit him?" I started for the door, prepared to track down and stop the attacker myself, if necessary.

Sharon grinned in spite of the attack. "You bet he does. Keith was part of Seal Team Six before he retired and joined the Secret Service. He's in his element with hand-to-hand combat. We laugh all the time about how guarding me is the most boring job he could have."

"Not anymore," Dr. White said.

"You're right, not anymore. The man who attacked him is under control," Sharon said.

"Toby?" It had to be. He had to have made a foolish move and been caught.

"You were right all along, Max. Toby tried to leave the hospital. He ran into Keith on guard duty at the loading dock and struck him with a bat or something equally solid."

Sharon's phone buzzed with a text. She opened the attached document and scanned it.

"Okay, Toby attacked Keith, but do we have proof he's behind the release of the pathogens?" I asked.

"We're almost there, Max. Let me tell you what my husband learned."

Milton Anderson had thrown his considerable political weight around to unlock a secret file of personnel clearances in the burnt-out lab. Volumes of information about each one included background checks, polygraphs, and fingerprints.

"He skimmed the bulk of the data but read the Robert Byers's file in its entirety," Sharon said. A congressional committee studying the incident found no anomalies in the clearance process. "The only lapse of security protocol occurred when the construction worker went looking for a bathroom, but that in and of itself was not enough to put the lab in lockdown."

The committee raised the red flag when an unauthorized person was discovered in the lab itself. According to the report, this person breached the uppermost floor where the most critical weapons research was being conducted.

"How do you know this? If the lab was demolished, wouldn't all evidence turn into ash with it?" Dr. Klein asked.

"Not if there were closed circuit television cameras in the critical areas," Dr. White said.

"But—" Dr. Klein got no further. Sharon held up a finger for silence. I grinned, because three of us used similar gestures to command silence.

"The labs have built-in redundancies. Data is stored locally and at a remote site with acres of server farms," Dr. White said.

"A few days ago, Milt called in a favor from a friend in Justice, who subpoenaed the videos." Sharon smiled for the first time that day. "He says the images are fuzzy, but after they were enhanced, Robby is recognizable. At first, it appeared the intruder broke in or was let in by a worker with clearance. He might even have used a false or stolen ID badge. He was discovered in the frozen storage room packing samples into an ice cooler. When Byers tried to apprehend him, the intruder shot and killed him."

"I thought the body was incinerated. I thought it couldn't be identified," I said.

"That's what the redacted report said, but the secret report with the images from the closed-circuit cameras captured the murder." Sharon slumped in her chair.

"First, you said the report didn't identify the man in the lab. Then, you said people in the government or on the committee knew his identity. And now, you know he was shot because it was on television?" I plowed ahead.

"Welcome to Washington, Max. It can be harder than hell to get a complete, factual answer on anything. Even what my husband ate for breakfast this morning," Sharon said.

"Well, unless the body was completely incinerated, what was left would have been autopsied," Dr. Klein said. "Even with the most badly burned bodies, it's possible for some tissue to withstand the fire. And if that tissue held a bullet or traces of a bullet's path, we'd be able to tell if the body was shot and, therefore, murdered."

Dr. Klein beamed at the direction the investigation was moving. For the briefest moment, he reminded me of Alex, who was always ready to don his super hero persona and ride to the world's rescue.

"What about fingerprints?" My gut boiled overtime on possibilities we hadn't voiced. "Is there any way we can see if they match Toby's?"

"Why would they match Toby's? The dead man was Robby, wasn't he?" Dr. White hadn't followed the zig when my brain zagged.

"Was he? The man who had the clearance was Robby Byers." I swiveled to face Dr. Klein. "Was the dead man Robby? Jerry, can you lift prints from charred skin?"

Dr. Klein shook his head. "If it's too badly burned, we can't. But we can match prints from samples of people here in the hospital to those in the file. That would rule out Toby being Robby. His prints will still be on file, even though he lost his security clearance."

Keith's team had collected prints from all of the staff, family members, and the adult patients. The FBI had run them through their databases. What we needed should be in their read out. When the team took Johnny's prints he told them they'd find them in Department of Defense files. "I served eight years in the Army, he said"

"Let's go back to that unauthorized person in the lab. How did he get in, and who was he?" Dr. White returned to her concern with the origin of the pathogens. "And, if what the committee reported is true, why would he steal samples?"

"Were either of the Byers' brothers responsible for stealing them from the burned-out lab?" I asked. "In my mind, that's the key question. If we agree the origin of the pathogens traces to the lab, shouldn't we move to the next question? The *why*?"

While I loved peeling away the layers of the onion to solve a crime—God knows I'd done it more than I ever thought I would—it was time to move to the next step. "Why would anyone want to steal them in the first place?"

Dr. Gupta picked up the thread. "You wouldn't, unless you're going to continue research on them or release them into a community."

"So, the fire in the lab-that-wasn't happened in 1999?" Dr. White asked as she added more "supposes" to what we already knew on a flip chart.

Sharon consulted the wad of paper in her pocket. "That's right. October 1999."

"Where were those samples kept since October 1999? Were they properly preserved to avoid contamination?" The epidemiologist added a cryptic mark to a new section of her chart. "Wherever it was, without proper handling, it'd be a miracle if any of the pathogens were still viable. Jerry found a fair amount of degradation in the blood tests. Could that be explained away through improper preservation?"

"Who says these were the original samples? What if these samples were multiple generations away from the originals?" Dr. Gupta's face lit up as if she'd seized upon a major clue.

Dr. White added even more scribbles to her latest chart. "That would mean the thief has a lab where he could continue his research. If he works here, his lab has to be in the community or fairly nearby. We know it's not in the hospital itself."

"Keith and his team left no corner unsearched. Multiple times," Sharon confirmed.

"Not that a researcher works all day every day to modify bacteria. If I were secretly working on enhancing an existing organism, I'd want my lab to be near enough to visit every couple of days to see how the cultures were developing," Dr. White said.

"Wouldn't he need a climate-controlled facility?" I asked.

"As long as he has uninterrupted power to run his refrigeration units, he'd be fine." Dr. Klein almost pushed his nose against a chart, the better to read Dr. White's mouse-sized printing. "Look, all he'd need is a reliable generator and a fuel source."

"Some tests take weeks or even months to show results," Dr. Gupta said. "After all, modifying DNA takes patience, knowledge of what you're doing, and a whole lot of luck. Forget what you see on television. None of this work happens in forty-five minutes."

"Viruses and bacteria have DNA, too. With knowledge in microbiology and some good microscopes, hypothetically, someone in a garage lab could conduct the kind of gene-splicing research that led to these becoming larger pathogens. Especially if he's an expert in virology. I mean, it's not like he's sequencing the *Yersinia pestis* genome, after all."

"*Yersinia pestis?*"

"Plague."

Why would Toby, who was fired for protesting research on biochemical weapons, steal samples and work to make them more potent? I scratched my head. "What's his motive?"

"That's the crux of the matter." Dr. Klein turned his back on the flip charts and white boards. "If he worked with contaminated samples, though, it might explain why the incubation periods are so crazy."

"Yes, like Alex getting sick so quickly. We all noticed the accelerated incubation periods. It's all right here," Dr. White said, nudging a piece of paper with a toe.

Dr. Gupta shook her head. "That doesn't make sense. Toby weaponizing these pathogens would be in direct conflict with his earlier position." I was in her camp.

"He could have changed his mind after 9/11," Dr. White said. "My fellow virologists spent hundreds of hours speculating about terrorists having biological weapons of mass destruction at their disposal." The airwaves had been so flooded with alarm that half the population was scared witless and the other half was sick to death of the whole mess. Anthrax had indeed been weaponized and mailed to government officials, killing some innocents in the process. Speculation about dirty bombs replaced anthrax, as did claims that if the U.S. had biological and chemical weapons, we'd somehow be safer. It wasn't unrealistic to think a pacifist would change his mind under those circumstances.

Hysterical information over too long a period produced nation-wide ennui. The public didn't want to be barraged with scare tactics any longer, in spite of the fact that the U.S. faced real and present dangers.

Bunk. My brain flipped and flopped, flopped and flipped. I was getting nowhere and making myself dizzy.

"Let me get this straight," Sharon said. "We might have a scientist who hated biological weapons potentially being used on mankind, only to make a one-eighty after 9/11 and create his own biological weapons." She shook her head. "It does not compute, as Captain Kirk said. He stole the pathogens *before* 9/11. He must have already had plans for them."

"It wasn't *Star Trek*. It was the robot on the old television show, *Lost in Space* . . . What? I can't help it if I'm a science fiction geek," Dr. Klein said, laughing at Sharon's look of incomprehension.

Dr. Gupta said, "It does seem unbelievable, but we can all name people who changed drastically after 9/11. We became more patriotic, if only for a short period of time. In the research community, we tightened our security protocols to the levels we already had with our nuclear arsenal. Today, I'd say no one could steal pathogens, but the protocols weren't as stringent in 1999."

I paced, dodging anyone and anything that stood in my way. I momentarily ignored the *why* to ask the *how*. "What if he wanted to create new delivery mechanisms, like using aerosols to spread the diseases?"

"Aerosols . . . " Dr. Gupta's voice trailed off. "Like in a nebulizer."

"Alex received nebulizer treatments constantly. What if hantavirus was in the solution?" My face must have gone pale because Sharon moved over and took my pulse. "Don't worry. I'm too pissed off to faint."

"Delivery experimentation could help explain why Johnny got sick after inhaling droplets Toby sprayed in the ICU. Maybe he's testing mass dissemination techniques to infect a large part of the population," Sharon said.

"Have we heard what Keith's swabs of the ICU turned up?" I asked.

Sharon nodded. "He pulled traces of plague from the spray residue on the walls."

I was ablaze with questions. "What if he wanted to demonstrate how easily these ancient diseases could be resurrected, manufactured in bulk, and reintroduced into an under-protected population? What if his oversized ego led him to believe he was the only one who could alert the world to the danger?"

CHAPTER THIRTY

HEADS SWIVELED IN my direction—or directions because I hadn't stopped pacing. As I fit the next pieces of the puzzle together, I ignored my phone merrily buzzing in my pocket. I was certain it was a text from Emilie or Ducks, maybe even a happy face *emoji*.

"The terrorist attacks of 9/11 resulted in a lot of depression, panic attacks, and mental illness," Dr. Gupta confirmed. "Heavens knows, the sale of anti-depressants skyrocketed in the weeks and months afterward. Lots of scientists and regular people hoped we'd find a magic bullet to protect us."

"No silver bullet, huh?" I asked with the trace of a smile.

"No vampires, either," Dr. White said.

"I was thinking about the Lone Ranger and his silver bullets," I said. Her expression made me laugh. "Never mind." I waved both hands in her direction.

"Back to what's going on here. Do we have any indication Toby was looking for a new way to deliver enhanced pathogens?" Dr. White asked. "We don't know if he was trying to develop something to keep us safe or a new weapon to kill the maximum number he exposed."

Before we could say anything else, the door swung open. Leena entered, a tray of instruments and used syringes in her hands, and a very scared Nurse Paula trailing behind. "I was checking our inventory on Dr. Running Bear's orders, when I found this hidden at the back of the supply closet."

On the tray were multiple syringes with different labels, nebulizer masks and tubing, and spray bottles. Her jaw set, Leena nudged the trembling woman forward.

"Paula has something to tell us. Go ahead. Talk."

Dr. Running Bear, Dr. Duval, and Keith slipped in before Paula began. Toby was absent.

Keith caught my questioning look, sidled over, and whispered, "He's locked in an inner room. No windows, no way out except through one door, which Ben is guarding. He's not going anywhere."

I exhaled. I remembered Ben, the six-foot-five hunk of muscle who had spooked me when we first met. Once I got to know him, I realized he was gentle and would have looked perfect with a full beard and buckskins, if the Secret Service would have allowed it.

"Are you all right?" I could see a large lump on the back of Keith's head.

"No amateur is going to take me out."

Dr. Running Bear stopped in front of Paula, who quaked under his stare. "Do you want to tell me what you hoped to accomplish?"

Sharon opened her mouth, only to snap it shut when Dr. Running Bear held up a hand.

"I thought he was trying to find a way to prevent terrorists from using pathogens in a biological attack." Paula's voice emerged as a near croak.

"And how did you think exposing your colleagues and friends would prevent terrorism?" Dr. Running Bear, still as a granite statue, appeared to loom over the shorter nurse, even though neither had moved.

"He—he said he wanted to test delivery mechanisms that would make the diseases easier to spread throughout a contamination zone."

Toby had convinced Paula he was only interested in pneumonic plague, even after he released hantavirus and monkeypox in the ICU. He thought plague was more capable of being weaponized if a terrorist manufactured enough of it. Hantavirus and monkeypox weren't reliable enough for maximum spread of infection.

"If he could find a way to spray the pathogen in bulk, then people would contract plague without knowing the source. If he could show how easy it was, he thought our government would work on preventing terrorists from acquiring the pathogens rather than us working on turning them into weapons."

"That logic is so flawed I can't wrap my mind around it," Sharon exploded. "It's FUBAR: Fucked Up Beyond All Recognition."

Dr. Duval raised an eyebrow but remained silent.

"How does he know the government isn't working on just that? Does he have a secret source in the government feeding him information? Or a crystal ball?" Dr. Klein's face reddened, and he pounded one fist into his palm.

Dr. Running Bear shot a glance at the pathologist and shook his head. Dr. Klein's lips glued themselves together. He was left to stew without further verbal outlet.

"So, he wanted to spray a city with pneumonic plague much like we sprayed Malathion to prevent the Mediterranean fruit fly from spreading?" Major controversies broke out in Southern California when that particular invasive pest threatened to destroy the citrus crop.

"If Toby could prove plague could be distributed through repeated sprayings, he could get governments around the world to pay attention and develop ways to prevent infections," said Paula, biting a thumbnail that was already bleeding.

"And exactly how does he think he can distribute plague?" Dr. Duval asked. She had remained silent up to this point, but I could almost smell small synapses shorting out. Like Dr. Running Bear, she was as rigid as an obsidian obelisk.

"Drones." Paula cast her eyes downward. "He said if his experiments with spraying in and around the ICU worked, then nothing could stop a terrorist from putting canisters on military drones." She pointed to a common spray bottle used for holding bleach or window washing fluid.

"Diabolical," Dr. White said.

"Cool," Dr. Klein said.

"What a monster! So, he sprays Johnny and waits to see if he gets sick, huh?" I wanted to slap this fool silly, but I balled my fists and stuffed them inside the pockets of my scrubs. "That doesn't explain trying to kill him with an overdose of morphine."

Dr. Running Bear beckoned to Leena, who carried the tray of medical waste. He pulled on gloves before picking up some IV tubing. "Look at the pinprick holes. He administered morphine through this."

"Toby didn't do that. I did," a mousy voice squeaked.

Dr. Duval rose over the shrinking nurse, who shriveled in front of our eyes. "What did you say?"

"I injected morphine into Mr. Medina's IV port. You were half asleep when I came in." Paula stared at me. "Even though you spoke to me, you never really saw me, did you, Mrs. Davies? No one sees me."

"Why?"

"Toby said you were dangerous, that you were too close to discovering us. He wanted to stop you." Paula swiped at her snotty nose with a sodden tissue, tears flowing freely. "I gave Mr. Medina the overdose."

"What had he done to you?" I wanted to strangle her.

"Not him. You." Paula's red-rimmed eyes bored into mine.

"Me?" I'd dismissed Dr. Duval's suggestion that I was somehow in danger. She was right after all.

"I thought you'd give up if Mr. Medina died."

"Well, you thought wrong. I'll do everything in my power to be sure you never leave prison."

"Did you tamper with the nebulizer equipment?" Dr. Gupta asked.

Alex and several of the other ill children received daily treatments before their hantavirus symptoms suddenly worsened.

"Not all. Some children got sick on their own. I injected the virus randomly into the medicine packets. When I put them back on the shelf, I mixed them up. Some kids got regular medicine, others got the contaminated solution." Paula looked almost proud of what she'd done.

"I checked the supplies," Leena said. "Several unopened

packets show needle marks. I put them into a box where we couldn't grab one by accident. We'll send them to the CDC to see what, if any, pathogens have been introduced into the sterile environment."

Leena carefully placed the items in a box for the CDC facility. My overactive gut said the tests would show Toby's and Paula's fingerprints as well.

"You did all this for Toby? Why the hell would you?" Dr. Klein asked.

"Because he treated me with respect. He didn't look past me like all of you did." Paula smiled a little. "He said I was smart enough to help him with his research. I was the only person he could trust."

Keith opened the door and beckoned to one of his detail. "Take her away. Don't let anyone visit her, and don't leave her alone, no matter what she says."

"Copy that."

I waited until the door closed behind the agents and Paula before erupting. "She did this because Toby was *nice* to her?"

"I can see it happening," Sharon said. "We had a med student when I was a third-year. She was so quiet she faded into paint. She was as starved for attention as Paula was. She washed out in her first year because she couldn't interact well with patients."

"Still, even if Toby pretended to love her, why would she fall for his line? Couldn't she see through him?" My mind refused to accept Paula's motives, which confounded me.

"Maybe Toby was the first man who pretended to like her. That's the only way I can explain her falling for his bullshit," Dr. Gupta said.

"Meenu!" Doctors White and Klein protested as one.

Dr. Gupta shrugged.

"How did you trip up Toby, Keith?" Sharon asked.

"He tried to go outside for a smoke. I wouldn't let him," Keith said.

"Toby doesn't smoke," Leena said.

"I knew that. I'd never seen him outside with the other butt heads. He tried to push past me. I made a mistake when I turned my back to secure the door. He swung at me with an empty oxygen canister. Luckily, I ducked and only got a glancing blow before I drop-kicked him in his balls. He decided he didn't need a smoke after all."

"Way to go, Keith," Dr. Klein said.

Keith shook his head. "Damned stupid to turn my back. Not to worry. He's in custody well away from his lab. He can't destroy any evidence."

One thought breached like a whale, a thought so disgusting I could voice it only reluctantly.

"Please tell me Toby and Paula weren't—" I could go no further.

"No, Toby manipulated her into doing what he wanted. I interrogated Paula while we were walking from the ICU. He flattered her and made her feel important. She said no man ever made her feel so needed, maybe even attractive. He didn't need anything but his charm to rope her in. They weren't lovers," Leena said.

I couldn't fathom anyone being so gullible. My face once again gave me away. Sharon reached out a hand and took mine. "You've never been plain, Max. We don't know what this woman has been through."

"She's going to go through much more, little of it pleasant. She's facing homicide, attempted homicide, child endangerment, and terrorism charges. She's going to spend the rest of her life in jail," Keith added.

"Can't she turn state's evidence on Toby?" Part of me felt sorry for the waste of life, even though she had tried to murder Johnny.

"We don't need her. Toby's bragging like a fool. Everything he says, which we are recording, can and will be used against him in a court of law—federal law, of course. He's facing the same charges as Paula, plus the murder of two people in St. Louis. The FBI will compile a list as long as my arm." Keith held out one very long arm.

"My granddaughter sensed something was wrong when she met him. She kept warning me about him," I said.

"But she's not here," Keith protested.

I didn't bother explaining. "And my home-school teacher called him a phony. He said pretending to be gay was stupid. It would only make him stand out in a crowd rather than disappear into it."

"And how did your home-school teacher know this?" Dr. Klein hadn't met either Emilie or Ducks, so any revelations from them were new news.

"His *gaydar* didn't go off when they met right after Alex's accident."

"*Gaydar?*" Dr. Klein asked.

"Ducks is gay. He can spot a phony quicker than I can. He said Toby used his act to disarm people, but he didn't fool Ducks." I then explained a bit about how Emilie's and Ducks' gifts worked. "They're my spooks who keep watch over me."

"Speaking of pretenses, Toby couldn't get out to dye his hair. He had dark brown roots showing. When he clocked me, I noticed his eyes were different, too."

"Different how?" I asked.

"They were lighter. He must have had contacts." Keith stood, ready to leave.

"Contacts, huh?" Dr. Klein said.

"Yeah."

CHAPTER THIRTY-ONE

EVENTS MOVED QUICKLY. Dr. Running Bear called a meeting in the cafeteria. We hadn't had one in a couple of days.

"Hello, everyone. I have a lot of news for you."

Before he could say another word, grumbles broke out. Families were anxious to get out of the hospital and return to their normal lives. He held up a hand. "I'll answer any questions you have left in a few minutes."

He paused for dramatic effect, leaving me time to scan the room to see if anyone other than Toby, Paula, and two agents were missing. None were.

"First, after a lot of hard work from the CDC team, we know what's been happening here on the Rez." Much of what Dr. Running Bear had to say was old news to those of us from the diagnosis room. For the other families, it was new and bewildering. He told them that three deadly pathogens had been purposefully introduced into the community to infect the patients, five of whom had died as a result.

"We've been battling hantavirus, monkeypox, and pneumonic plague. Those of you whose children were infected with one of the organisms know which child had what. When this outbreak began, we only identified hantavirus. Since it's found in nature under certain circumstances, we weren't all that concerned. While there is no cure, we can treat the symptoms, which we did with moderate success. Unfortunately, four children died in spite of our best efforts."

He moved on the monkeypox. "I know this looks like smallpox, but it's not. Let me repeat: We did *not* have smallpox. Monkeypox is from the same family of viruses, but is not as deadly. If you had a smallpox vaccine, you are probably protected. If you are worried, the CDC will make the vaccine available. Let us know if you would like one."

Plague was last. "I don't know which word, pox or plague, is more highly charged, but as far as I am concerned, I would rather have plague. It's a bacterium. That means standard antibiotics knock it out.

"I'm sorry we had anyone die, but we did. But we know how the pathogens—sorry, organisms—came into the hospital. Someone, one of our own, was experimenting with new ways of transmitting very dangerous diseases. He used the hospital as a real-life laboratory."

Voices raised in anger. Scraps of accusations flew.

"You know who he is?"

"Yes."

"How did he get in?"

"He worked here," Dr. Running Bear said firmly.

"Why did he choose this hospital?"

"We don't know yet, but we will. We confirmed our suspicions when Mr. Medina suffered an overdose of morphine, something none of us would have prescribed. Mr. Medina has plague. Morphine can reduce respiration, and his respiration was already compromised. As a result of the injection, he nearly died."

Parents turned to stare and glare at me. I hadn't done anything wrong, but anger didn't seek a logical target. It just sought a target. I sat straight and nodded to those with whom I made eye contact. I was in the same mess the parents were. They needed to remember I had two people I loved in the ICU, where none of them had more than one.

"I can't tell you everything about where the organisms came from, but I can tell you that Toby, our lab technician, and Paula, the neo-natal nurse, released them into our community."

"Not Paula. She nursed my preemie for two months until I could take her home. She can't be involved," one mother protested.

"Much as I hate to believe it, she was. They spread the diseases through injections using contaminated needles, respiratory therapy, and aerosol mists. The FBI has them in custody. In due time, they will be prosecuted at the Federal level and, when found guilty, will face long prison terms."

"Why didn't you use tribal police?" shouted the most vocal father, whose son had been there a full week.

Keith stepped forward. "Dr. Anderson was threatened verbally by Toby, and he attacked me. We are responsible for her safety. The charges both are facing go beyond the extent of tribal law, even though what they did occur here on tribal land."

"Like what?" the father challenged.

"Terrorism, for one. Murders in Missouri, for another. Tribal laws don't cover multi-jurisdictional crimes, neither do they cover terrorism. You don't want them to go free, do you?"

The man shook his head.

Dr. Running Bear held up a hand. "Not to worry. There will be plenty of justice for all of us."

Questions flew from every corner of the cafeteria. Dr. Running Bear answered those that were within his purview, with the CDC doctors answering others. An hour later, after the last of the questions were put to rest, Dr. Running Bear stepped forward and beckoned Leena by his side. She pushed a cafeteria cart in front of her. As a final act, one agent raised the blinds, allowing sunlight to flood the room. I blinked in the unfamiliar brightness.

"I have discharge papers. Once we brief you on how to take care of your children, you are free to leave. The CDC is lifting the quarantine."

Chairs scraped. People stood. Women hugged each other. The vocal father came over to tell me he was pleased Johnny and Alex would be going home.

I called my leasing agent and told him to prepare my jet before I texted Whip, Emilie, and Ducks with the great news.

###

After I called upstairs to tell my boys to get ready to leave, I processed Johnny's and Alex's paperwork. I could almost hear Alex's joyful shout in the diagnosis room, where the team met for the last time. Doctors White and Gupta were busy rolling up the flip chart pages, wiping the boards clean, and making sure they left nothing behind.

I thanked them for their work and for trusting me to keep the secret about what was going on. I turned to leave just as Dr. Duval, Dr. Running Bear, and Sharon entered. Dr. Running Bear waved us to sit.

"The FBI found Toby's lab," he said.

Dr. Duval nodded. An old trailer out on the reservation, "completely unsecured, with only rudimentary safeguards. I'm surprised he didn't die from accidental exposure."

"Do we know why he killed his brother?" For me, the fratricide issue was still unresolved.

"He told us he'd pilfered viral samples for more than a year because he'd lift his brother's ID badge at night. He let himself into the lab and took what he wanted." Keith went on to explain that Toby had never worked directly with pathogens in his previous positions, so he didn't know how to preserve them. "He lost a lot of 'product' in the early days."

Dr. Duval took up the narrative. "Once he researched preservation techniques and how to handle and transport the frozen samples, he was more successful." One night, Toby entered the lab as he always had, unaware that the badge he used had been reported lost. "That set off silent alarms minutes before the construction worker went looking for the toilet. Toby's brother Robby was working late. Your turn, Keith."

Keith nodded. "Robby confronted Toby, and they fought. Toby had a gun—remember, this was before the days of metal detectors everywhere—and shot his brother. He took more samples, ran down the back stairs, and set the building on fire using cans of gasoline he'd hidden outside in case he needed them. He killed the construction worker who died taking a—on the toilet."

"So, the official report spoke of an explosion, not arson, of an unauthorized entry, of the constipated construction worker, and nothing else," Sharon said. "The redacted portion of the report was silent on the lost ID badge, the murdered man, and his identity. It didn't divulge the missing pathogens because the lab was destroyed. Authorities had no way of inventorying the contents, so it was assumed all had been destroyed in the inferno. No one figured on samples being stolen prior to the fire, until after the video was discovered. By then, the story had been safely put to rest. The official report stood as written."

"And if anyone was ever arrested for murder, knowledge that was held back, namely the videos, would have been introduced at trial," Keith said. I felt only vaguely reassured about our government's opacity.

"Why did Toby do it?" We had the *how* and the *who*.

"Because he could." Sharon gave me a hug and promised to stay in touch. "Oh man, we have so much to tell Eleanor. Too bad we can't. I'll call you for lunch soon. I need a new friend." With that, the Secret Service escorted her to the front door and her waiting limo.

I asked Dr. Running Bear and Dr. Duval to wait. I had the utmost respect for the hospital staff, which had struggled to conquer an enemy they were total unprepared for and initially had no way of confronting.

"I watched what you all did to treat Johnny and Alex, as well as the other children. I can't tell you how grateful I am for healing my family and letting me take them home safely." I swallowed hard.

Dr. Running Bear put his hand on my shoulder. "Max, we just did our jobs. I'm really sorry Alex and Johnny got caught up in this insanity."

"Me too, but they survived."

"I cannot thank you for all your help with the other parents and with helping us think though the twists of this case." Dr. Duval took my hand in hers. "I wish we had met under different circumstances. I want to learn more about your *spooky watchdogs*."

I squeezed her hand. "They'd be happy to meet you at your leisure. And now, I need your help one more time. I'd like to make a special donation to San Felipe." I'd had my assistant back in New York City research what the hospital needed to set up a state-of-the-art lab, but I wanted Dr. Duval to double-check the list. I handed it over. She scanned it.

"This is very generous, Mrs. Davies," Dr. Duval said. "Very generous indeed." She handed the list to Dr. Running Bear.

"This is too much, Max." Dr. Running Bear pushed the list toward me.

"That is for saving Johnny." I pulled a second list from my pocket. "And this is for saving Alex."

He took the second list and whistled.

"If you're going to continue using this room for education, you need more than white boards. This equipment will make it easier to teach faculty and the community."

"You don't have to do this," Dr. Running Bear said.

"I want to, please." I grasped Dr. Running Bear's hand. "We made a formidable team. I'd like to do something to help this community. Besides, Dr. Running Bear, the equipment for this room is already sitting in a warehouse in Albuquerque, where it's been waiting for the quarantine to lift."

"Max, you're a force of nature." Dr. Running Bear put his arm across my shoulders and gave me a hug.

"So I've been told."

ACKNOWLEDGMENTS

So many people helped with this book that I'm sure I will forget a few. If you aren't named, please know I value your support and assistance.

First, of course, my dear husband Terry deserves credit for helping me sort through the various diseases available to infect San Felipe. He is my sounding board for vast chunks of the narrative.

Mark Young, my wicked critique partner, still never lets me get away with a bit of delightful purple prose, a misplaced sentence, or a gap in the narrative, even though he doesn't know a comma from a semi-colon. Thanks for working through the narrative multiple times.

My agent and publishing team have been with me since the first Mad Max book. Dawn Dowdle of Blue Ridge Literary Agency, and John Koehler and Joe Coccaro of Koehler Books, make a good team. Thanks for continuing to believe in Mad Max.

My two writers' groups, Lake Writers and Valley Writers, suffered through multiple readings of sections I struggled to get right. Without their honest input, I probably would have made many more bone-headed mistakes.

To a cadre of unnamed virologists, microbiologists, epidemiologists, and infectious disease experts who patiently answered questions, any mistakes in this manuscript are solely mine. You gave countless hours of advice. I hope I captured it correctly.

To my special friends at the CDC and Secret Service, thanks for helping me work out protocols in a quarantine situation. Without being able to trap the vice president's wife in the hospital, many of the character interactions would have fallen flat.

Last, but never least, my readers keep me writing about Mad Max and her family. I hope this book entertains you as much as the first two did.

WHERE I HANG OUT

Contact me through my website to reserve time for your book club or to chat about anything on your mind:

http://betsy-ashton.com/contact-me/

Sign up for my newsletter to receive advanced notifications of new books, contests, and other rather cool stuff

http://betsy-ashton.com/

I blog twice a month on the home page above as well as at **www.rosesofprose.blogspot.com** on the 17th and 27th of each month.

Follow me on social media. I'm Betsy Ashton on each of the sites below:

Facebook
Twitter
Pinterest
Instagram
Goodreads
LinkedIn

CPSIA information can be obtained
at www.ICGtesting.com
Printed in the USA
LVOW12*1626050318

568695LV00009B/210/P